SKIN AND BONES

LECTOR HOUSE PUBLIC DOMAIN WORKS

SKIN AND BONES

THORNE SMITH

9 789353 367312

ISBN: 978-93-5336-731-2

First Published: 1933

SKIN AND BONES

BY

THORNE SMITH

1933

FOR HORRID AND HIS WIFE,
EUPHEMISTICALLY KNOWN AS FRANK R. AND LORNA ADAMS,
IN FOND RECOLLECTION OF NUMEROUS FESTIVE OCCASIONS,
SUCH AS EARTHQUAKES, BANK HOLIDAYS
AND HOLLYWOOD ON HALF PAY.

CONTENTS

CHAPTER 1.

BLAND IN THE FLESH

When Quintus Bland set out to enjoy the evening he had not the vaguest idea he was destined to become a skeleton. Yet that is exactly what he did become—an impressive structure composed entirely of bone as far as the eye could reach.

Had fate vouchsafed the man some small warning of the radical departure from his customary appearance, there is no doubt he would have stopped where he was and become a skeleton comfortably in the privacy of his own home, assuming for the moment one can comfortably become a skeleton while still alive and active.

There were many persons who wished he had pursued this course and remained at home. Life for them would have still retained a little of its zest.

Indubitably this would have been the more agreeable course not only for Mr. Bland and his friends, but also for a number of unfortunate individuals who through no fault of their own were forced to undergo the ordeal of gazing on Quintus Bland in far less than the nude—in, perhaps, the most disturbing form a man can present to his fellow men.

Although to become a skeleton is a noteworthy achievement it is not an admirable one. If a man must so disport himself he would show far more consideration by enjoying his horror in solitude instead of in the heart of a populous city. The metamorphosis from flesh to bone is not one especially designed to be regarded affectionately by the average observer.

In extenuation of Mr. Bland's slight lapse it must be recorded that he had neither the intention nor the inclination to become a skeleton. Such an ambitious undertaking never entered his mind. Bones, in appalling number, were thrust upon him, so to speak. Or, inversely, flesh was removed. In the long run it made little difference how the change occurred. Bland suddenly and confoundingly discovered he had turned to a skeleton. He discovered also that it is the rare individual indeed who regards a skeleton either as a social equal or a desirable companion.

By way of explanation it should be known that Quintus Bland literally sniffed himself into his skeletonhood. For long hours at a time he had been inhaling the potent fumes of a secret chemical fluid with which he had been experimenting for some months past. It was his somewhat revolting hope that some day by means of this fluid he would be able to produce a fluoroscopic camera film. Why any normal man should wish to create such an intimately revealing commodity is difficult to conceive. Possibly Quintus Bland was not quite normal.

But before we take the man in his bony structure it would perhaps be a gentler approach and show better taste to consider him first in the flesh.

Quintus Bland was the sole owner and active head of one of the largest and most successful photographic studios in the city of New York. Like a versatile undertaking establishment the Bland Studios, Inc., could handle any job no matter how unappetizing. No face, not even the most murderous in character, ever took itself off the premises without feeling that it was quite a good face to look at.

As a small boy Quintus had made clicks with his camera while his companions were making pops with their guns. He was an essentially gentle little boy, and consequently was known as a queer duck, a mamma's boy, and a 'fraid cat. Eventually when he fell upon his tormentors and inflicted upon their quick healing bodies severe and humiliating punishment he gained the local reputation of being an embryonic homicidal maniac.

The truth of the matter was that these violent reprisals of the youthful Bland had not been undertaken in his own behalf, but rather in the best interests of a besieged turtle the other boys were attempting to open with the same ruthless enterprise they applied to clocks, watches, and other diverting bits of mechanism. Doubtless the boys considered the turtle as being nearly if not equally inanimate. Not only did young Quintus save the life of the turtle, but he also won the lasting admiration of a small female child with long golden hair who had witnessed the rescue. Later he married the girl.

At the moment when we take up Mr. Bland actively he had just turned thirty-seven years of age. There were days when he looked every bit of that, and others when in some surprising manner he appeared to have recaptured the breath and body of his youth. One could never be sure about Quintus Bland. He was never quite sure about himself. His age fluctuated most bewilderingly. If the conversation bored him he gradually became haggard and enfeebled, to the intense irritation of his wife. Should the talk turn to more diverting matters, he made a rapid recovery and attacked the subject with vigor and animation. His eyes had always been old, very old and wise. And there was a far-away quality in his smile that gave one the impression of mental reservations. It was a disturbing but not an uninteresting effect. He was a tall man and a dark man. Like the rest of him his hair was straight and dark. The word "lank" well covered the impression Mr. Bland created. And he made a lanky skeleton, which is, of course, one of the most demoralizing types of skeletons to encounter. He had a surprisingly snappy pair of dark eyes. Occasionally they glittered wickedly. At other times they smoldered morbidly into vacancy. His wife found it difficult to decide whether her husband's eyes were more annoying when they saw nothing at all or when they saw everything. He had a way of regarding her darkly for an interminable moment, then grunting suddenly as if from sheer disgust. She found this most disturbing.

At present he was having his full share of wife trouble. On her part the little blonde girl of years ago had come to rue the day she had ever witnessed the dark youth rescue the turtle from the grubby talons of the village boys. She blamed that turtle with all the blind unreason of her sex. She wished she could find the slow-witted creature and give it a piece of her mind. She would have liked to point out to it in terms of passionate reproach that if he had only kept on turtling instead of parking provocatively in the exact middle of a dirt road she, Lorna Bland, sometimes called Blondie because of the inevitable alliteration, would not now be married to a long-legged, grunting maniac, capable of seeing life only through the lens of a camera. Yes, that turtle had plenty to answer for when presently he stood in the presence of his God. That would be a long time off, she speculated gloomily. Turtles, she had been given to understand, lived practically for ever, provided that they escaped the attentions of small boys.

Blondie Bland was about as pretty as any reasonable man should require a woman to be. Pretty of face and pretty of figure, with a quantity of unlived hell still flickering near the surface of her great blue eyes. She was all that a woman should be and much that one should not. But the worst that could be said of her was that she was tarrying a little overlong on that stage of her development in which the capture of men through partial surrender seemed a matter of prime importance. Quintus was a most satisfyingly jealous husband. Lorna did not endeavor to make things any easier for him. His long legs done into joints frequently made her unreasonably furious. There were times when she wished she could kick his shins, but remembering the fury of the dark youth in action she suppressed this dangerous impulse.

When they were first married, Lorna Bland had been seven years younger than her husband. Gradually the years separating them had increased until by now they had become ten. At the present rate of speed, Quintus Bland reflected sardonically, theirs would soon assume the aspect of an April-October union. This set him to wondering why Lorna loved youth instead of life, why she wallowed in repetitive experience instead of questing fresh adventure. In a sense she was older than he was, more settled in her ways, more reconciled with the set routine of her existence. The lovely but benighted creature still approached a tea, flirtation, or dinner party with the same eager anticipation of her first year out. He hated to believe that women were instruments of torture or pleasure according to the occasion. Yet Lorna did much to further this belief. He often wished he had the courage to shake her blonde head off her smooth, firm shoulders.

In much the same state of unsatisfied hostility couples drag themselves along to regret their golden anniversaries. Neighbors call with congratulatory words. A festive to-do is made. The venerable couple, cynically despising the whole affair, have their picture taken together, the nearest physical contact they have had in years. In the local paper a paragraph appears. Then the neighbors, after singing "Auld Lang Syne," depart, vowing they will presently return to celebrate with equal gusto the diamond anniversary. Sometimes the old battlers are actually fooled by public approval into believing they really care for one another, but this mood is speedily dissipated when presently they retire to bed to lie in the darkness, wondering why they had not given each other pulverized glass somewhere between the paper and the wooden, when they still had a chance to carry on with a mate who would have understood them.

In the majority of cases a golden anniversary is in reality a gathering of friends to celebrate the fact that a man and a woman have miraculously succeeded in living together for fifty years without committing murder. There are not many such occasions. There was little likelihood that Quintus and Lorna Bland would ever celebrate theirs. Long before that time one or the other of them would have succeeded in escorting his or her mate to the grave. Already much of the man's innate gentleness was being replaced by strong homicidal impulses. Frequently now he found himself contemplating his wife and thinking how pleasant it would be to drag her about the house by her hair. He even speculated whether it was long enough to afford a good grip. So far, however, physical conflict had been avoided.

The highly desirable Blondie consistently feigned a vast contempt for cameras, their works, and those who worked them. To irritate her husband still further she was frequently seen at art exhibits, where she bored herself insufferably by looking at paintings she neither understood nor appreciated. It must be said for her that she took her punishment with fortitude worthy of a better cause.

On the evening when Mr. Bland set forth in search of enjoyment his wife returned to their fashionable suburban home with a painting she had acquired at no small expense. As far as she could judge, it was a picture of a cow in convulsions. In her mind's eye she had already selected the exact spot on the library wall where this atrocity would do the most harm, that is, where her husband's eyes would be forced to fall on it most frequently. Having hung the daub to her infinite satisfaction, she fluffed out her golden hair, sighed happily, flexed her supple torso like a cat preparing to pounce, then curled herself up in a chair with a book which she did not read. Presently Quintus Bland arrived from the city with a bundle under his arm.

"Ah, there," said Mr. Bland, defensively flinging the words in the general direction of his wife. "I've brought home a new study—wheels, all wheels."

"Ah," welcomed Lorna Bland, "an X-ray of your negroid head, I take it."

"What?" asked Mr. Bland in a preoccupied voice as he busily unwrapped the bundle. "You were saying?"

"Never mind," his wife replied, feeling that under the circumstances minor insults were superfluous. "It really doesn't matter."

Humming under his breath in a peculiarly irritating manner, Quintus, with his new study of wheels, approached the exact spot on the library wall on which the cow was having her convulsions. Blondie, not missing a move, decided that this little affair was going to turn out even better than she had anticipated.

Bland raised his eyes to the wall and met the cow face to face. Both faces expressed acute agony. The man looked as if the cow had gored him in some vital spot. He, too, seemed seized with convulsions. Then, as if suddenly realizing that the eyes of his wife were hatefully studying his reactions, Bland rallied gamely. Once more he endeavored to hum as if his mind was quite serene, but this time there was a noticeable quaver in his voice.

As if he had grown up in daily association with the stricken cow, he removed her from the wall and carelessly scaled her across the room. By this action his humming was definitely improved. It swelled to a note of triumph.

From her coiled position in the chair Lorna shot like a maddened spring. She grabbed the cow from the floor, pressing it to her heart. In her eye flashed the light of battle.

"You beast," she said in a tragic voice. "You long-legged butcher."

"Why shouldn't a butcher have long legs?" her husband inquired mildly.

"I don't care whether a butcher has any legs at all," Mrs. Bland heatedly flung back.

"A butcher would hardly chop off his own legs," the man pursued thoughtfully. "That wouldn't make any sense."

"What do I care about butchers?" cried Mrs. Bland.

"I don't know," replied Mr. Bland. "What do you care about butchers?"

"Nothing!" snapped the lady. "I don't care a damn about butchers."

"I'm glad to learn," said Quintus Bland, "that there is one class of male that fails to attract you. Is it because they hide their trousers beneath their aprons?"

Mrs. Bland blinked.

"You're a vulgarian," she told him.

"Admittedly," agreed Quintus Bland. "But I'm not a butcher. Were I one, I would have hacked that obscene beast to bits."

"If you keep going on about butchers," Lorna Bland assured her husband, "I'll do something desperate."

"You'll be sorry when you're hungry," Mr. Bland warned her. "For my part I am very fond of butchers. I fully appreciate the dignity and importance of their calling."

With this observation he hung his study of wheels in the space recently occupied by the convulsive cow.

"And besides," said Mrs. Bland, hovering round the spot, "that isn't an obscene beast. It's a cow—a swell cow."

"I hope she swells until she bursts," remarked Mr. Bland. "If you hadn't told me I would have carried away the impression it was a composite picture of all the most objectionable features of the animal kingdom."

With his head cocked on one side he stepped back and stood admiring his weird study of wheels.

"Do you imagine that horror is going to remain there on the wall?" asked Lorna Bland in a low voice.

"Of course it is, my dear," replied her husband. "Can't you almost see those wheels turn, hear the purr of the dynamos, feel the reverberations of—"

His sentence was never finished. Already there had been too much of it for Blondie Bland. The man's complacency had completely unbalanced her mind. Snatching the picture from the wall, she sprang to a footstool and brought the framed photograph down on the cocked head of Quintus Bland. In less time than it takes to think of it, the head protruded through the wheels with the frame around its neck. Across the face there flickered momentarily an expression of surprise, then the features became impassive. In silence they confronted each other; then Mr. Bland, with a polite smile, helped his wife to step down from the footstool. With elaborate courtesy he removed the convulsive cow from her possession, raised it aloft, then brought it down with great force and deliberation upon the sleek blonde head. Being stretched on canvas, the convulsive cow bounced up with a snap, but not so Mrs. Bland. With a gasp of astonishment she found herself squatting on the floor, literally driven into that position in which she remained, all thought of dignity forgotten.

"Go on," she said at last in a dull voice. "Finish me with the frame. It's the only thing left to do."

"There was glass in yours," observed her husband. "You might have cut my throat."

"I wanted to cut your throat," Mrs. Bland retorted. "I still do. From ear to ear," she added.

"Indeed," sneered Mr. Bland. "Well, just observe this cutting."

Lorna Bland, still squatting, looked up with sudden interest. Her husband had taken a knife from the long library table. With this weapon in one hand and the convulsive cow in the other he placed himself before her so that she could enjoy a clear and unobstructed view of his actions. Even at that tense moment the squatting wife could not refrain from dwelling on what a fantastic picture her husband presented, standing ceremoniously before her, his framed head protruding through a mass of wheels, a knife poised dramatically above a picture of a cow. It would be a crisp moment for the entrance of a neighbor. The dramatic solemnity of the man suggested a priest of some ancient religion on the point of making vicarious sacrifice to his bloodthirsty gods.

"You wouldn't dare," breathed Mrs. Bland. "That cow cost one hundred dollars."

"I'd pay twice that amount to cut her to ribbons," Mr. Bland informed her. "Watch. See, I slit the creature's throat from ear to ear as you would have slit mine." This he proceeded to do with one deft stroke of the knife. "Next," he continued, "I swish off her hind legs, or quarters." The legs were neatly severed from the body. "And not content with that," he added grimly, "I disembowel the beast like this. Observe!" Mrs. Bland observed and saw exactly how it was done. "And now, my dear," resumed her husband politely, "here is your hundred-dollar cow. Have you any more funny pictures?"

"Thank you a lot," replied Lorna sweetly, rising from the floor and accepting the tattered ruin. "I think I'll hang it back where it was. When callers want to know what has happened to the picture I'll explain in full detail."

"Very well," said Mr. Bland, delicately removing his head from the frame. "If you are going to do that, I am going to do this, and when callers inquire about the jagged state of this photograph I'll simply tell them you tried to cut my throat with it—from ear to ear."

Thus speaking, he placed the shattered study of wheels in the center of the mantelpiece.

"They'll be sorry I didn't succeed," said his wife, eyeing the picture critically. "It certainly looks like hell up there."

"Your cow scarcely adds to the attractiveness of the room," Mr. Bland reminded her.

"In trying to dash my brains out," said Lorna Bland, "you succeeded in giving me a terrible headache. I must take some aspirin."

"It's merely good luck I'm not standing in a pool of blood," observed Mr. Bland. "As it is, I, too, have a headache."

"I wish to God you were standing in two pools of blood," commented Mrs. Bland. "One foot in each."

Having voiced this pious wish, Lorna Bland rang for the maid, Fanny, a small, desperately passionate-looking girl, slightly oversized in the right places.

"Aspirins, Fanny," said Lorna. "It may interest you to know that your master has just beaten me over the head in an attempt to dash my brains out. Tell the cook."

"And it may further interest you to know, Fanny," put in Mr. Bland calmly, "that your mistress has just attempted to slit my throat. Tell that to the cook. It would have been from ear to ear," he added, drawing a long finger across his throat to make himself clearly understood.

There was no doubt that Fanny was deeply impressed. She looked first at Mrs. Bland's head, then transferred her dark gaze to Mr. Bland's throat. There was such a lot of Mr. Bland's throat. Fanny was just as well pleased it was not slit. Fanny took care of the rugs.

"I'm sorry, madam," she said respectfully. "Is there anything I can do?"

"Yes," replied Madam bitterly. "You might get a gun and shoot me and get it over with."

"Or," suggested her husband, "you might ask the cook to step in for a moment with the carving knife and cut my throat for the edification of Mrs. Bland. I'll endeavor to bleed in two separate pools, my dear, and place a failing foot in each."

Mentally confronted by this ghastly picture, Fanny hurried from the room.

"Have you no pride?" asked Quintus Bland when the passionate maid had gone.

"None whatsoever," his wife coolly replied. "In the presence of a stalking murderer there is no room for pride."

Fanny returned with aspirin and water. Lorna took one tablet and washed it down with a small gulp.

"Will you have one?" she asked the stalking murderer.

"Thanks," he replied. "Two."

"Your headache is no worse than mine," said his wife. "I'll take three."

"How petty," remarked Mr. Bland, enjoying Lorna's efforts to get the tablets down. "How, how petty."

"You started it," said his wife, passing him the box.

"Might as well finish them off," he said, glancing at the contents. "There are only four left."

Even for his long throat the swallowing of four aspirins presented some difficulty. Nevertheless he succeeded in flexing them down. With thwarted eyes his wife watched her husband's neck until the last spasmodic ripple had subsided.

"You should have been a sword swallower," she commented; then, turning to Fanny, "Are there any more aspirins in the house?"

"No, Mrs. Bland," said Fanny. "Shall I send for some?"

"Do," replied Mrs. Bland. "A large box."

"How petty," murmured Mr. Bland. "How very, very petty."

"I hope your heart stops beating," snapped his wife.

"Fanny," said Mr. Bland, disregarding this hope, "where is my dog? A man must have some companionship."

"If that dog shows his stupid face in here," Mrs. Bland announced in a voice of cool determination, "I'll pull his tail out by the roots."

"I think you mean off," corrected her husband.

"Off or out," cried Lorna Bland, "it doesn't matter which. If that dog comes in here he'll leave the room with his tail in my hands."

"So you would carry the warfare to dumb animals," said Mr. Bland with a sneer in his voice.

"I started it with one," Mrs. Bland replied with evident satisfaction.

At this moment the dog whose tail had been under discussion, and whose correct name was Busy, came on little bounces into the room. Busy was about a foot high, a trifle less than a foot wide, and a little more than a foot long. It was quite obvious the dog had made a brave attempt to make himself as nearly a cube as possible. He was all white and woolly. Two black eyes like washed grapes danced vividly in a large square head. Such was Busy. Both Quintus and Lorna Bland were always on the point of looking up in a book to find out just what sort of dog he was, but what with one thing and another they had never quite got round to it. Nominally Busy was the property of Mr. Bland, although his wife was equally fond of the dog. Now, however, it pleased her to consider the animal entirely his, realizing that the best way to attack her husband was through this odd-looking beast.

Therefore, the moment the blonde woman's eyes fell upon the unsuspecting dog she swooped down upon him and began to tug lustily at his tail. Busy gave tongue to a sharp yelp of indignation. This was quite enough for Quintus Bland. He rushed across the room and seized his crouching wife by the hair.

"Let go of that dog's tail," he threatened, "or I'll drag you about by the hair."

"See," said Lorna Bland triumphantly, as she went over backwards, dragging the dog with her. "What did I tell you, Fanny? The man's a stalking murderer. This probably will be the end. Run for your life."

For a moment the situation remained static. Mr. Bland had his wife by the hair while she had his dog by the tail. Fanny could not recall ever having seen anything quite like it. Neither seemed willing to let go first, although Busy would have been only too happy to wash his hands of the whole affair. The ring of the doorbell broke the deadlock. Quintus Bland released his wife, who in turn released his dog. Struggling to her feet, she began to fluff out her hair. As Fanny with a backward glance hurried to the door, the master of the house assumed a dignified attitude while his consort fixed a smile of greeting on her lips.

"Will you help me to get through college," hopefully inquired a voice, "by subscribing to one of these popular magazines?"

"Certainly not!" shouted Mr. Bland to the unseen aspirant.

"No!" passionately elaborated his wife. "Not if you remain ignorant to the end of your days, which I hope are numbered."

Feeling definitely certain that this was a poor portal indeed through which to enter into the realms of higher education, the youth withdrew, and Fanny hurried back to the room, hoping to witness the resumption of hostilities. But for that day active hostilities were at an end. Mrs. Bland was busy with the telephone. Her husband was watching her with a pair of brooding eyes.

"Is that you, Phil?" said Lorna Bland after a short pause. "Yes, of course, it is. Certainly this is Blondie. I simply wanted to let you know that my husband has just attempted to dash my brains out, then drag me round by my hair. Pretty, isn't it?"

"She brutally assaulted my dog," thundered Quintus Bland over his wife's shoulder, "and tried to pull his tail off."

"That was the voice of the murderer," said Lorna into the telephone. "No, no, not mine. He was referring to the dog's. [Pause.] Listen, Phil, I want you to take me out to dinner. I'll pick you up in the car. [Pause.] How sweet of you. Yes, yes, yes. [Another pause.] And after? Oh, I don't care what happens after. Better that than death."

She replaced the instrument and glanced significantly at her husband.

"Better that by far," she said as if to herself.

"What do you mean by that?" he demanded.

"Don't tell me you were born yesterday," she retorted.

"So that's how the crow flies," said Mr. Bland nastily.

"I don't care whether the crow flies or crawls along on the flat of his belly," was his wife's indelicate rejoinder. "You look like a crow yourself. How do you fly?"

"If I fly into a rage," said Quintus Bland, "you'll be sorry you were ever born."

"I'm sorry you ever were," Mrs. Bland flung back at him as she rose to quit the room. "And if I could lay my hands on that turtle I'd wring his horrid neck off."

"Animal baiter," muttered Quintus.

"Fanny," called Mrs. Bland from the stair-way, "come up here and help me find my black underwear with the lace."

A look of consternation took possession of Mr. Bland's features. He gathered the assaulted dog in his arms and sat down with him on the sofa. In a surprisingly short time Lorna Bland was down again.

"Good-bye," she said, looking in at the door. "I have it on, the black underwear with —"

"I know," Mr. Bland interrupted. "With the lace."

For a moment the small blonde creature lingered undecidedly in the door. She was sorry she had said he looked like a crow. It was too close to home. And she had lied about the black underwear, what little there was of it. Phil Harkens was not worth black underwear, especially with lace. Sitting there in the shadows, her black long-legged husband did look for all the world like a dark bird of ill omen—an old crow huddled on a sofa with a square dog on his lap. Still, he might say something friendly. She wanted only a word or so to call the battle off. But no word was forthcoming. Feeling a little hollow inside, she closed the front door slowly behind her. Shortly after, the man on the sofa heard the expostulations of her motor. He listened until the spluttering had turned to an ingratiating purr which grew fainter and died away. So she really had taken herself off with her black underwear with the lace. Now he had the house to himself, and he did not want it. Damn her, anyway, and damn her black underwear. Damn the lace, too. He removed a strand of blonde hair from his vest. Yes, damn her blonde hair.

For a long time he sat there quite motionless with the square dog. The battle had left him deflated. Idly he examined the tail of Busy. It was an odd hook of a tail not unlike a jigsaw piece with hair on it. It seemed to have escaped injury. Its permanent hook was undamaged. Mr. Bland decided it would be difficult to pull off a tail as strongly affixed as Busy's.

Darkness drifted into the room and piled up in the corners. Bland was too listless to switch on the lights. The far-away drumming of a scooting express train throbbed across the gloom. The sound made him think of the city. Lorna in her black underwear was spending the evening with that rotter, Phil Harkens. Why should not he, Quintus Bland, make a night of it also? The city was congested with good-looking women. His acquaintance among models was extensive.

"Busy," said the man to the square dog, "I feel very much like hell. All washed out, you know. Should I or should I not go to the city?"

The dog was far above the battle. He slumbered heavily on his master's lap and made gross noises about it.

Fanny's dark eyes glittered in the doorway.

"I'm going out, Fanny," said Quintus Bland from the sofa. "Pass the word to the kitchen. There will be no dinner."

Fanny's expression revealed the fact that she was sorry her master was going out. She had certain ideas of her own in which he was rather intimately involved. She wished she had the courage to tell him there was no need for him to stir farther afield in search of amorous diversion.

"Will you be back late, Mr. Bland?" she asked.

"If at all," Mr. Bland replied.

He removed the dog from his knees and placed him gently on the sofa. The square animal snored peacefully through the transition. Accepting his hat and stick from a reluctant Fanny, he moved out into the dusk, quitting the comforts of his suburban home in favor of the city, where he later became a skeleton, which was even worse than wearing black underwear with lace on it.

CHAPTER 2.

BLAND IN THE BONE

Quintus Bland became a skeleton at exactly eleven forty- five that same evening. After the consumption of much bad alcohol he was endeavoring with the aid of a female companion to pull himself together in a private room of a popular speakeasy situated just off Washington Square.

In an adjoining room two other couples belonging to his party were carrying on in a manner which, to put it mildly, was not quite becoming. Having been deprived of amusement by the poor quality of the play they had attended earlier in the evening, they were now endeavoring to find diversion in various other questionable directions.

It will never be known definitely what chemical combination wrought the amazing change in Mr. Bland's physical composition. Quite possibly the fumes of his strange concoction, together with an overdose of aspirin invigorated by the reaction of much raw liquor, were sufficient to create a fluoroscopic man instead of a fluoroscopic film. The explanation is really not important. Mr. Bland was far more concerned with the social aspects of his predicament than with the scientific ones. He regretted that like Mr. H. G. Wells's Invisible Man he had not made a good job of it and disappeared entirely. There is no place in the social scale for an animated structure composed wholly of bones. No matter how convivial and responsive strong drink makes individuals, they still remain unreconciled to skeletons who carry on quite as if nothing untoward had occurred. And Quintus Bland became the most disconcerting sort of skeleton a man could become. He became a recurring or sporadic skeleton. He became a skeleton in fits and starts. One could never be sure where one had him. At one moment he would find himself devastatingly deprived of his flesh only to discover a few minutes later that he was once more a complete man down to the last detail. This fluctuating condition of being made any continuous line of conduct almost impossible. Even when he was completely himself, his friends could not refrain from regarding him with fear and suspicion. And there were some who looked upon him with loathing not unmixed with awe.

Lulu Summers, a luscious hose-and-underwear model whom Mr. Bland had occasionally employed as a subject for his camera, was the first to discover that her present partner was not all or even a part of what a perfect gentleman should be.

It was regrettable in the extreme that Lulu, in order to further her partner's interests, had found it necessary to remove nearly all of a not over-burdening attire. Being a model and at the same time thrifty might possibly be advanced as an excuse for her conduct by charitably-minded persons, of whom there are too few.

She, together with a somewhat comatose Quintus, was reclining on a large divan when stark tragedy entered her young if not innocent life. In an attempt to ameliorate the discomfort of her occasional employer, she was stroking his long black hair when gradually it was borne in on her consciousness that, instead of ministering to a head with hair on it, her hand was caressing a smooth, round surface. Interested but not yet alarmed, she glanced at the head to discover the reason for the change. Luckily for the girl, Mr. Bland was lying with his face turned to the wall. At first glance Lulu's eyes encountered what they mistook for an extremely bald head. That alone would have been enough to revolt the average beholder, but Lulu was made of ruggeder stuff.

"Quinnie," she said in a reproachful voice, "why didn't you tell me you wore a wig? I've been rubbing your head for ages."

"Don't call me Quinnie," grumbled Mr. Bland, happily unaware of the change that had come over him. "I don't like it at all. What's that you said about a wig?"

"You're as bald as a bat," the lady replied. "I've never seen anything like it. Your wig has fallen off."

"What!" exclaimed Quintus Bland, placing a fleshless hand on his skull. "My God, you're right! No hair at all. What's happened to my head?"

Nervously his fingers drummed upon the bony surface, producing a hollow tapping sound most unpleasant to the ear.

"What's that?" he asked with increasing alarm. "Am I making that noise?"

The shriek that greeted this question made him turn suddenly round on the divan. In the middle of the room Lulu was trembling in all of her beautiful limbs. Upon looking at his face the shriek was automatically repeated. Resting a bony hand on what used to be a cheek, he gazed at the girl in astonishment.

"For heaven's sake, stop that screaming," he commanded. "People will think I'm murdering you."

"You are," declared the girl. "You're doing worse than that. You're scaring me to death. Please don't be like that. It's not at all funny."

"Like what?" asked Mr. Bland, his mystification increasing.

"The way you are," said the girl. "How can you bear to do it?"

Thoughtfully Quintus Bland stroked his face. The peculiar scraping sound accompanying this gesture was not reassuring. Once more Lulu gave a cry of distress. Mr. Bland glanced hastily at his long bony fingers, then looked at the rest of himself. He was unable to recognize anything familiar. As he snapped up in the divan, he, too, began to tremble, but his limbs were far from lovely.

"By God," he said, "I'm a skeleton."

"You certainly are," fervently agreed Miss Summers. "And I'm clearing out. I might have my moments of weakness, but I draw the line at fleshless men."

"Come on back," called Mr. Bland as the girl made for the door to the adjoining room.

"Like fun," said Lulu. "What for?"

"I might get my body back," he suggested.

"Yeah?" she replied, skeptically. "While I lose my mind watching those bones turn to flesh? Nothing doing."

Rising from the divan, Quintus Bland strode across the room. This was too much for Lulu. With a wild shriek she disappeared through the door. The man stopped in his tracks and glanced at himself in a long mirror; then, unleashing a shriek of his own, he, too, disappeared into the next room, where a chorus of shrieks greeted his arrival.

"Give me a drink," he cried, desperately. "Somebody give me a drink."

"What would you do with it?" Chunk Walling managed to get out. "What you need is a coffin."

"Or a closet," put in Sam Crawford. "Isn't that where skeletons belong?"

"Don't ask me," replied one of the young ladies, "but I wish to God he'd hide himself somewhere."

"If you ask me," faltered the other young lady, "a sight like that just doesn't belong anywhere."

"And to think that I was in bed with the thing," Lulu Summers murmured.

"O-o-o," breathed the first young lady, known in the trade as Elaine. "How disappointing!"

"If I wasn't in such a shocking condition," said the other girl, who operated under the name of Flora, "I'd be almost home by now. Look! It's actually drinking."

Mr. Quintus Bland removed the bottle from his lipless mouth.

"Don't call me It," he said, reprovingly. "I am still Quintus Bland even if my flesh is gone."

"If I were you I wouldn't admit it, old chap," Sam Crawford told him. "A performance like this isn't going to do you a bit of good."

"Do you imagine I'm doing it for fun?" asked the indignant Mr. Bland.

"Fun for who?" demanded the girl called Flora. "It's certainly no fun for us. Why didn't it splash all over your ribs?"

"Why didn't what splash?" asked Mr. Bland.

"That hooker of gin you just drank," said the girl.

"Oh, that," Mr. Bland replied. "I'm sure I don't know. As a matter of fact I know less about myself than you do."

"I know more than enough," said Flora.

"There's nothing like a skeleton to break down maidenly reserve," Mr. Walling remarked.

"I find this conversation most objectionable," declared Mr. Bland.

"I object to the whole damned business," expostulated Chunk Walling. "You're positively indecent."

Mr. Bland sat down and crossed his legs with a click.

"Gord," breathed Flora. "Did you hear that? My blood is just one curdle."

"Do you think I like it?" snapped Mr. Bland, making another click, this time with his teeth.

"I don't see how you can," replied Sam Crawford. "We actually hate it. Can't you go back?"

"How do you mean?" asked Quintus Bland. "Go back where?"

"Go back to your flesh," explained Sam. "Be yourself for a change."

Mr. Bland laughed suddenly and bitterly. It was not a nice sound. The two couples and Lulu moved to the other side of the room, where they huddled together for comfort.

"Don't do that," pleaded Lulu. "Make some other noise. I can't stand that one."

"Someone will have to send for a doctor," said the young lady called Elaine. "That's all there is to it. I must have either a hypodermic or a bottle of whisky or something."

"Think of me," commented Quintus Bland. "Imagine how I feel."

"You're asking too much of flesh and blood," replied Flora. "No one wants to imagine how you feel."

"Well, don't stand over there all huddled up," said what remained of Mr. Bland. "I'm not going to do anything to you."

"You've already done it," put in Lulu. "I'll never be the same woman. When I think of what might have happened my blood runs cold."

Mr. Bland rose from the chair and, lifting his arms above his head, stretched himself and yawned. Had he deliberately set out to torture his companions he could not have proceeded more effectively. A gasp of sheer horror came simultaneously from five pairs of lips.

"What is he going to do?" quavered Elaine. "Attack us?"

The framework of Bland moved shockingly across the room. One bony hand clutched the gin bottle, which emitted a clanking sound. Placing the bottle where his lips should have been, he polished off its contents, then unconsciously wiped his teeth with a fleshless arm. The grating noise this made caused even the skeleton to shudder.

"Horror upon horror," murmured Flora. "And he's drunk up all the gin."

"Why his backbone isn't even moist," observed Sam, "is still a mystery to me."

"I'm not at all interested to find out," Chunk Walling replied. "The details of that skeleton are overshadowed by the whole."

"And we were going to have such a jolly evening," Lulu regretfully observed.

"It's not too late," said Mr. Bland, reseating himself on the chair. "We can still have a jolly evening. Come over here, Lulu, and sit on my lap."

Lulu gave vent to a slight scream.

"Did you hear that?" she asked in a shocked voice. "Did you hear what he wants me to do?"

"I'd rather sit on a nest of hornets," said Elaine.

"Much," added Flora, with conviction.

Quintus Bland, in spite of the critical condition of his anatomy, found himself growing pleasantly drunk. He had consumed nearly a whole bottle of gin and felt a great deal better for it. He began to feel that his fleshless condition lent him a touch of distinction. After all, what was a skeleton among friends?

"Come on over," he said to Lulu. "I'm not going to do anything to you."

"What do you mean by anything?" asked Lulu. "You've already done enough."

"Go on, sit on his lap," urged Sam. "He might get mad if you don't. I'd hate that."

"Yeah?" retorted Lulu, sarcastically. "And I'd go mad if I did."

"But what can a skeleton do?" said Chunk Walling.

"He might try to kiss me," Lulu replied, "and twine me in those arms."

The other two women made noises of distress.

"All right. All right," said the skeleton of Mr. Bland in a disgusted voice. "Order a couple bottles and I'll stand the treat."

"That's far more reasonable," put in Flora. "I'm beginning to like that skeleton."

"You're even more depraved than I thought," said Elaine.

"Is that so?" snapped Flora. "Well, I'd rather have a skeleton for a boy friend than some of those fat swine you lug about."

"Okay, sister," replied Elaine. "There's your skeleton. He's all yours."

"Please stop discussing me as if I were not present," protested Mr. Bland.

"You're only partly present," said Chunk Walling.

"Yes," agreed Lulu. "And the least desirable part, at that. The man is virtually speaking from the grave."

"Don't you feel at all dead?" inquired Chunk Walling.

"Not at all," Quintus Bland replied. "I feel very much alive— raring to go."

"Why don't you go?" suggested Elaine. "I, for one, won't bar your way."

"Is that nice?" asked Mr. Bland.

"Perhaps not," the girl replied, "but you don't seem to realize that you're a total skeleton—a fleshless man—an animated boneyard."

"Some day," said Mr. Bland, maliciously, "you'll be just like me."

"Oh, no, I won't," Elaine assured him. "When I get in your terrible condition I'm going to cut out night clubs and all other social contacts."

"The grog will be right up," Sam Crawford announced, turning from the telephone.

"Those are the first agreeable words I've heard to-day," said Quintus Bland. "Now we can settle down and take life easy."

His five companions received this remark in skeptical silence. They were all wondering how life could be taken easily in the presence of a skeleton.

"I long to get drunk," observed Lulu, "but I'm almost afraid to do it. Wouldn't it be just awful to forget one's self with a skeleton?"

"I'd call it impossible," said Flora, running a critical eye over the uninviting frame of Quintus Bland.

"Is this discussion quite necessary?" he asked in a pained voice.

"If you were a lady you'd say it was," Elaine replied with a slight tilt of her fine eyebrows.

"The fact that you can envisage such a contingency," remarked Mr. Bland, "hardly qualifies you to consider yourself a lady."

"I'm more of a lady than you are a gentleman," Elaine replied. "You're merely a beastly old stack of bones."

"Admitted," said Mr. Bland, complacently. "I don't have to be a gentleman. I'm just a drunken skeleton with no moral obligations."

"I don't like the sound of that," declared Lulu. "If old Mr. Bones over there gets amorously binged and starts making passes at me you're going to have a dead model on your hands."

Mr. Brand's indignant rejoinder was interrupted by a knock on the door.

"Come in!" Sam Crawford thoughtlessly called out.

A chorus of squeals from the girls and a smothered exclamation from Bland greeted this invitation. Leaping across the room, he hurled himself clatteringly against the door.

"Oh, momma," breathed Flora, her eyes popping wildly, "modesty isn't worth it. Did you see that nightmare move?"

"Yes," murmured Lulu. "And I heard him dash. I'm not going to be able to stand much more of this sort of thing."

In the meantime Quintus Bland had partially opened the door and thrust out a bony hand and arm, hoping that in the half-light of the hall the waiter would not notice their fleshless condition.

"You can give me the bottles," he said. "We'll settle up later. I haven't any clothes on."

The statement concerning Bland's lack of attire was not at all a novel one to the waiter, but the appearance of that ghastly hand with its long clutching fingers was something altogether new and unexpected.

"What sort of a hand is that?" the waiter wanted to know. "I don't like the looks of it."

"It's a trick," replied Mr. Bland, not knowing what else to say. "A simple trick."

"It's a damned dirty trick," retorted the waiter. "I wouldn't play it on a dog."

"Well, I haven't played it on a dog," Bland declared. "Give me those bottles and go away."

"I'll go away fast enough," said the waiter, "but it will be a long time before you'll get me back. Nor will I hand you the bottles. Pick 'em up yourself."

Placing the bottles at a safe distance from the door, the waiter hurried away. He did not look back to see a long skeleton arm slide through the slit in the door and gather in the bottles. It was just as well for him he missed this petrifying experience.

Quintus Bland closed the door and confronted his five companions. There was a bottle in either hand.

"I'm not getting used to you," Lulu Summers told him. "No matter how hard I try, you remain just as awful."

"If you want any of this grog," he answered with a grim click of his teeth, "you'll have to make the best of it."

"What I want to know," said Chunk Walling, "is how did you get that way. It's incredible to me. I'd suspect my own eyesight were it not for the fact that four other persons are seeing the same thing."

"I'm not sure," replied Mr. Bland, removing a cork from one of the bottles. "I've been experimenting with some rare and exceptionally potent chemicals lately. Perhaps they turned the trick."

"Well," observed Elaine, "like that waiter said, it certainly is a dirty one."

"But where are all your organs?" Flora wanted to know. "You must have something or you'd be a dead skeleton."

"As he should be," put in Elaine. "Even in times of depression a girl shouldn't be expected to associate with skeletons with or without organs."

"I say don't let's talk about his organs," suggested Lulu. "What we can see of him is bad enough."

"I know," declared Flora, "but he must have a stomach or else he wouldn't be able to gulp down liquor the way he's doing."

"Maybe he has invisible organs," said Sam Crawford. "You know, they're there but we can't see them."

"Who wants to see them?" Elaine demanded.

"I would, for one," replied Mr. Bland. "Being a skeleton is damn' lonely business."

"You're not lonely enough to suit me," declared Elaine. "You should be dead and buried."

"I'd like to wring your neck," said Quintus Bland, dispassionately.

"I'm surprised he hasn't wrung all our necks," remarked Lulu, "and left us strewn about the room. He looks mean enough to do it."

"Do you realize that I'm paying for your night's enjoyment?" asked Mr. Bland, who had lost most of his gentlemanly instincts together with his flesh.

"Enjoyment!" cried Lulu with a wild laugh. "That's a hot number. Why, if you kept me to the end of my days you'd never be able to repay me for that moment on the divan."

"Sure," agreed Elaine. "He turned a skeleton on you. I'd sue him for mental anguish, and make him pay through the nose, or where it used to be," she added, glancing with a shudder at the skull of Mr. Bland.

"Look here," said Sam Crawford. "Stop panning our friend, even if he is a skeleton." But Mr. Bland at that moment was beyond panning. Having consumed nearly all of one of the new bottles, he now found himself overcome with a desire to sleep. Accordingly he staggered over to the studio couch and collapsed clatteringly upon it.

"Is he dead or just asleep?" asked Flora.

"That's difficult to say," replied Chunk Walling. "You can't very well feel a skeleton's pulse."

"I don't want to feel any part of him," said Lulu.

"Let's get dressed and go downstairs," Elaine suggested. "Can't have any fun with a dead or drunken skeleton at one's elbow."

"The couch is all his," agreed Lulu. "I hope he never wakes up."

"All right," said Crawford. "We'll blow for the time being."

A few minutes later Mr. Bland's five companions slipped noiselessly from the room. Flora was thoughtful enough to place the remaining bottle within easy reach of the couch.

"Now," she said, "if he happens to wake up he won't come barging downstairs in search of a drink."

Then she switched off the light and quietly left the room.

"God protect us," she informed the others in a low voice. "I think he's snoring a little."

CHAPTER 3.

THE WHITTLES ARE NOT ALARMED

Nearly an hour later Mr. Bland awoke.

Sleep had neither improved his appearance nor refreshed his soul, if a skeleton can be said to possess a soul. From the adjoining room a shaft of light streamed in through the half-opened door. His companions, Mr. Bland decided, were in there enjoying themselves. A sleeping skeleton had probably cramped their style. Accordingly, they had shifted the scene of their unhallowed operations, leaving him quite alone and in comparative darkness.

Sitting on the edge of the couch, Quintus Bland began to feel no end sorry for himself. He was cut off from all human contacts. He was one man against the world. He was not even that. He was an unsightly structure of bones unfit for any strata of society this side of the grave. Also, he was far from sober. He tried to rest his elbows on his knees. The result was not satisfactory. His elbows kept sliding off the bony ridges. When he attempted to clutch his distracted head in his hands, the hollow sound his skull gave forth made him shiver in every bone.

"Firecrackers," he muttered. "My skull is full of firecrackers. I hate myself from head to foot."

Perhaps, he mused, if he put on some clothes he might appear more acceptable in the eyes of his fellow men. This might even apply to women, which was much more important. He desperately desired female companionship. He desperately desired his wife, Lorna, but she, the jade, was out somewhere disporting herself licentiously in her black underwear with the lace on it.

This disturbing reflection drove him up from the couch. Women were never able to keep a good thing to themselves. Buy them lovely underthings and they promptly tuck them away for an occasion more interesting than a mere husband. Engaged in these profitless reflections, he passed into the next room. This he found deserted save for a huddled bundle of bedclothing which looked as if it might be concealing an equally huddled body.

Mr. Bland refrained from investigating. In his present condition he felt a little delicate about arousing a slumbering person. The shock might prove too great for an alcoholic heart. Instead he set about searching for his hastily abandoned garments. How terribly things had turned out. Just as he had been about to find consolation in the arms of a beautiful woman this thing had happened. In the twinkling of an eye the beautiful woman had been equally in need of consolation herself. In spite of his unalluring appearance Bland could not help being slightly amused by the memory. What a trying situation. Lulu had accused him of wearing a wig. A wig indeed. For once a woman had been guilty of understatement. No doubt the recollection of her close shave would cure the wench for ever of interest in light alliance. But women were hard to discourage. He hoped so.

In the act of dragging his drawers from beneath a pile of clothes Mr. Bland was arrested by the sound of a voice. Considering the circumstances, it was a surprisingly mild voice. It addressed Mr. Bland with the casualness of a boon companion. Even as he listened, the thought flashed through his mind that the speaker must have lived for years in close association with skeletons.

"I beg your pardon," said the voice. "Would you mind telling me if I am having the disagreeable distinction of watching a skeleton holding a pair of drawers?"

Quintus Bland turned and gazed on the large pale face of a perfect stranger. Written on this innocent countenance was an expression of intense concentration from which all traces of fear were amazingly absent.

"Yes," replied Mr. Bland. "I'm afraid you are. Why do you ask?"

"Why do I ask?" repeated the man on the bed. "Wouldn't you ask? Isn't some small scrap of explanation due me? What, my dear sir, would you do if you were suddenly confronted by a skeleton holding a pair of drawers?"

"I don't know," faltered Mr. Bland, "but I don't think I'd stop long enough to ask many questions."

"Probably not," reflected the stranger, "but I'm locked in, and you're standing between me and that other door."

"Would you like to leave?" asked Mr. Bland.

"Not if you remain calm," replied the man. "Not if you act within reason. Of course," he continued, thoughtfully, "a man in my position doesn't often run into this sort of thing."

"Of course not," agreed Mr. Bland. "There are few positions in which a man does run into this sort of thing."

"I can't think of any," said the stranger. "Not that I haven't seen lots of bones in my time—a skull here and a thigh there. Once while visiting a museum I was far from pleased by the skeleton of a dinosaur, but he had been extinct for some time, and, I suspect, part of him had been filled in—like a broken fence."

"I don't follow you," remarked Mr. Bland.

"Neither do I," replied the man. "I rarely if ever do. But please remain reasonable. You are the first real skeleton I've ever had any dealings with."

"Do you mind?" asked Mr. Bland.

"Not at all," replied the man. "I'm relieved you're not a pink monkey or a blue dragon or a flock of loathsome reptiles. I've seen all of those things in my time, but I like the last least. They upset me terribly."

"They do me, too," Mr. Bland agreed. "I think they're even harder to bear than skeletons, don't you?"

"Far," said the stranger. "Much. But you're not any cinch. Are you a domesticated apparition or do you stalk by night?"

"Tell me," asked Mr. Bland, "aren't you more than a little drunk?"

"I am," admitted the man. "But I don't know how much more. I'd like to get lots."

"So would I," agreed Quintus Bland, and there was no mistaking his sincerity. "I haven't been a skeleton long, you know."

"You've been one long enough," declared the stranger. "A little of a skeleton goes a long way with me."

"You know," Mr. Bland suggested, "I might look more like myself if I put on some clothes. What do you think?"

"Not knowing what you looked like to begin with," said the stranger, "it would be hard for me to say."

"I wasn't so bad," Mr. Bland observed rather wistfully.

"You mean, so bad as you are now?" asked the man. "That would hardly be possible. However, if you wear clothes they'd have to be perfectly tailored. And then again you'd have to catch the tailor. Even if you succeeded in cornering him—getting him at bay, so to speak—his hands would be shaking so he'd be quite unable to measure your bones with any degree of accuracy."

"You do love to run on," remarked Quintus Bland. "Do you think my old clothes would bag on me?"

"They wouldn't look smart," the other replied. "And a man in your position can't afford to make a bad impression."

"No," agreed Mr. Bland. "I should try to look my best. Anything would look better than a skeleton though."

"Almost," admitted the stranger. "Except loathsome reptiles."

"I dare say my old clothes would fall off my body," Mr. Bland reflected aloud.

"Your bones," corrected the man, who was evidently a stickler for accuracy. "You might tie 'em on with bits of string, though. You wouldn't look exactly natty, but you might succeed through sheer charm. You might even become the vogue."

"You're too optimistic," declared Mr. Bland. "A man in my condition gets scant opportunity to exercise his charm. People don't wait long enough."

"I can well understand that," said the other. "I'm only standing you myself because I might easily be seeing much worse sights—loathsome reptiles, for instance. They always get the best of me."

"By the way," Mr. Bland inquired, "speaking of reptiles, have you seen anything of my friends?

"Have you any friends?" asked the stranger in a surprised voice. "It seems hardly possible."

"I guess I haven't," Bland said, bitterly. "When a man loses his flesh his friends disappear with it."

"When a man loses as much flesh as you have," observed the stranger, "more things disappear than friends."

For a few moments the skeleton and the man considered in silence the various losses sustained by the former. At last the stranger looked up.

"Skeleton," he said, "is there a drink in that next room? A little something might do us both a world of good."

"Don't call me skeleton," protested Quintus Bland. "It sounds so bald."

"But you are bald, skeleton," the stranger insisted. "You're about the baldest object I've ever seen. There's not a hair left anywhere. How did you come to die?"

"What!" exclaimed Quintus Bland. "Good God, man, I'm not dead."

"Oh, aren't you?" replied the stranger. "I wouldn't mind if you were, you know. Even that would be better than loathsome reptiles, the appalling creatures. But if you're not dead, this situation is even odder than I thought. You should be, you know."

"I almost wish I were," muttered Mr. Bland. The stranger on the bed pondered over this for a while.

"Skeleton," he said at last, "to return once more to that drink: is there any in that next room?"

"I'll look," Bland answered, impatiently, "but I do wish you'd stop calling me just simply skeleton like that. It makes me feel so—so removed."

"Then what shall I call you?" the stranger asked, equably.

"My correct name is Bland," Mr. Bland replied. "Quintus Bland. Possibly you may have heard of me."

"I have," declared the stranger. "You're the photographer chap. Your people took a picture of my wife once. It gave her young ideas."

"Did it do her justice?" asked Quintus Bland, his professional interest overcoming his low spirits for the moment.

"More than," said the stranger, briefly. "Much. That picture ruined her morals—not that she ever had any."

"Sorry," remarked Mr. Bland. "My wife has young ideas, too."

"They're not so good when they get that way," the man on the bed confided. "And they never seem to realize how silly they're making themselves as well as their husbands." He paused to scratch his thin, rather washed-out-looking hair. "Wives are awful, anyway," he resumed. "I suspect mine is having me incarcerated in here simply because I got too drunk to sit on my chair."

"It wasn't a bad idea," observed Mr. Bland.

"But poorly executed," replied the stranger. "She should have stood by to keep me company. How do I know what she's doing?"

"I hate to think of what mine's doing," said Mr. Bland, sombrely. "She left me flat for another man."

"Is that why you turned to a skeleton?" asked the stranger. "Or did she leave you flat because you had turned to one already?"

"A person can't turn to a skeleton," Bland retorted, "just because his wife leaves him flat."

"I can't," admitted the stranger, "but I thought maybe you could just to spite her, you know."

"That," declared Quintus Bland, "would be as bad as cutting off your nose to spite your face."

"It would be even worse," commented the stranger. "You've cut off lots more than your nose.

"I'll look for some drink," said Mr. Bland a little coldly.

"Do, skeleton, do," urged the stranger. "If you bring old Whittle a drink he'll never forget you—not that he ever could."

"Is that your name?" asked Mr. Bland, pausing in the door to the next room. "Is it Whittle?"

"It is," admitted the gentleman on the bed. "That's actually my name, and I think it's quite a funny one. The first part is Claude, but that's not so funny. In fact, it's very disgusting."

"They're both funny," observed Mr. Bland, switching on the light in the adjoining room. "Mine are funny, too. Quintus is a very poor name even for a skeleton." His voice trailed away as he glanced about the room. "Whittle," he called out in a happier voice than he had used for some time, "I've discovered a whole bottle. We seem to be in luck."

"We seem to be," said Mr. Whittle when Bland appeared with the bottle, "but I'm not at all sure. There seems to be someone at that door. Will you see to it?"

Mr. Bland cast a look of pitying contempt at the man on the bed.

"How would you like to open a door in the face of a grinning skull?" he coldly inquired.

"Are you grinning?" asked Mr. Whittle, greatly interested. "Your skull looks awful but expressionless to me."

"Does it matter?" demanded Bland. "Would you like to have this skull thrust in your face?"

"A thousand times no," declared Mr. Whittle. "Better that, however, than the skull of a loathsome reptile."

"To hell with your loathsome reptiles," clicked Mr. Bland.

"All right," retorted the man on the bed, childishly annoyed. "I hope yours burn to a crisp."

The sound of a key turning in the lock took the two gentlemen's minds off their respective loathsome reptiles. Mr. Bland turned and gazed into the eyes of a strikingly good-looking woman. She was tall and reasonably slim. Studying her somewhat avid lips, Mr. Bland received the impression that there were few experiences of the pleasanter nature that this fair creature had not tried at least once.

"Gracious goodness," murmured Mr. Whittle, observing the woman's bellicose expression. "This is much worse than a loathsome reptile, skeleton."

After glancing chillily for a moment at the two men, the woman advanced into the room, slamming the door behind her.

"Whittle," she said in a hard flat voice which seems to be automatically endowed upon all wives the moment the ring is on their finger, "Whittle," she repeated, "what are you doing with this repellent-looking object in your room?"

"Nothing at all, my dear," mildly replied Mr. Whittle. "Nothing at all. Simply chatting, you know. Don't you notice anything odd about him— different?"

"Everything's odd about him," said the woman. "It's disgraceful. Can't I leave you alone for a moment without your taking up with some abominable freak of nature?"

"But," pursued her husband, hopefully, "aren't you a little bit scared? He's a real skeleton, you know—fresh from the grave."

"Whittle," said the woman, "you should know me better. Why should I be scared by a measly collection of bones? How did he get in here to begin with?"

"Quite casually," replied Mr. Whittle. "Just dropped in, you know."

"You're incoherent," she said, briefly; then, turning on Mr. Bland, "Well, sir, what have you to say for yourself?"

"What would you like me to say?" he asked.

"As little as possible," replied the woman. "I don't care for the way your teeth click. Is it necessary?"

"Always with skeletons," said Mr. Bland.

"Then why don't you return to the morgue," she demanded, "and pick up some more suitable companions? I can't have my husband associating with a thing like you—not while he's still alive, at least, which I hope will not be long."

"But I'm not dead myself," objected Quintus Bland. "I'm quite as alive as he is."

"Which isn't saying a lot," she observed. "What have you got in that bottle?"

"Drink," said Mr. Bland.

"That's something, at any rate," the woman conceded. "It would be better if we drank. You've nullified the libations of an entire evening."

"By the way," interposed the man on the bed, "you two haven't been properly introduced yet. Mr. Bland, this is Pauline, my wife. Pauline, this is what is left of Mr. Bland, Mr. Quintus Bland. He's the swagger photographer chappie."

"He should have a picture of himself now," observed Pauline Whittle. "If he could induce anybody to take one."

"I don't want a picture of myself," retorted Mr. Bland. "I'd tear it up. However," he added, gallantly, "when I see such a beautiful woman as you I greatly regret so much of my former self is absent."

"What do you suppose he means by that?" Whittle inquired, uneasily.

"I'd hate to explain," his wife replied, "but I gather Mr. Bland is not quite as dead as he looks."

This time she turned with more favor on the skeleton and accepted a drink from the clawlike hand.

"Here's to the speedy return of my flesh," proclaimed Mr. Bland, raising his glass aloft.

"What for?" asked Whittle, suspiciously. "Are you by any chance making passes at my wife?"

"Whittle," said Pauline Whittle, "don't be jealous of a skeleton. I assure you it's quite impossible even if I were interested. Mr. Bland is as sexless as a retired madam."

"I don't understand how he even sees," Mr. Whittle replied. "He hasn't any eyes, yet he doesn't miss a trick."

"What do you use for eyes, Mr. Bland?" asked Pauline. "There isn't one in your head."

"Search me," replied Mr. Bland.

"That wouldn't be hard," put in Whittle, "but it would be damned unpleasant."

"I know," thoughtfully agreed Pauline, "if this skeleton has invisible eyes he may all be present though unseen."

"Are you interested?" asked her husband, coldly.

"Not greatly," retorted his wife. "I was merely wondering about it, that's all."

"I wouldn't if I were you," replied Whittle. "It's hardly a proper line of speculation for a married woman, or a single one, for that matter."

"Well, one would like to know where one has one's skeleton," remarked Pauline Whittle.

"You don't need to have him by anything," snapped her husband. "Leave him entirely alone."

"Let's have another drink," Quintus Bland suggested. "I object to this conversation."

"So do I," agreed Mr. Whittle. "Isn't it just like a woman? Never willing to let well enough alone."

"But I don't see what's so well enough about him," Pauline objected. "As far as I can see he's sheer waste of time."

"Your wife appears to possess a romantic disposition," Mr. Bland observed dryly.

"The correct word is 'bawdy,'" replied Mr. Whittle. "Romance to her is strictly horizontal."

"How would you have it?" asked Mr. Bland.

"Oh, don't ask me," snapped the man on the bed irritably. "You're both lewd persons. Don't go on about it."

"I'm not usually lewd," observed Mr. Bland, "but being a skeleton seems to bring out the worst that's in me."

"What's in you?" Pauline Whittle asked, quickly.

"Mr. Bland," interposed her husband, "she's lower than a loathsome reptile. Will you please pull some trousers over those fleshless legs of yours? They seem to be exerting some obscene influence over this bestial wife of mine. I'm so glad I'm sober."

Pauline Whittle laughed coarsely.

"None of us is sober," she cried, taking another drink. "Let's jump in bed with Blandie."

"You must be drunk," said her husband, "if you can even entertain the idea of jumping into bed with that."

"I mean you, too," Pauline explained. *"En masse* like—you know—loathsome reptiles together."

"Oh, you're very drunk," declared Mr. Whittle. "Very drunk indeed. What difference would that make?"

"That's up to you," said Pauline. "Couldn't we huddle up together and leave the world behind?"

"Hear me," declared Mr. Whittle in a decided tone of voice. "If I huddle up with that skeleton I'd leave more than the world behind."

At this the skeleton giggled. It was a peculiar sound.

"Then let's yank on his trousers," suggested Mrs. Whittle.

"They wouldn't stay on," said Mr. Bland.

"Then a necktie would," put in Pauline. "It would dangle from his spine."

"Wouldn't that spoil the effect?" asked her husband.

"Not as much as trousers," observed his wife. "If you yank trousers on that skeleton you'll be spoiling one of the most astonishing effects I've ever witnessed."

"But I fully intend to get dressed all over," Quintus Bland assured them. "From head to foot."

"What about your face?" asked Mr. Whittle. "No matter how smartly dressed you are, that face will cause a panic."

"Why not put a mask over it?" suggested his wife.

"A pillowcase would be better," said Mr. Whittle. "A pillowcase with slits for his funny eyes."

"It would cover his lower jaw," agreed Pauline, "and, God knows, that jaw needs covering."

"Sometimes when it wags at me," solemnly observed Mr. Whittle, "I feel too discouraged to answer."

"It's good we don't mind this skeleton," declared his wife. "I mean not much. I like him because he's so unattainable."

The whisky which Mr. Bland had been drinking so copiously now began to manifest itself in tears. He was deeply touched by the friendship of these two strangers. At the same time he was sorry for himself. Silently the tears streamed down his bony face. With intense interest his two companions concentrated their blunted faculties on the sobbing skeleton. Even in this fuddled condition this phenomenon was somewhat baffling.

"Where do they come from," Pauline asked In a hushed voice, "all those tears? I don't see any ducts."

"Ducks?" inquired her husband, stupidly. "What's all this about ducks?"

"There's nothing at all about ducks," said his wife. "There are no ducks."

"I didn't ask for any ducks in the first place," Mr. Whittle replied in a hurt voice. "A tearful skeleton is quite enough to bear."

"I said ducts, not ducks," Pauline Whittle retorted.

"Oh," exclaimed Mr. Whittle. "You mean tear ducts. They haven't any feathers." For a moment he considered Mr. Bland. "You know," he resumed, "this skeleton is more versatile than I thought. If he has hidden ducts —I mean, if tears can come out of his eyes—he might have other ducts and things concealed about his person. He might even —"

"Please," protested Mr. Bland. "For goodness' sake, don't go on."

Having thus rebuked Mr. Whittle's sordid curiosity, Quintus Bland arose and walked with a certain show of dignity from the room. The man on the bed looked significantly at his wife.

After an interval, Mr. Bland, swaying slightly in his gait, returned to the room.

"Well?" inquired Mr. Whittle.

The skeleton nodded briefly.

"I must have," was all he said, "or something."

"How intriguing," murmured Pauline Whittle.

"It shouldn't be to you," snapped Mr. Whittle. "Don't think about it."

"I can't help myself," said Pauline, simply.

"Please pass that bottle and stop discussing my probable parts," Mr. Bland cut in, reprovingly. "I find it most disconcerting."

"Then tell me," asked Mrs. Whittle, "do you like to dance?"

"In my present mood I'd like to do anything," he told her.

"Well, see that you stop at dancing," said Mr. Whittle.

"For the present, at least," agreed Pauline. "One must grow acclimatized to a skeleton; even to such a gifted one as Mr. Bland. Would one call him a skeleton of parts?"

"I wouldn't," replied Mr. Whittle, "but I dare say you would, and consider yourself amusing."

"Shall I get dressed now?" asked Mr. Bland.

"We'll help you," replied Pauline.

"He'll need it," said Mr. Whittle, rising from the bed.

They put shoes on Mr. Bland's feet and stuffed them to fit with old pieces of paper.

Mr. Whittle was busy strapping the trousers round Mr. Bland's thighbones.

"I think they call this the pelvis," observed Whittle. "It looks like a pelvis."

"Don't waste any more time naming me," protested Mr. Bland. "You're not giving a lecture on the bony structure of man."

Next came the shirt and collar. The coat was held sketchily in place by bits of string. Finally a pillowcase with slits in it was dropped over his head.

"There," exclaimed Pauline, stepping back to observe the results of their joint efforts. "You don't look much like a man, I'll confess, but no one would know you were a skeleton unless some woman gets too friendly."

Whittle dubiously shook his head.

"That hardly seems possible," he said.

"You can't be sure," replied his wife. "Some women are morbidly attracted by sheer horror."

"Thank you both so much," cut in Quintus Bland, acidly. "After all your kind words I won't even trouble about looking at myself in the glass. Is the bottle empty?"

"It is," replied Pauline.

"And you emptied it," said her husband. "Let's go."

Taking the weird figure by either arm, they proceeded unsteadily towards the door. Here Mr. Bland halted.

"I haven't any drawers on," he said.

"Neither have I," Pauline informed him, "and you don't hear me complaining."

CHAPTER 4.

PANIC IN A NIGHT CLUB

"To think," breathed Mr. Whittle in the hallway, his mild eyes growing round with realization, "to think," he continued, "that we're actually going to sit at a table with a real live skeleton. It should be enough, my dear, to make us forget our differences. It should draw us together—sort of, what?"

"I don't know about that," vouchsafed Pauline, "but if Quinnie falls down that flight of stairs nothing will draw him together. He'll resemble a jigsaw puzzle."

Mr. Bland shuddered at this and pictured himself in fragments. It was not inspiriting. His clutch tightened on the banister.

"And all the king's horses and all the king's men," cheerfully quoted Mr. Whittle.

"Wouldn't dare approach him," announced Pauline. "Quinnie is the very antithesis of Humpty Dumpty. More awful."

"Yet equally fragile," commented Mr. Whittle.

"I can't understand how some persons can be so callous," observed Mr. Bland, "so utterly blind to the misery of others. In fact, they seem to enjoy it."

"We're not enjoying you," Pauline Whittle answered him. "We're doing our darnedest to tolerate you. And that takes some doing."

Suddenly Mr. Bland stopped and stood swaying perilously on the stairs as he held up for their inspection a pair of bony hands.

"My poor hands," he muttered brokenly. "My poor, poor hands. Look at them."

"They're awful," admitted Mr. Whittle. "Don't rattle them under my nose."

"And my trousers," continued Bland. "They feel as if they were going to drop off at every step. What if they did?"

"What if they do?" replied Pauline. "It would take an expert to establish your sex."

"It's his pelvis," explained Mr. Whittle. "In life he must have been able to whirl on a dime."

"In life!" exclaimed Quintus Bland. "Hang it all, man, I keep telling you I'm far from dead."

"Perhaps you're not as far as you think," Mrs. Whittle remarked, enigmatically. "You've merely anticipated the worm."

Once more Mr. Bland shuddered.

"And," he said, bitterly, turning on the woman, "as far as my sex is concerned, I wish you'd leave it entirely alone."

"I don't want any part of it," Pauline emphatically assured him.

"Oh, very well," replied Mr. Bland, a trifle tiffed by this unflattering announcement. "If that's the way you feel about it, we'll let my sex drop."

"Can't you two ever stop bickering about sex?" Mr. Whittle complained, wearily. "Let's get on with it. I'm parched for a drink."

"So am I," agreed his wife. "Perhaps if we feed this skeleton he might begin to grow some flesh."

"But what about my hands and trousers?" persisted Quintus Bland.

"I have it!" exclaimed Mr. Whittle. "If he put his hands in his pockets and sort of sauntered carelessly—you know, lounged along—he'd be able to hold up his pants and at the same time hide his hands. Two birds with one stone."

"Whittle," said his wife, an unfamiliar note of approval in her voice, "I never suspected I'd accept any suggestion coming from you, but that one is almost inspired. Try it, Mr. Bland."

The fleshless photographer balanced himself carefully against the banister and thrust his hands in the pockets of his trousers.

"How's that?" he asked, a little self-consciously.

"Terrible," replied Pauline Whittle. "Simply awful. It won't work at all. The absence of your stomach becomes much too apparent." She snapped open her handbag and produced a pair of white wash gloves. "Here," she continued. "Try these on. You look so unusual already, it really doesn't matter what you wear."

"Women's gloves," muttered Bland, unhappily, as he slipped them over his fleshless fingers. "To think I have come to this. How do the damned things look?"

Once more he held up his hands for their inspection.

"It's the final touch," said Mr. Whittle. "It makes the whole world mad. Let's proceed."

By careful if critical stages they descended the stairs and stood in the door of the dining-room. At one end was a long bar in full blast. In the middle of the room lay a small polished surface upon which a number of men and women were engaged in making a public demonstration of a strictly private operation. Shrill, meaningless laughter cut through a hanging pall of smoke. The ceiling was low and the voices were high. The results of the Noble Experiment were being consumed openly and in great gulps.

"You know," said Mr. Bland, in a low voice, "when I watch all those people swigging down that poison I understand why this country is called the land of the free and the home of the brave. It takes guts to do it."

"That's what puzzles me about you," replied Pauline. "I don't see where you put it. You haven't any —"

"Don't go on," Mr. Bland interrupted, with dignity. "We'll let them drop, too, together with my sex."

The entrance of the Whittles, flanking the extraordinary figure of Mr. Bland, did not pass unnoticed. In their vicinity conversation died down. The diners at the tables became all eyes. At a table in the far corner of the room Mr. Bland's previous companions sat up and considered the figure apprehensively.

"Gord," breathed Lulu, penetrating Mr. Bland's disguise. "It's his nibs. If he happens to catch sight of us he might try to pull some funny stuff."

"That guy," declared Flora, "couldn't pull anything funny if he tried, but he might pull something very, very nasty."

"That's what I mean," said Lulu. "It wouldn't take much from him to make me throw a fit. Wonder who his playmates are?"

"Don't know," replied Crawford, moodily, "but they've shown more courage than we did. After all, old Quintus is a friend of ours, with or without flesh. We should have stuck by him."

In the meantime, while the ethics of their treatment of Mr. Bland was under discussion, Bland himself was busy with his trousers, which were showing an alarming inclination to make startling revelations. Fortunately this difficulty so occupied his thoughts that he was momentarily unaware of his surroundings and the unpleasant impression he was making on all beholders. While Pauline was regarded with admiration, the glances directed at him were eloquent with astonishment and disgust. Mr. Whittle was scarcely observed at all. He was merely another male of indifferent aspect.

However, he appeared to have a way with head waiters, an irreproachable specimen of which immaculate clan imperturbably escorted them to a highly desirable table on the border of the gleaming dance floor. Mr. Bland tenderly lowered himself into a chair and peered unhappily at life through his pillowcase.

"Why didn't he put us out there right in the middle of the floor?" he asked, ungraciously. "Then everyone could have had a look."

"Don't mind him," Pauline explained smoothly to Charles, the head waiter. "He's paying off an election bet, and I, for one, think he's showing a very mean spirit about it."

"He could be showing much worse," observed her husband.

The head waiter smiled sympathetically.

"If you'll pardon me," he murmured, "I can hardly blame the gentleman. I have never seen anything quite equal to it before. His costume is most impressive."

"The man means revolting," snapped Quintus Bland. "I know how I look."

"I doubt if his mother would know him," said Mr. Whittle.

"I doubt if she'd care to," said his wife, Pauline.

"Not even his wife would know him," continued Mr. Whittle.

"In a place like this," remarked Charles, "there are certain advantages in that."

Pauline let her gaze drift round the tables circling the dance floor. Finally it rested on a couple occupying a table directly opposite them.

"Charles," she said to the head waiter, "who is that small good-looking blonde on the other side of the floor?"

But Charles was never given the opportunity to answer. Mr. Bland, having followed the direction of Pauline's casual gaze, had half risen from his chair. In his need for emotional expression his teeth were clicking together like a sewing machine in full cry. It was a terrible exhibition. Even Charles, as accustomed as he was to terrible exhibitions, felt himself deeply moved. Mr. Bland, apparently stifling for lack of breath, was clutching frantically at the pillowcase in a mad endeavor to bare his skull to the world. Equally determined that no such horrifying revelation should be made, Pauline Whittle and her husband were clinging grimly to the edges of the pillow-case, and so successful were their joint efforts that, by the sheer weight of their bodies, Quintus Bland was borne off center and crumpled clatteringly back in his chair. There he sat puffing, panting, and chattering so vigorously that the pillowcase billowed and surged like a sail flapping in a stiff breeze.

"By God," he gibbered at last, "that woman's my wife, and she's wearing black underwear with lace on it."

"Look here," said Pauline, "in addition to your other quaint ways, have you also X-ray eyes? How do you know she's wearing black underwear with lace on it?"

"She told me so herself," muttered Mr. Bland.

"But couldn't she have changed her underwear?" Mr. Whittle inquired, mildly. "People do, you know."

"Don't quibble," snapped Mr. Bland. "I'm going to polish off that chap with her. His name is Phil Harkens."

"Remember your pelvis," warned Mr. Whittle. "You don't want to lose your pants."

"To hell with my pants and my pelvis," retorted Mr. Bland.

"Do you feel that way about them when you're a whole man?" asked Pauline Whittle.

"What's that to you?" was the discourteous reply.

"Is there anything I can do?" put in Charles in a polished but puzzled voice.

"Yes," said Mr. Whittle. "Six double brandies, Charles. My friend has a bit of a chill."

"Has he also a cold in his head?" asked Charles, looking thoughtfully at the pillowcase.

"Yes," replied Pauline, "and the poor thing is as bald as a bat. We have to keep him out of draughts."

"By rights," said Mr. Whittle, "he should be home and in bed."

"By rights," amended his wife in a low voice, "he should be mouldering in his grave."

"Enough of that," clicked Mr. Bland. "I'll murder the whole room— everybody!"

"What a man," said Whittle, feebly. "I fear for the success of our evening."

"As long as that sheik of the suburbs is with my wife," asserted Mr. Bland, "the evening is busted wide open."

With a clever, appraising scrutiny, Pauline Whittle considered the gentleman under discussion.

"Can't say that I blame you," she commented at last. "I know the type. He's one of those strong, confident men, the overpowering sort. If there's a springboard handy he'll swan-dive and jack-knife for you *ad nauseam*. I hate their guts, myself."

"Pauline," interposed her husband, "are you deliberately trying to egg our friend on?"

"No," replied Pauline, "but I wouldn't much mind."

"He owns an aeroplane," said Quintus, moodily. "I haven't any aeroplanes."

"Neither have we," Pauline told him, soothingly. "But, of course, he would have one—the rugged bum."

"Pauline," protested her husband, "your language—it's lousy."

"I'll endeavor to model it after yours," said Pauline, sweetly.

While this marital exchange was in progress, Quintus Bland relaxed a little in his chair, but his gaze still remained fixed on his wife and her hateful companion. She was the prettiest woman in the room, he decided. There was no doubt about that. Why did they always have to quarrel so? he wondered. And why did she have to bring home that objectionable daub of a cow in convulsions? That painting had started all the fireworks. Had it not been for that shocking example of bad taste they might still be at home together, enjoying a pleasant evening. For his part, he did not want any other woman. He was perfectly satisfied with her, provided that she revised both her habits and her temperament a little. Then he suddenly remembered his condition. A feeling of utter hopelessness overcame him. He would have to revise himself more than a little to be acceptable in the eyes of Lorna. Even his dog would object to him, not to mention that passionate maid, Fanny. As he watched his wife through the pillowcase, the conviction was gradually borne in on him that she was not having the jolliest of evenings. Even a stranger could tell that the couple were not hitting it off any too well together. Phil Harkens, a splendidly proportioned he-man with glossy dark brown hair, was talking to Lorna with the confidence and complacency begotten of his awareness of his strength and beauty.

Lorna was doing her best to look as if she were listening while thinking of other things. From her politely bored expression it was not difficult to gather she was finding the deception irksome. Of course, had the lady been aware of the fact that her husband was observing her from across the way, she would have fawned upon her companion, hung on his slightest word; but believing, as she did, that she was no longer able to torment her long-legged mate, the situation was robbed of its spice. After an evening spent in the company of Phil Harkens she was beginning to realize that he was God's own gift to hard-pressed matrons who were themselves over-anxious to give. Lorna was growing up. She longed to return home and have even a better fight with her husband. In spite of his faults, there was something different about him, something that set him apart from other men. She suspected it was an inherited streak of madness. A reminiscent smile momentarily touched her lips. She was hearing her husband saying, "And not content with that, I disembowel the beast..." What a fool. The smile faded. She was sorry she had left him flat. In walking out on him she had taken an unfair advantage. It would have been more loyal to stay at home and fight it out to a finish. She would have won anyway. She always did. He was such a simple-minded dolt she could always confuse the issue without his realizing the fact.

"Pardon me," she said sweetly to Harkens, "it's so noisy here. What were you saying?"

"I was saying," replied Harkens, "that a husband is a fool to expect a beautiful woman to confine herself entirely to him. It just isn't being done. Wives are waking up."

"How true. How true," murmured Lorna. "All over the world wives are waking up. Some of them are even getting up, don't you think?"

"And returning home to virtuous couches," said Harkens with a nasty grin.

Observing this grin, Mr. Bland grunted unpleasantly in his pillowcase.

"She's having tough sledding," he said to his companions. "The trouble with that woman is, she doesn't realize she adores me."

"That's the trouble with all wives after the first few months," Mr. Whittle heavily asserted. "Take Pauline here. She's mad about me, simply mad. If I died, I doubt if she'd ever marry again. It would be a terrible blow to her. As it is, though, the poor creature isn't intelligent enough to analyze her own emotions."

With pitying contempt in her eyes, Pauline regarded the speaker.

"Not excluding this ass of a skeleton," she said with great clarity, "I have the most repellent and all-around worthless husband yet unpoisoned. An error," she added, "I hope to rectify at the earliest possible moment."

"Don't trouble yourself, my dear," declared Whittle with a bland smile as he reached for a double brandy. "I'll poison myself for you— pleasantly. Here's to your weeds."

One gulp and the brandy was gone. Pauline followed his example. Before they were able to stop him, Mr. Bland had raised his pillowcase and tossed a drink through his fleshless lips. A girl at the next table emitted a low, gurgling gasp of horror, then slid from her chair to the floor.

Mr. Bland cocked his pillowcase in the direction of the crumpled body and peered at it through the slits.

"What did she want to pop off like that for?" he asked the Whittles. "Makes me nervous to have women popping off. Wonder what's the matter with the poor creature."

"You are," said Pauline, coldly.

"What do you mean?" Mr. Bland demanded.

"The next time you take a drink," the lady explained, rather wearily, "please be so good as to slip it up under the pillowcase instead of disclosing to the world that shocking object that serves for a head."

"Oh," muttered Quintus Bland, a trifle taken back, "was that what did it? I didn't realize."

This time, when he took his brandy, he followed Pauline's advice. His white-gloved hand, clutching the glass, disappeared under the pillowcase, which for a moment became a thing of life, then the hand and glass reappeared. From the pillowcase came the muffled sound of lips being smacked as if in satisfaction.

"That's good," grunted Quintus Bland. "Get some more."

"What I'd like to know," said Mr. Whittle, addressing himself to his wife, "is how he can smack his lips when he hasn't any lips to smack?"

"I'm afraid I can't help you there," Mrs. Whittle told her husband, "but I wish he wouldn't do it."

"Don't know how I did it myself," Mr. Bland informed them. "Just felt like smacking my lips and there you are. That's all there is to it. They smacked."

"We heard them," said Pauline Whittle, briefly.

The young lady who had been privileged to catch a glimpse of Mr. Bland's skull had by this time been restored to her chair. She was now reclining limply in it, her eyes studiously averted from the hooded figure at the next table. She told things to her escort in a low strained voice which, nevertheless, conveyed conviction. When this gentleman had heard the reason for her sudden collapse, he drank deeply, then drank again. With an expression of resolution, he turned to Mr. Whittle.

"Pardon me," said the gentleman, "but may I ask if that—er— synthetic-looking object under the pillowcase is real or just fun? What I mean to say, is it alive?"

"Unfortunately it is," replied Mr. Whittle, "and it's no fun. But why do you ask?"

"Well," continued the gentleman in a troubled voice, "this young lady says there's a skull under that pillowcase. That's why she fainted, she claims. It grinned at her—horribly."

The pillowcase suddenly became agitated, and a voice issued therefrom.

"It's a lie," said the voice. "A lie. I couldn't grin if I tried. I can't even smirk."

"How much has the lady been drinking?" asked Mr. Whittle, with an un-called-for lack of tact.

Naturally this remark was not well received by the lady's companion. His troubled expression was replaced by one of intense hostility.

"Do you mean to imply that this young lady has been drinking too much?" he demanded.

"That would be the more charitable view to take of her astonishing allega-tion," replied Mr. Whittle with the courage of two double brandies. "Otherwise she must be insane—plain crazy."

The young lady's defender stiffened in his chair. His eyes began to boggle with anger. Chivalry was gripped tightly in his large fists. Mr. Whittle watched these warlike manifestations with a kindling eye.

"Come on. Come on," he challenged. "Hit me a crack. I'd love it."

At this stage in the controversy Quintus Bland deemed it necessary to inter-vene. Leaning over to the unreasonably enraged Whittle, he rapped him sharply on the shoulder.

"Ugh," came from Mr. Whittle as he shrank back. "Don't do that. Don't do it. Your fingers are like rivets."

"I'll handle this little matter," Bland told him with great composure. "That person will have to answer to me for his unwarranted conduct. Observe."

Both Pauline Whittle and her husband did observe. They were well rewarded for the restraint they placed on their own actions. Yet what Mr. Bland did was in no way spectacular. He merely removed his gloves and shook his fleshless fingers in the face of the gentleman at the next table. From beneath the pillowcase issued a succession of low, hollow groans mingling with the chattering of teeth. Even the imperturbable Pauline admitted later that she had never heard a more depressing sound.

On this occasion it was the young lady's escort who slid from his chair to the floor, but he didn't even want to gurgle. One shocked, petrified look at those crazily shaking hands had started him on his downward course. The groan had finished him off. As he slid from his chair his girl friend with a choking gasp tossed the tablecloth over her head and followed him to the floor, upon which both bod-ies lay inert. Having more than achieved his purpose, Mr. Bland delicately adjust-ed the gloves on his talon-like fingers, then dashed off another brandy.

"How's that for a mere skeleton?" he asked, unable to repress a note of pride.

"Pretty darned good, I'd say," replied Mr. Whittle. "I'm glad you're on our side, because if you'd done that to me I'd be on the floor too."

Naturally, this little diversion did not pass unnoticed. A score of guests were peering stupidly at the fallen couple. Charles, the head waiter, was doing his stuff in another corner of the room. Even from the back of his neck one could tell he was smiling ingratiatingly and suggesting champagne. However, when he faced about at the whispered summons of a waiter, perturbation had replaced the smile. Swiftly he moved to the center of interest, where he stood looking down at the prostrate figures, a puzzled expression in his eyes. He had a dim suspicion that this unfortunate incident was in some way associated with that weird hooded figure at the next table. For a moment Charles was rattled. Seldom if ever had he seen a couple pass out simultaneously. Could it be a suicide pact? He glanced at the Whittles' table, to discover that Mr. Whittle was alone in his glory. His wife and the hooded figure were behaving queerly on the dance floor. Before Charles could think of anything useful to say, Mr. Whittle spoke impressively.

"Charles," he said, "isn't it about time you removed those objectionable persons? They have done their best to make our evening decidedly uncomfortable. Why don't you drag 'em out?"

"Sorry, Mr. Whittle," replied Charles, deferentially, "I had no idea they were getting that way. I'll have the bodies removed at once. Are they alive?"

The bodies themselves answered the question. The man sat up and looked fearfully about him, then, extending a shaking hand, violently shook the young lady.

"It's gone," he said in an unsteady voice. "Come on. Let's hurry."

The girl opened her eyes, uttered a piercing shriek, then flung herself on the man who, in his weakened and nervous condition, fell back on the floor with a gasp.

"What's gone?" asked the distracted Charles.

"Is this any time to ask questions?" the man managed to get out as he floundered on the floor. "Take this woman off me. She's trying to crawl into one of my pockets."

With the aid of several waiters the two struggling bodies were lifted from the floor and placed on the perpendicular, which they maintained with the utmost difficulty.

"Where is he?" asked the young lady. "Or whatever it was. Where is it?"

"Will you kindly explain, madam?" Charles almost pleaded.

"The man with the skeleton hands," said the girl. "He moaned and chattered his teeth."

At this moment a wild cry from the dance floor turned all eyes in that direction. Incredulously, they beheld the rear view of the hooded figure frantically endeavoring to pull a pair of trousers up over a bony structure which Mr. Whittle had dubbed a pelvis.

"It has more than skeleton hands," one onlooker remarked with a crude chuckle. "That object has a skeleton —"

The end of his observation was drowned in a babble of voices, which was just as well for those who objected to calling a spade a spade.

"What is it, Charles?" asked the lady. "What can it be?"

"Madam," he replied, wearily, "how should I know? I have never seen anything like it before."

"I hope never to see anything like it again," another voice declared, emphatically, "as God is my judge."

In the meantime Quintus Bland was having troubles of his own. So was Pauline Whittle. She was vainly struggling to drag her partner from the glaring publicity of the dance floor.

"Don't pull me like that," Mr. Bland was pleading. "If these trousers trip me up I'll smash to powder."

"I wish to God you would," Pauline assured him. "I'd love to blow you into oblivion."

Even in his dire circumstances Mr. Bland felt a thrill of horror. The possibility was by no means remote. How could this woman think of such things at a time like this?

"It's the knot," he explained. "Can't you see? We can't yank the trousers up without untying the knot."

"How do you mean we?" Pauline demanded. "I wouldn't drag my husband's trousers up, let alone a relative stranger's, and a skeleton's, at that."

"You don't have to go into it so," protested Mr. Bland. "Just untie the knot. I'll drag them up."

With hands that trembled Pauline Whittle grimly attempted to loosen the knot which was located just below her partner's pelvis.

"I mustn't go mad," she muttered. "I must remember to keep calm. Do stop clicking your kneebones together."

"I can't," replied Mr. Bland. "Never have I been so nervous."

"Whee!" said Pauline Whittle as another thought struck her. "Wouldn't it be shocking if you got your body back now?"

Mr. Bland stepped backward and snatched at his trousers.

"Don't come near me," he pleaded. "Keep your hands to yourself. I won't have you fumbling about with such depraved ideas in your mind."

With a convulsive wriggle of his pelvis, which brought a gasp from the spectators, Mr. Bland succeeded in shifting his trousers back into place. Holding himself rather girlishly by the waist, he walked towards his table with as much dignity as he could muster under the circumstances. Mrs. Whittle trailed behind. No one attempted to interrupt Mr. Bland's progress. He seated himself in his chair, and Pauline followed his example.

"Rather a lively dance," commented her husband. "When he wriggled his pelvis into his pants I thought he was doing the rumba."

It was at this moment that heaven-sent inspiration descended upon Charles, the prince of head waiters. "Ladies and gentlemen," he announced, "let me introduce to you Señor Toledo, the world's most baffling magician."

With a graceful sweep of his arm, he bowed to Quintus Bland, sitting dumbfounded in his chair.

There was general handclapping throughout the room, mingled with cries of approval.

"Don't let me down," Charles whispered. "Would you mind giving them a bow?"

"Clever of you, Charles," murmured Pauline; then, turning to her recent partner, she added, "That will explain everything. Go on, Quinnie, and make a nice bow."

Snapping down another brandy, Mr. Bland rose with reluctance and bowed to his admiring audience. Unfortunately the knot that Pauline had loosened took this opportunity to become untied entirely, with the result that Mr. Bland's pelvis was once more on public view. He sat down abruptly and busied himself with the string. The spectators, thinking it was all a part of the show, cheered enthusiastically.

"Why does Señor Toledo show only his middle section?" a voice called out.

"Oh," replied Charles, suavely, "the Señor thought it would be more convincing."

"You mean more indecent," another voice rang out.

"Señor Toledo should be ashamed of himself," announced a lady. "What a way for a magician."

"But what has the Señor to be ashamed of, madam?" Charles inquired, with a significant tilt to his shoulders.

"That's just the point," contributed the lady's escort. "This young lady means that Señor Toledo should be ashamed because —"

"I meant nothing of the kind," retorted the young lady, indignantly.

"Well," replied Charles, a trifle disconcerted as he observed Señor Toledo writhing in his chair, "it would be better not to go too deeply into all that. Later, perhaps, the good Señor will show us even more."

"I've seen quite enough already," a gentleman declared. "That's no way for a world-famous magician to act. He might get away with it in Spain but not in the U.S.A."

Charles turned gratefully to Mr. Bland, slapped him heartily upon the shoulder, then, uttering a low cry of pain, examined his tingling fingers. With a startled look at the hooded figure, he made a formal bow, hurried down the long room, and disappeared through the service doorway. There was certainly something radically wrong with the physical composition of Señor Toledo. He fervently hoped that his strange guest would not attempt any further and more elaborate exhibitions. In this Charles was doomed to disappointment, for even while he was breathing this hope to the patron saint of all well-deserving head waiters, trouble was brewing at the Whittles' table. To be strictly accurate, trouble had already brewed. This trouble was caused by a resounding slap administered by Lorna Bland upon the beautiful burnished face of Mr. Phil Harkens. She was about to deliver another one when Harkens, smiling tolerantly, caught Lorna's wrist, twisting it so deftly that she was rendered impotent with pain and anger. A sharp little cry escaped her lips as she helplessly looked about her.

Quintus Bland, who had been jumping spasmodically in his chair during the first part of this engagement, sprang to his feet at the sound of his wife's cry and instinctively tossed off his coat. Not content with ridding himself of this encumbrance, he violently discarded his pillowcase and trousers, thus disclosing himself to the world for what he was, a skeleton in ill-fitting shoes and gloves.

Quintus Bland was truly a heart-chilling object. His bones seemed to snap and crackle with the venom and potency of his fury. For the first time since the change had occurred he gloried in the fact that he was a horrible-looking skeleton. Even the Whittles, who up to that moment had thought they had seen him at his worst, pushed back their chairs from the table and regarded their friend in alarm. Here was a force more difficult to deal with than a tidal wave or an earth-quake. Once more the young lady and her escort at the next table slid unprotestingly to the floor. Cries of horror and astonishment rose from all parts of the room. Various inebriated gentlemen stamped on the floor vigorously and shouted words of drunken encouragement to Señor Toledo, the world's most famous magician.

Heedless of the panic he was creating, the Señor clumped recklessly across the dance floor. That he was far gone in double brandies in no way impeded his progress. If anything, the brandies had given him confidence. He no longer cared whether or not he dashed himself to fragments. His sole purpose in life was to destroy utterly and for ever the body and person of Phil Harkens. As he hurried across the floor, couples preparing to dance scattered before him, the orchestra found itself unable to draw an effective breath and stopped on a series of shuddering wails. Diners rose from their tables and huddled against the walls of the room. Several women fainted and lay forgotten on the floor. Their escorts had troubles of their own.

Quintus Bland, however, was blind to all this. The smug, tolerant smile on Phil Harkens's lips alone attracted his gaze. And even though the smile became glazed and fixed with horror as the skeleton neared the table, it was just as hateful to Quintus Bland. Luckily for Lorna's nerves as well as for her reason, she was far too angry with her escort to be bothered much by the sudden and infuriated appearance of a mere skeleton. She was interested but not alarmed. Having lived for years with a long, gangling structure of skin and bones, she saw little to choose between her husband and Señor Toledo. The difference was merely one of degree—a matter of a few pounds.

Mr. Bland now stood towering over the unhappy Mr. Harkens, who had half risen from his chair. He was still clinging to Lorna's wrist, but now he was clinging to it for comfort and protection. Stretching his bones to the limit of their expansion, Mr. Bland drew the glove from his left hand and slapped Phil Harkens with it across his mouth. As the man collapsed in his chair, a fleshless hand grasped him by the throat, and five relentless talons dug into his flesh.

"Take your hand from that woman's wrist," Bland commanded, grinding his teeth to add effectiveness to his words. "Down to the grave you come with me to moulder with the worms."

There had been wild cries before in the room that night, but none to equal in earnestness and volume the cry that tore itself from Mr. Harkens's tortured throat when he heard about mouldering with the worms. He could not conceive of a more unalluring prospect. In his anxiety to escape the talons clawing at his neck, his chair toppled over backwards with a crash and he found himself floundering on the floor with a gibbering skeleton on top of him. With a desperate effort he wriggled free from the clutches of the skeleton, scrambled sobbing to his feet, and staggered to the nearest door. This led to the kitchens of the establishment, in which pandemonium broke out immediately upon the devastating arrival of Mr. Bland.

"Mon Dieu!" shrilled Henri, the chef. "Señor Toledo outdoes himself. I part for my life."

And that was exactly what everyone else proceeded to do in various directions. Trays were dropped by waiters, and pots by underchefs. There was the sound of crashing dishes and the babble of foreign tongues.

In the midst of this confusion, Mr. Bland paused and looked about for Harkens. That worthy gentleman was nowhere in sight.

"Where is he?" cried Bland. "Somebody tell me where he is."

"He parted through the *porte,*" came the voice of Henri from behind an overturned table, "also as if for his life."

Snatching up a carving knife, Quintus Bland ran jerkily to a door that gave to a backyard from which an alley ran out to the street. Down this alley Phil Harkens was speeding as if pursued by all the demons in hell. Mr. Bland halted his impassioned pursuit and stood watching the fleeing figure until it had disappeared from view, then he turned slowly back into the yard. Finding a rude bench he sat down and gazing up at the dark sky, rested after his labors. He felt coldly indifferent now about the fate of Phil Harkens. After all, it had not been the man's fault so much as Lorna's. Harkens had merely answered her summons. Any man would be a fool to overlook such an opportunity. Bland felt almost sorry he had been so rude to Harkens, but then again he should not have manhandled Lorna. Quintus Bland felt sick, tired and disgusted. His head was dizzy, the roof of his mouth parched. It had been the worst evening in his life. Had he not turned to a skeleton in the nick of time, he might be sitting there now, an unfaithful husband. He almost wished he were one. Lorna deserved to be taught a lesson. She was too damned headstrong. He very much wanted a drink, but he had no desire to return to the restaurant.

"Somebody bring me a bottle of brandy," he shouted.

Henri, who had emerged from behind his barricade, promptly produced a bottle and handed it to the nearest waiter.

"Convey this with my compliments to Señor Toledo," he said. "He is pushing screams for it in the yard."

"Oh, yeah," replied the waiter, who had been crudely born and bred in the Bronx. "And if I came face to face with that bone-naked bozo, I'd be doing more than pushing screams. I'd be fairly flinging them about."

"Is it that you lack in courage?" demanded Henri.

"It certainly is," admitted the waiter, almost proudly.

"But so do I," said Henri. "Me, I am a nervous collapse."

In the midst of this perplexity a small blonde woman, whose lovely figure immediately restored the nervous collapse to the pink of condition, took the bottle from the waiter's hand and disappeared through the back door.

"Señor Toledo," said a small voice in the darkness, "I have brought you a bottle of brandy."

Mr. Bland started and looked nervously up at his wife.

"Thanks," he said shortly, reaching out for the bottle. "Sit down, if you don't mind skeletons."

"I don't mind some," Lorna Bland answered demurely as she seated herself by her husband.

"Have a drink," he said, passing her the bottle.

\

CHAPTER 5.

ON A BACKYARD BENCH

"In life," observed Lorna Bland, after several reflective pulls on the bottle," you must have been a very gallant gentleman."

"What do you mean—in life?" the bogus Toledo demanded, removing the bottle from his wife's hand.

"When you were," explained Lorna.

"But I still am," Mr. Bland assured her.

"You still are what?" asked Lorna, innocently.

"In life," replied Quintus Bland.

Lorna laughed tolerantly, then reached for the bottle.

"You're dead," she told him, simply. "Part and parcel of the grave. Don't tell me. I know."

"But I do tell you," Mr. Bland insisted. "I'm very much alive."

"Oh, you're active enough," his wife admitted, "but they get that way, you know. They always do."

"What are you talking about?" her husband roughly demanded.

"Psychic phenomena," she retorted, calmly. "You're a psychic phenomenon, you know—a manifestation—a—a—a phantasmagoria." She paused to tilt the bottle, then smacked her pretty lips. "They're always active," she added.

"Madam," said Bland, coldly, "I am none of those things. Let me once more assure you I'm just as alive as you are."

"Married?" asked Lorna, briefly.

Mr. Bland nodded.

"And is she a skeleton, too?" she asked, then continued without waiting for an answer: "Naturally she must be. The children must be cute—a lot of little baby skeletons crawling about the floor. Think of it. You all must be no end careful not to chip and crack each other. And all your chairs must be padded—heavily padded. I —"

"Please don't go on," Mr. Bland broke in on his wife's musings. "That bottle is getting the better of you. We have no children."

"Perhaps it is just as well," sighed Lorna Bland.

"Why?" demanded Quintus. "I've always wanted a child."

"But," Lorna reasonably pointed out, "think of introducing a perfectly normal doctor into a household of skeletons. Why, the poor man would be a mental case before he could open his bag."

"You're either drunk or mad," said Quintus Bland, disgustedly.

"Perhaps a little of both," his wife admitted. "Were it not for this bottle I might find you a trifle difficult—macabre, I think, is the word. Some people call it horrid."

From the window of the kitchen the chef's eloquent eyes peered at the pair on the bench.

"Mon Dieu," he observed in wonderment, "the chic madam still sits *en tête-à-tête* with the fleshless Señor Toledo. Me, I could not do it."

"No," observed a waiter, sarcastically. "You would push plenty cries."

"I am a man of courage," declared the chef. "A lion in the fight, but I do not converse with bones. Far better to sit *en tête-à- tête* with a soiled camel."

"Well," said the waiter, "I'd just as soon not sit *en tête- à-tête* with either, although a soiled camel wouldn't upset me much. Far better to push cries and run like hell, say I."

"In that there is wisdom," agreed the chef. "The mere knowledge that out there on that bench sits an object so incredibly horrifying makes it difficult for me to turn my back on the door. We must drink of wine."

"No," declared the waiter. "We must drink of whisky. Wine is far too weak to get me used to that bony party out there."

"In that also there is wisdom," said the chef, turning from the window. "Let it be of whisky."

Meantime Mr. Bland and Lorna were doing their best with the bottle, and their best was not so bad.

"You know," said Lorna, confidingly, "if you had about ten pounds of flesh distributed about those bones of yours I fancy you wouldn't look unlike my husband."

"Ha!" said Mr. Bland. "Your husband."

"Yes," went on Lorna. "You even sound like him, only more hollow, of course."

"Naturally," agreed Mr. Bland. "Your husband must be thin, I take it."

"No, it's my turn to take it," protested Lorna, reaching for the bottle. "You've just had it." After a delicate gurgle she once more smacked her lips and resumed. "Is my husband thin?" she asked, rhetorically. "Señor, you're the only man that's got him licked. Why, he's so thin people pity him in the streets."

"They do, eh?" said Quintus Bland. "I almost pity him myself, but I dare say he's a nice man."

"He's a dirty man," said Lorna.

"What!" exclaimed the skeleton. "A dirty man?"

"Yes," said Lorna, simply. "My husband is a dirty man."

Quintus Bland was thoroughly outraged.

"How dirty?" he asked in a low voice.

"Oh, very dirty," replied Lorna, warming to the subject. "And he has a dirty dog. In fact, they're both dirty dogs. I tried to pull his tail out."

"Any luck?" asked Mr. Bland.

"No luck," said Lorna, moodily. "No luck at all. Did you ever try to pull a dog's tail out—or off?"

"No," admitted her husband. "Why?"

"It's impossible," said Lorna, bitterly. "Can't pull a dog's tail out. They're like that with their tails." Here she held up two fingers closely pressed together.

"I didn't know," murmured Mr. Bland. "But I'm sorry your husband's so dirty."

"Oh, yes," replied Lorna, eagerly reverting to the subject. "He's a very dirty man. Just like his dog. My husband's a dirty dog."

"And thin," added Quintus.

"And thin," agreed Lorna. "He's a thin dirty man or a dirty thin man, whichever way it goes."

She lapsed into silence, as if brooding over the lamentable dirtiness of the emaciated Mr. Bland. Her husband, morbidly moved by an impulse to learn the worst, broke in upon her thoughts.

"Would you say he was a filthy man?" he asked with an attempt at diffidence.

"Sure, I'd say he was a filthy man," she replied without a moment's hesitation. "My husband is a filthy man." Something caused her to glance up at the object beside her. "What's the matter with you, Señor Toledo?" she inquired. "Got a chill?"

Señor Toledo's actions fully justified the question. He looked as if he had been seized by a violent ague. He had stood more than flesh, and much more than bone, could bear. To be called a filthy man in the third person by one's own wife was truly a devastating experience. With an effort he pulled his bones together.

"I'm all right," he said, huskily. "Guess I need a drink."

"That's better," commented Lorna, passing him the bottle. "You were rattling something awful."

"I'll try to do better," he promised. "It's a shame about your husband."

"No, it isn't," she answered, surprisingly. "I like him as filthy and as thin as he is. He's such an awful fool. I can twist him about my finger and get him angry whenever I like."

"Do you think that's so nice?" asked Mr. Bland.

"Oh, no," she answered, promptly. "I'm a dirty dog, too, only I'm a small dirty dog and not at all thin. At that, neither of us is as dirty as Phil Harkens."

"The chap I scared from the scene?"

"The same," replied Lorna, nodding. "He's dirty in the worst sense of the word. Only went out with him to get my husband mad." She laughed a little ruefully. "I guess we're both a little mad," she continued. "I pretended I was going to put on my black underwear with the lace on it. You should have seen the poor man's face. It was nearly as bad as yours. What a face "

"Hey, in there!" shouted Mr. Bland with sudden violence. "Bring me another bottle."

"Name of God!" exclaimed the chef. "One thousand thunders. Did you attend? Not only does he demand a bottle but also he wants it brought to him."

"I'm pushing cries right now," said the waiter, hurrying with his tray from the kitchen.

"My brave," pleaded the chef, turning to another waiter, "Señor Toledo calls for a bottle. He is a man of distinction of the utmost. He is also an amiable man. To him you will carry the bottle, is it not so?"

"It certainly is not so," said my brave with the calm of a mind in which lurked no indecision. "The distinguished and amiable Señor Toledo is wasting his breath on me. Did you hear that whoop he let out?"

"It came as if pushed from the grave," breathed the chef.

"If you ask me," asserted the waiter, "that voice was shoved clear up from hell."

At this moment Señor Toledo himself bounded into the kitchen. With no less agility everyone else bounded out. The chef alone was unable to make the grade, being spiritually as well as professionally linked to his cauldrons. To that extent he was a man of courage, as he had claimed.

"Do I get that bottle or don't I?" clattered Mr. Bland.

"Remain tranquil," pleaded the chef. "You do, Señor, you do. That bottle is virtually in your hands. May you enjoy it to the full."

"Snap to it," said Mr. Bland.

The chef snapped. Like a magician he produced a bottle, which he placed on a table within easy reach of the terrible figure in the doorway.

"Señor," said the chef, "it is I who present the bottle."

"Thanks," replied the Señor, tartly. "Shall I bite the cork out?"

"Would you like to?" asked the chef, endeavoring to be agreeable. "I should consider it an honor to watch the magnificent feat. I shall form myself into an audience of one."

"Bah!" exclaimed the skeleton, explosively. "Pull out that cork."

In his anxiety to comply, the chef almost wrung the neck off the bottle. Quintus Bland snatched the brandy and retired to the bench.

"Got it," he said to the small figure sitting in the semi-darkness.

"Good," returned Lorna in a subdued voice. "It's hard to wait for liquor."

"One of the hardest things I know," replied Bland, "but see here, you've been drinking too much to-night."

"It's remorse," said the woman.

"What are you sorry about?"

"I'm sorry I left him home, sitting in the shadows."

"You mean the dirty dog?"

"Yes, the dirty dog. I called him an old crow or something."

"Why didn't you call him a buzzard?"

"Didn't think of it," she replied, truthfully.

"Make a note of it for further reference,"

Mr. Bland suggested, sardonically. "Maybe he stepped out himself."

"He would never do a thing like that. He's the straightest man I know — straight but thin."

Quintus Bland reflected that she little realized how appallingly thin her husband was.

"You can never tell," he remarked. "Even the dirtiest dog will have his day."

"Perhaps you're right," said Lorna. "He deserves some sort of a day." For a moment she fell silent over the new bottle. Then: "Tell me, Señor Toledo, are passion and romance one and the same thing?"

Mr. Bland pondered, not because he did not know the answer, but more because of the established inhibitions existing between him and his wife. At last he spoke.

"The only honest reply would be, *Yes*," he said. "By that I mean you couldn't have one without the other."

"Then," declared Lorna, "there should be some device to stimulate passion in the home."

"I think," replied Mr. Bland a little pointedly, "that there should be one to confine it to the home."

"But the American woman does not like to confine her charms to a mere husband," Lorna asserted. "I know because I'm an American woman. We all crave to be desired by other men. Especially if there are other women around. Bad, isn't it? And so small. When I was engaged to Quintus—that's my husband's depressing name—I thought only of him. I dressed for him, did my hair for him, and perfumed myself for him. Other men were not in it —they had no place. That kept up even after we were married— for a while. I wanted to look intriguing for him at all times. Lovely under-things and all that. Then gradually I found myself tucking my most abandoned garments away and not caring so much how desirable I appeared in his eyes. Of course, he always looked like hell, but funny. I liked him."

She paused and gazed into. the shadows, then continued: "Romance or passion were already packing up, and for no apparent reason. Now for whom do you suppose I was saving all of my pretty things? I had no definite man in mind. Just men. Women always have the consciousness of men in their minds. If you have a decent husband you know he's safe. Then some devilish impulse prompts you to play with a man who is not quite so safe, and that almost nearly always leads to trouble, unless you're both lucky and clever. A woman constantly needs reassurance that she is desirable. She is willing to risk and pay a lot for that. You see, Señor," she broke off, "it's not only a matter of passion. It's some inner need or craving a woman requires to hold her to her youth, to keep her from slipping over the borderline of romance into the placid, unexciting backwaters of domesticity. Some women are built for that. I envy them in a way."

"Children help," suggested Mr. Bland in a rather strained voice.

"Not today they don't," asserted Lorna, with a scoffing little laugh. "You should see some of the mothers I know. Why, the very knowledge that they are mothers seems to drive them to more frantic and disgusting endeavors. They'd mix it up with almost any man who shows them a little attention, especially after a couple of snifters."

"Pretty tough on their husbands," observed Mr. Bland.

"Sure," agreed Lorna. "They can't be fist-fighting all the time, and a gun is a trifle too drastic."

"Then why don't they beat their wives?"

"Half the time they can't get anything concrete on them. They know but they can't prove. It's quite a mess, this modern mix-up."

"You don't seem to hold your sex in high regard," remarked Quintus Bland.

"I don't hold this member of it in any regard at all," replied Lorna. "just a creature of impulse, of low impulse, at that."

"There is such a thing as tenderness," said Mr. Bland.

"I've shown the dirty dog very little of that," replied Lorna. "Wouldn't know how to begin now. He'd become suspicious."

"Well, let's not worry too much about all these things," her husband said in a heartier voice. "As I see it, the woman is not wholly to blame. Believe me, when a woman gets out of hand some of the fault can be traced to the husband. Then, again, it might be the weather."

He laughed a little falsely and elevated the bottle.

"Is Mrs. Toledo very fond of you?" Lorna asked, somewhat haltingly. "Do you have a happy love life?"

"You'd have to ask my wife about that," answered Mr. Bland. "A man only knows how his wife is acting, never how she is thinking. God has spared him that final humiliation."

"I'd love to have a long talk with Mrs. Toledo," declared Lorna, musingly. "I suppose she's much like you, only smaller?"

"She's smaller," admitted Quintus.

"Well, if I can stand you," she observed, "I should be able to stand her, but I doubt it I'd be quite comfortable with both of you together—on either side of me, so to speak."

"Not to mention a lot of little skeletons squirming about the floor," offered Mr. Bland.

"That would be bad," admitted Lorna. "Pass me the bottle, Toledo. I've been too long depressed."

"Do you intend to drive home to-night?" asked the skeleton.

"Sure," she said, then stopped. "How did you know I had a car?" she asked him.

"Señor Toledo knows many things," quoth Mr. Bland, enigmatically.

"For some reason you keep on reminding me of my husband," his wife said in a puzzled voice. "We had such a devil of a row. He must be feeling rotten about it."

"He is," remarked Bland without thinking. "How do you know?" she asked him.

"I have ways of knowing things," fenced Mr. Bland. "But suppose you don't find him home?"

"Oh, he'll be there," she answered, confidently. "He never steps out unless I'm along."

"But still," persisted her husband, "he might not be. You drove him pretty far, you know."

"Then I'll go to bed alone," declared his wife.

"That would be a pity," he observed.

"Señor Toledo," said Lorna, "not only are you a skeleton, but you're a dirty skeleton, at that. No wonder you remind me of my husband. I'm going now."

She rose and handed Mr. Bland the bottle, while she stood a little unsteadily, testing her appearance in various quarters, as women have a right to do.

"Will you be good to the dirty dog if you ever get him back?" Mr. Bland asked in a hesitant voice.

"How do you know I've lost him?" she demanded.

"Somehow I've a feeling you have," said Bland, slowly, "but I don't know for how long."

"Do you mean to say that dirty dog has left me?" Lorna asked, furiously.

"Not of his own accord, perhaps," Bland replied in a mollifying voice. "Wherever he is, he is probably wishing he were home with you."

"Señor Toledo, you're getting me frightened,' breathed Lorna. "I like that dirty dog, but if he's done a bunk I'll claw him to shreds when he gets back home."

"He might find even that diverting," said the skeleton of Bland. "I wish I had some shreds to be clawed. It's not much fun being like this, you know."

"I'm sorry," replied Lorna. "It hadn't occurred to me. You seemed to be such a natural-born skeleton, so self-possessed and competent. It must have its difficult moments."

She swayed a little and clutched his hand and bony arm for support.

"Bur-r-r," she gasped, hastily withdrawing her hand. "Wow! Oh, dear me. What an excruciating sensation. I'm almost shocked sober." She regarded Mr. Bland with new interest. "You know, I've been sitting here in an alcoholic haze not caring much whether you were a skeleton or not. At any moment I expected my brain would clear and I'd wake up to find you a real person. But that arm! It's real and it's all bone. No flesh at all."

"Would you like me to go away?" asked Mr. Bland, humbly.

"Where would you go?" asked Lorna.

"I—I scarcely know, myself," admitted Mr. Bland. "I'd forgotten about that. There doesn't seem to be any place for me to go, does there?"

"Yes," replied Lorna, decisively. "You've been decent to me, decenter than a flesh-and-blood man. Now I'm going to bring you home to my husband. You can stay there for the night, then we'll think of something."

"Oh, no," Bland protested. "I could never do a thing like that. I might frighten your husband to death if he's so thin."

"Nonsense," snapped Lorna, now all efficiency and determination. "He'll merely think he's found a long-lost brother who needs a bit of feeding. Where are those things you were wearing?"

"Distributed about the dining-room, I dare say," replied Mr. Bland.

"Wait here and take a drink," she commanded. "I'll be right back."

And strangely enough she was right back with all of Mr. Bland's clothes, which in her haste she failed to recognize.

"There's a cap in the car and glasses," she said when Bland had covered himself as well as possible, considering the circumstances. "If you slump down in the seat you'll be able to get away with it easily. The car is at the end of this passage. We won't have to go back through the speak."

"But the bill and all that?" protested Mr. Bland.

"Charles assured me everything would be okay with him," said Lorna, "so long as you refrained from mingling with his patrons."

"A generous and resourceful man," remarked Mr. Bland.

"Bring the bottle along," commanded Lorna. "We'll need it on the way, although there's lots more at home, thank God."

From behind his window the chef was witnessing these preparations with no small show of interest. As he saw the couple head for the alley, he breathed a sigh of relief.

"Señor Toledo parts," he observed, "in company with that chic madam." He paused, thought deeply, then eloquently shrugged his shoulders. "Señor Toledo is a man of many parts, but still I don't quite see... no, I should have thought... *eh bien,* why puzzle oneself about such baffling amours?"

Señor Toledo had parted. That was good. That was to be desired. Nevertheless, as the chef busied himself over his various recondite rituals he found himself still perplexed by the apparently pointless choice of the chic, petite madam. The most distinguished of skeletons could hardly be a satisfactory lover. Again the Gallic shrug.

CHAPTER 6.

THE INTERMITTENT SKELETON

Quintus Bland had only the most fragmentary memory of that mad drive home through the night. Yet even as he slumbered beside the small figure at the wheel he had a vague consciousness of a vast and steady beat of wind, of heavy darkness occasionally interrupted by onrushing rivers of light, and of terrible, terrible speed. He wanted to make some remark about this unnecessary hurtling through space, to interpose a mild objection, but found the effort altogether too much for him. In a single night he had taken aboard more liquor than he had consumed in the course of a whole year. Also, he had lost, perhaps for ever, all of the little flesh he had possessed. The double shock had numbed his faculties. He was no longer able to carry on as Señor Toledo. Let Lorna take charge. Even if she was two-thirds binged herself she at least had all of her flesh.

One fact he realized vividly. He was going home. He was withdrawing from the public eye, finding sanctuary beneath his own roof. For the moment he had forgotten that he was playing the part of Señor Toledo, presumably a mere visitor to his own home. He was simply a fleshless Quintus Bland, and he was sitting by his wife. That thought comforted his slumbers. He was no longer in the hands of libidinous friends and strangers.

At the New York entrance to the Holland Tunnel he nearly dragged his trousers from his much-discussed pelvis in a polite endeavor to procure change with which to pay for the ticket. The man at the booth accepted the money, slipped the ticket into the skeleton fingers, paused and stared in stupefaction at those fingers, then followed them up until his dilated eyes rested on the weird face confronting him. With an incoherent exclamation he jumped back into his little house, the change rattling over the floor.

"Look," he managed to say to the agent directly behind him. "'That lady's driving a skeleton through our tunnel."

"Wish they were all skeletons," commented the man, "and deep down in their graves." He paused to sell a ticket, then continued passionately, "I hate all motorists. How do you know she was a lady? Sounds more like a ghoul to me."

"What's a ghoul?" asked the other.

"Something horrid," said his colleague, a trifle misty himself.

"I know," declared the other, brightly. "I've heard of them—ghoul birds they're called."

"That shows how much you know," said the second man. "You're thinking of jail-birds. There ain't no such thing as a ghoul bird."

"Well," replied the first ticket vendor, not to be wholly squelched, "when I played basketball at the settlement house I used to make ghoul after ghoul, if that's what you mean."

"You poor lug," said the other. "A ghoul is a body snatcher."

"A ghoul didn't have to snatch this body," the first man replied. "This body could snatch for itself. There wasn't no flesh on it at all. I saw its bony fingers wiggle. Gord, I even touched the awful things. And its head was just a skull."

"If you're going to talk like that," said the second man, "I'm clearing out. Motorists are nutty enough for me. I don't want to be cooped up with no madman."

The first man relapsed into silence. He realized the utter futility of attempting to make himself understood. The more he tried, the madder people would think him. No one would ever believe. Nevertheless deep within him the man felt fundamental craving to find at least one person somewhere in all the world who would credit his incredible story. Furthermore he was dead certain he had made ghoul after ghoul in basketball.

Mr. Bland next remembered being awakened by the stabbing beams of a flashlight. From the darkness behind the light came an awed ejaculation.

"Holy Mother preserve us," said the voice. "What a sight on a lonely beat. Lady, you've got a grinning corpse beside you."

"He's not grinning, officer," came the cool voice of Lorna. "He's grimacing."

"Whatever it is," said the officer, "I wish he'd give it up."

"That's why I was driving so fast," explained Lorna. "He's desperately ill. I've got to get him home."

"Mean to say you're going to take that thing into your own house?" demanded the officer.

"Certainly," answered Lorna. "He's a sick man. "

"I'll say he is," agreed the officer. "He's wasted away something shocking. You can drive on, lady. You've got me all upset."

So they left the officer to his thoughts and drove on to the open country. Here by the roadside they drew up to take a drink. This was one of Mr. Bland's pleasanter memories. A car was parked directly ahead of them. The car was dark but not quiet. There were certain sounds. Mr. Bland and his wife exchanged significant glances, then Lorna raised the bottle. As she did so the door of the other car slammed and a man came aggressively up to them.

"Say," he began, "what's the big idea in parking your car next to mine? Ain't this road long enough?"

Slipping off his coat, Mr. Bland half rose and extended two long, deathlike arms towards the aggressive gentleman.

"Not long enough for you," he croaked. Not long enough for you, old boy, old boy."

The man did not run. He was incapable of co-ordinated action. Jerkily, as if motivated by clockwork, he swayed back to his car. No sound had escaped his lips. For the moment his lungs had ceased to function. Whatever had been taking place in that car was indefinitely postponed. The man threw the motor into action and resigned his soul to God. The poignant disappointment of the girl beside him was swallowed up by her anxiety for the safety of her life and limbs, especially for her limbs, for without those attractive members there would be no life at all worth speaking about.

Quintus Bland expanded his ribs and emitted a howl like a drunken Tarzan, then drank deep of the bottle. A moment later he was once more slumbering peacefully beside his wife.

He was still slumbering when the little roadster hunched itself through the doors of the garage directly behind his home.

"Señor Toledo," Lorna sang out, "we are here! Wake up and stir your stumps."

"Eh?" muttered Mr. Bland. "What's this about my stumps?"

"Shake a leg. Get a move on," she told him. "Come in and meet the dirty dog. We'll yank him out of bed."

But when they looked for the dirty dog all they found was a wriggling Busy who was not at all the right sort of dirty dog. Lorna was crest-fallen. Her high spirits plunged without brakes and splashed in a puddle of disappointment. She tried to become very angry, to work herself up to a rage, but her heart would not respond. She had planned to show her husband that she was not wearing the black underwear with the lace. And her plans had not stopped there. They were much more elaborate. But now—what? The dirty dog was gone. He had done a bunk on her, and she was left in the house with a male skeleton she had met that night for the first time.

They turned away from the door of the empty bedroom and went downstairs. At any rate, she thought as they descended the stairs, she could not be compromised by a skeleton. How fortunate it was that she had not brought a real man home. That would have been difficult at this hour of the night, or rather, morning.

After a few drinks in the living-room she suggested they retire to bed. Her husband, who amid familiar surroundings had forgotten he was supposed to be Señor Toledo, readily agreed. Not only did he follow Lorna upstairs but also into her bedroom. Once there the routine of years swam through the fumes of alcohol. Automatically he began to prepare himself for bed. The first indication Lorna received of her guest's clubby intentions was when she saw him sink into an easy chair and wearily remove his shoes from which fell several wads of paper.

"Had to stuff my shoes to keep them on," he explained casually to his wife. "The Whittles thought of that."

He rose, went to his closet, and produced a pair of slippers, then he began to attack his trousers.

"Just a moment," said Lorna in a crisp voice. "What is the big idea?"

"We're going to bed, aren't we?" asked Quintus Bland.

"Certainly," replied Lorna, "but not together."

"Why not?" inquired Bland.

"Your wife is one reason and my husband is another. Added to those I have various reasons of my own. Those are my husband's slippers, by the way."

"Nonsense," scoffed Mr. Bland. "Don't tell me. I know whose slippers they are." He moved to a chest-of-drawers and extracted a pair of pajamas therefrom. "I suppose," he challenged, dangling the objects before his wife's puzzled eyes, "you're going to say these aren't mine."

"Of course they're not yours," declared Lorna.

"Ha!" laughed Bland, sarcastically. "I suppose I have no rights in this house at all."

Lorna's hands moved ominously to her hips. One small foot was steadily tapping the rug.

"Listen," she said, her voice gone frosty. "Listen, Señor Toledo. I let you take your shoes off in this room because I couldn't stop you. It was a horrid sight. I'll even go so far as to allow you to borrow my husband's slippers. If you insist you can have a pair of his pajamas. But I'll be damned from here to Harlem if you're going to take your pants off in my presence. Don't interrupt. I know it wouldn't mean anything if you did, but just the same, the idea is repellent."

"But where shall I take them off?" asked Mr. Bland, desperately.

"Anywhere but in front of me," said Lorna. "We've a perfectly good guest room."

"Damned if I'll sleep in the guest room," said Bland.

"Damned if you'll sleep in here," said Lorna.

Mr. Bland was once more fiddling with his trousers, this time with an air of grim determination.

"Stop that this minute," cried Lorna. "Señor Toledo, keep those trousers on."

"See here," replied Mr. Bland, "you get along with your own undressing and let me take care of mine."

"Do you expect me to undress with you in the room?" his wife demanded.

"I hope you don't want to sleep with your clothes on," said Bland.

"You get out of here, Toledo," said Lorna in a dangerous voice. "Apart from all considerations of morality I am not going to sleep with a skeleton, and that's that."

"But didn't you say," Mr. Bland demanded, "that your husband was nearly a skeleton?"

"Toledo," said Lorna, primly, "there's a world of difference between a skeleton and a thin husband."

"Don't know what you're getting at," Mr. Bland grumbled.

"It's just as well you don't," said Lorna. "Leave those trousers alone and get on out of here. I want to go to sleep."

"You've got nothing on me," her husband replied, dragging his trousers down over his pelvis. "And sleep it's going to be."

Lorna gasped, gathered up a few garments of her own, and hastened to the door.

"You've forced me to watch you taking your trousers off," she said with great dignity, "but I won't remain to see you put those pajamas on. I'll sleep in the guest room." She slammed the door behind her, then promptly opened it again, struck by a new thought. "Toledo," she said, "I thought you were a gentleman, but you've proved yourself to be merely a filthy skeleton. I hope you fall out of bed and break every bone in your body."

"Sweet lady," Bland retorted, bitterly, "your husband's a filthy skeleton himself."

"Is that so!" said Lorna. "Well, if my husband comes home and finds you in here you won't have to fall out of bed to break every bone in your body. He'll do it for you."

Bland laughed nastily as she again slammed the door and betook herself to the guest room. When she fell asleep a short time later it was with a sense of solitude and separation. Also, she was exceedingly put out with Señor Toledo, who by this time was slumbering vociferously where she by rights should have been.

In the morning she was up just in time to catch Fanny, the passionate maid, on the point of entering the marital bedchamber with two cups of coffee and the morning papers. Lorna, still a trifle fuddled, emitted a small scream.

"Oh, no," she called to Fanny. "Don't do that. There's a skeleton in that room."

A little startled, but more curious, Fanny cautiously opened the door and peered in at the still form in the bed. Then she closed the door and came up to her mistress.

"He doesn't look any thinner than usual," said Fanny. "He's sleeping like a babe."

"What!" exclaimed Lorna. "Like a babe, did you say?"

Fanny nodded her dark head.

"Yes, ma'am," she replied, quite seriously. "Like a babe."

"Where's the skeleton?" asked Lorna. "Didn't you see a skeleton? A skeleton by the name of Toledo?"

Fanny considered her mistress suspiciously. Had Mr. Bland at last succeeded in driving his wife mad?

"Could I bring you some aspirin?" she asked, solicitously.

"Yes, Fanny," said Lorna in a preoccupied manner. "Lots."

Still carrying the coffee, Fanny departed on her errand. The moment the maid was gone, Lorna approached the door behind which she had left a skeleton putting on her husband's pajamas. There was no doubt about that. One could not be mistaken about a skeleton, no matter how much brandy one had consumed. Nevertheless something was radically wrong. Fanny had said that her husband was sleeping in there like a babe. Lorna found it difficult to conceive of either her husband or Señor Toledo sleeping like a babe. They might sleep like a beast, but certainly not like a babe.

Quietly she opened the door and looked in and caught her breath with a little gasp. There lay her husband sleeping, if not like a babe, at least like a log. Unconscious of the change that had taken place in his anatomy, Quintus Bland in the flesh lay inertly in his bed. In some mysterious way the potent fumes of the chemical mixture he had created had become dormant during his slumbers, with the result that Bland's flesh had once more reappeared. He was no longer a fluoroscopic man.

Having satisfied herself that her husband had returned, Lorna closed the door and retreated to the guest room to think things over. She had seen no broken bones about the room, yet quite obviously something had happened to Señor Toledo. She wondered if her husband had chased him from the house.

While she was pondering over this mystery, Bland himself awoke and sprang from the bed.

He had a confused but strong impression that he had turned to a skeleton. And even as he stood by the bed struggling to collect memories of the previous night, his body began to fade until he was once more a fleshless man. His pajamas slipped from him as he moved across the room to a long mirror. Mr. Bland did not care. What good were pajamas to a skeleton? What good was anything to a skeleton? A drink, Mr. Bland decided.

Fanny, having provided her mistress with aspirins, was moved to take another look at Mr. Bland. Accordingly she armed herself with fresh coffee and the paper, then quietly approached the door. This she opened and looked into the room. The next moment Lorna was summoned to the hall by a series of screams. Her own nerves were so jumpy she was screaming a little herself. The sight of Fanny served to calm her. The maid was in a bad way. Never had she looked less passionate or felt less so.

"What is it?" demanded Lorna.

"It's Toledo," gasped Fanny.

"Is he back again?" exclaimed Lorna.

"I don't know about that," said Fanny, "but there's a skeleton in there and he's looking at himself in the mirror."

"Why shouldn't he look at himself in the mirror, Fanny?" said Lorna. ` Do try to be reasonable."

Fanny laughed hysterically.

"Reasonable?" she retorted. "I don't think it's reasonable for a skeleton to look at himself in the mirror. If I was a skeleton I'd want to see as little of myself as possible."

"Did you see anything of Mr. Bland?" asked Lorna.

"No, ma'am," replied Fanny. "Perhaps Toledo, the skeleton, has destroyed him."

Without further words Lorna hurried to the door and rapped sharply upon it.

"Toledo," she called, "where is my husband?"

"Search me," was the indifferent reply.

"Oh," breathed Fanny, "I'd hate to do that."

"Toledo," repeated Lorna, "tell me this instant what you have done with my husband."

"He's gone," said Mr. Bland. "He took one good look at me and then he went away."

"Did he say where he was going?"

"He didn't even say how-do-you-do," complained Mr. Bland. "He just went away—fast."

Exasperated, Lorna threw open the door. The skeleton of Bland stepped out into the hall. Once more curiosity overcame Fanny's fear. She placed herself behind her mistress and awaited further developments.

"Don't be afraid," Lorna reassured her. "Señor Toledo can be most annoying, but he is quite harmless."

"I wouldn't touch a hair of your head," Mr. Bland told Fanny, "except for amusement."

"It wouldn't amuse me," said Fanny. "Think of something else to do."

"I wonder," said Lorna, "why my husband left the house without saying a word to anyone."

"Perhaps," Mr. Bland suggested, "he didn't want to become involved. Look at his situation. He comes home late at night and finds a skeleton in his bed. Quite naturally he concluded that you had gone in for skeletons and brought one home with you to take his place. Knowing you as he does, he doesn't put anything past you. From Phil Harkens to a skeleton is merely a —"

"That will do, Toledo," Lorna hastily broke in. "Go downstairs and get yourself a drink. Fanny will bring you some coffee. And do stop gossiping like an old woman."

Fanny, who delighted in gossip, felt a little more favorably disposed toward this amazing freak of nature. Perhaps from him she might be able to learn all sorts of interesting things about the events of last night. With a queer, uneasy sensation at her back she allowed Señor Toledo to follow her downstairs. A short time later Lorna appeared dressed for the street. She found the skeleton of her husband sitting in an easy chair. He was contentedly sipping a highball.

"Hope you don't mind my not dressing," said Mr. Bland, politely, laying aside the paper.

"Not at all," replied Lorna, taking a drink herself. "I don't believe in half-measures, Toledo. If you're going to be a skeleton, I say whole hog or nothing. You either should beseen not at all or seen at your best, or rather, your worst. I'm going out to think things over. Make yourself at home."

As Lorna left the house, Mr. Bland poured himself another drink. He continued to repeat this operation until finally he fell asleep in the chair, the newspaper abandoned on his lap.

Some time later Mr. Bland was awakened by a small, quickly smothered cry. Whether it was a cry of fear or appreciation, he was unable to decide, so confused was his state of mind. Fanny, the maid, was standing before him. Fear could hardly account for the expression on her face. Her eyes were large and wild-looking, and when Mr. Bland discovered he had regained his flesh his eyes looked as wild as Fanny's.

"Why, Mr. Bland," she said in a hushed voice, "you're all naked."

"Not quite," replied Mr. Bland, taking a firm grip on the newspaper on his lap.

To his great consternation Fanny leaned over and scanned an advertisement.

"My," she sighed, wistfully, "they're having such a lovely sale at Macy's. Have you finished with the paper, Mr. Bland?"

CHAPTER 7.

THINGS GET NO BETTER

Taking an even firmer grip on the newspaper, Quintus Bland looked defiantly at the passionate maid.

"Fanny," he said, "I have long suspected there was little good in you. Now I know it. Clear out, you trull."

"Half a moment," said Fanny. "I want to take just one more look at those cute little scanties in that advertisement."

"Wish I had a pair on myself," muttered Mr. Bland.

Fanny laughed merrily.

"Wouldn't you look funny?" she said, bending over the newspaper.

"Are you near-sighted?" asked Mr. Bland, pressing back against the chair. "Don't come an inch nearer."

It was in this somewhat unconventional position that Lorna Bland found the two of them when she quietly entered the room on her return from her walk. To make matters even worse, she had also heard Fanny's merry laughter. Busy, the square dog, added to the complications. On seeing his naked master he emitted an excited yelp and, with one of his most springy pounces, landed heavily upon the newspaper. As the dog established contact Mr. Bland gave a grunt of dismay.

"Take him away," he called to his wife. "Yank him off me. Can't you see this fool dog is destroying my last shred of decency?"

"I don't care if he claws it to pieces," declared Lorna, sounding as if she meant every word she had said.

"But I do," protested her husband. "I'm in a hell of a fix."

"I suppose," observed Lorna, "there's no need to ask the meaning of this lovely little tableau I so thoughtlessly interrupted? Had I waited a bit longer it would have broken into frantic action, no doubt."

"Honest, Mrs. Bland," said the now no longer passionate maid, "it wasn't that. It wasn't what you mean."

"What minds you women have," said Bland in a despairing voice. "All the time evil."

"Shut up, you senile wreck," snapped Lorna, then added, turning on Fanny,

"What was it, then, you trollop?"

"I was just taking a look at an advertisement," was the trollop's lame reply.

Lorna gave a little snort of disgust.

"It's a sweet and pungent way to be looking at an advertisement," she said. "And that's about one of the stupidest lies I've ever been told."

"I tell you," Mr. Bland put in, desperately, "we'll all be sorry if Busy digs a hole through this paper."

Lorna laughed mirthlessly.

"I should worry," she flung at her husband. "It doesn't matter to me if he claws all the skin off your bones." She stopped abruptly, then turned to Fanny with a glittering eye. "And that reminds me," she continued. "Where's that skeleton got himself to? What's become of Señor Toledo?"

"I don't know, ma'am," the maid replied. "After you left he fell asleep over his drink. Later, when I came to ask if he wanted a cup of coffee, there sat Mr. Bland as naked as a babe."

Lorna looked at Mr. Bland and shivered.

"So instead of withdrawing like a modest, self-respecting woman," she said, "you just ambled up to the naked babe and began to read advertisements off him, laughing merrily the while." She turned furiously on her squirming husband. "Speak up, you dirty dog," she snapped.

"Then call off this other dirty dog," Bland pleaded. "I can't use my hands."

Lorna collected Busy and stood looking down at her husband.

"Well?" she said. "Go on."

"When I got to the station," he began, "I suddenly came over sick, as they say, so I returned home and went directly to bed."

"Then what did you come down here for?" asked Lorna.

"To get my pipe," said Bland at random.

"You don't smoke a pipe," said Lorna.

"Eh!" exclaimed Mr. Bland. "What? I don't smoke a pipe? By Jove, so I don't. Now isn't that odd?"

"Yes," answered Lorna. "It's impossible. Did you see a sleeping skeleton in this chair?

"Sure," lied Quintus Bland. "He was just leaving. He sent you his regards. And I saw him when I first got up. That's why I went away. I'm not so used to skeletons." Here he laughed falsely. "Funny things, skeletons. This one called himself Toledo."

"It's strange," observed Lorna, looking thoughtfully at her husband, "I can never get you two together. There's some funny business going on."

"You're right, there is," agreed Quintus Bland, taking the offensive. "The minute my back is turned, you pop a skeleton into my bed. What's the meaning of that? What does this Spanish atrocity mean to you? Where did you dig him up?"

"That's what I'd like to know," put in Fanny, following close on Mr. Bland's lead. "Whoever heard of a real live skeleton? It's against nature, say I."

"Fanny," said Lorna in a quiet voice, "the next time you want to seduce my husband I'll appreciate it if you don't pick out the most public room in the house."

"Didn't try to seduce your husband," retorted Fanny. "I've got all my clothes on."

"That isn't saying much," replied Lorna, "if you wear as little as I do."

"But it's your husband that's naked," protested the girl.

"He's more thorough about it than you are, Fanny," Lorna told her. "That's the only difference. I suppose he chased you downstairs?"

"That's just what he did," lied Fanny. "He ran after me making noises."

"What sort of noises?" asked Lorna.

"You know," said Fanny, significantly. "Those sort of noises."

"I'm afraid I don't," replied Lorna. "You'd better explain."

"Passionate whoops," said Fanny. "You know, passionate whoops."

Lorna looked mildly surprised.

"Mr. Bland has never whooped passionately at me," she said. "I should think it would be most disconcerting."

"She's lying," broke in Quintus Bland. "I was too sick to whoop passionately at anybody. Besides, I don't know how to whoop that way. It never occurred to me to try."

"I hope it never does," said Lorna. "I'd forget what it was all about."

"And along the hall he came bounding and pounding," Fanny continued, elaborating her story. "His great arms were thrashing about. Oh, Mrs. Bland, it was terrible."

"And when he had chased you downstairs," said Lorna, "he promptly forgot what he was chasing you for, so he sat down and began quietly to read the paper. Is that it?"

"Yes, ma'am," replied Fanny. "He came over sick like and collapsed in that chair."

"She's a liar," said Mr. Bland.

"Of course she is," said Lorna. "You're both liars."

"Am I to sit here all day naked?" her husband demanded, "or will you send that Jezebel away and let me get upstairs? She's feasted her eyes quite enough."

"I'd like to know what on," said Fanny, coolly surveying the naked man. "It would take some eye to pick a feast off you."

With this parting shot she flounced away to the door.

"Is that so?" Mr. Bland called after her. "Why don't you tell your mistress you wanted me to give you the newspaper?"

The maid did not deign to answer as she sailed out of the room.

"Well," said Lorna with a philosophical shrug, "what with lecherous husbands, disappearing skeletons, and nympholeptic maids it's a charming little household."

"You'd better include yourself in the picture," Mr. Bland retorted. "You and your black underwear with the lace."

Lorna studied him darkly.

"Get upstairs, you passionate whooper," she said. "I'm through with you for good." And she too sailed from the room.

"Nice women," Mr. Bland muttered moodily to space. "Charming creatures, the both of them."

For a few minutes he sat brooding over the respective exits of Fanny, the passionate maid, and Lorna, his incensed wife. Then he did the best thing a man could do under the circumstances. He took a drink. Feeling somewhat better, he relaxed in his chair and considered the situation. Here he was back in the flesh again. But how long would he stay that way? Mr. Bland had lost all confidence in his body. It seemed to be in a constant state of flux. This made any consistent line of conduct well-nigh impossible. He was either coming or going. At one moment he might be Señor Toledo, an animated skeleton, at the next Quintus Bland, a naked photographer. In either form he was equally embarrassing to himself and disconcerting to others. One ray of hope—perhaps these rapid changes in his physical composition were due to a gradual diminishing of the potency of the fumes he had inhaled. Mr. Bland heartily hoped so. He took another drink. He got up and surveyed his body to make sure it was still there. It was. He went upstairs and covered it with garments. Then he returned to the bottle. By the time he had finished with this he did not much care whether he was Quintus Bland in the flesh or Señor Toledo in the bone. He even found himself missing Toledo a little. A skeleton had its points, although Bland could not think of any good ones at the moment. Feeling more cheerfully disposed towards life than he had in the last twenty-four hours, he collected his hat and stick, then quietly left the house with Busy at his heels. Mr. Bland had decided to walk to the village for the purpose of getting a shave, his own hand being too unsteady to attempt that delicate operation. From an upper window Lorna watched the lank figure of her husband as he walked down the drive. What was he up to now? she wondered. Strange things were going on in the house. She strongly suspected Mr. Bland of being at the bottom of them. Stripped of flesh, he would look exactly like Señor Toledo, she decided, yet did not all skeletons look almost exactly alike? Lorna found herself sorely perplexed in mind as well as physically jaded. Accordingly she did the best thing a woman could do under the circumstances. She went downstairs, called for a fresh bottle, and took a drink. It did her a world of good.

In the meantime Quintus Bland had pursued his way to the village. He was now reclining in a barber's chair with a steaming towel covering his face. Busy, having growled defiantly at a glittering boiler containing more steaming towels, had curled himself up in a corner with an eye cocked on this object lest it should attack him unawares.

The shop was owned by a small, dark, emotional Italian known as Tony — perhaps the only Tony in existence outside of a speakeasy. Mr. Bland had known him a long time. He was fond of Tony. And Tony was fond of Mr. Bland. Mr. Bland was a very fine gentleman. Tony would shave him well, as if his skin were made of the most perishable fabric. Little did the Italian realize how perishable Mr. Bland's skin really was.

In the next chair the local mortician was having his cheerful face shaved. The local mortician's name was Brown. In the lives of the families thereabouts Mr. Brown played rather an intimate part. He was literally with them from the cradle to the grave. When they were alive he sold them beds, and when they were ready for more permanent repose he provided them with coffins. Consequently he had come to regard births and deaths in the light of dollars and cents. An old gentleman with a bad cough or a young matron in an interesting condition was equally dear to his heart. Both were prospective clients. As a matter of business expediency Mr. Brown had developed two totally different personalities. The Brown who sold a crib was not at all the Brown who sold a coffin. The Brown of cribs and furniture was a jovial, amusingly insinuating man of the world. The Brown of coffins was as lachrymose and gently morbid as the most bereaved widow could wish to encounter.

Although Mr. Bland had never purchased either a crib or a coffin from Mr. Brown, they had known each other for years, having gone to school together. For some time past Mr. Brown had been looking on Mr. Bland with growing disappointment. Quintus Bland would neither die nor propagate the race. It was Mr. Brown's belief that a good citizen should constantly be doing either one thing or the other. To his way of thinking, Quintus Bland was a sheer waste of time.

After having exchanged greetings with Tony and Mr. Brown, Mr. Bland, what with the liquor he had consumed already that morning plus the residue of the previous night, relaxed in the chair and promptly fell into a doze. A portly, florid-faced stranger arrived and seated himself in a chair. Later a second customer came in and seated himself in another chair. Tony beamed happily upon the towelled face of Mr. Bland. Business was picking up. Tony was pleased. He removed the towel from Bland's face and proceeded to cover it with lather. With deft, solicitous strokes he then shaved off Mr. Bland's current crop of whiskers. So far so good. A fresh towel and a gentle massage. Tony began to look puzzled. Gradually his fingers slowed down their action until they remained motionless on Mr. Bland's chin. Here they made a final convulsive effort and stopped. Tony looked down. His fingers, stiff with horror, leaped from the chin. He had the remarkable presence of mind to hide what he saw with a fresh towel. He covered Mr. Bland's face gently and with reverent fingers which trembled a little. Then he approached Mr. Brown as that gentleman was just heaving himself out of his chair. "Come," said Tony, mysteriously, taking the mortician by the arm, "I have a little business for you. Mr. Bland, our very good friend, he's dead in that chair. You must take him away and bury him. That fat-faced man is waiting."

Fully believing that Tony's fine Italian mind had suddenly gone bad, Mr. Brown moved over to the other chair and considered the motionless figure stretched out in it.

"Watch," commanded Tony with the air of a magician. "Gaze upon the face of our very old and very dead friend."

With a slight flourish he flipped the towel from Mr. Bland's face. The mortician found himself looking down upon a naked skull. In spite of his long association with all sorts and conditions of corpses, Mr. Brown was not prepared to meet a skeleton face to face. For a moment he stood blinking at the skull, then he transferred his blinking to Tony. The Italian, under the impression that blinking in the presence of a skeleton was an old American custom, followed the mortician's example. He blinked down at the skull of his erstwhile customer, then blinked upon Mr. Brown.

"There is no doubt, I suppose?" said Tony with a rising inflection. "This is a dead?"

"That is a dead," replied Mr. Brown. "By the looks of him a very old dead."

"But," protested Tony, "he was all alive when he sat down in that chair. You spoke to him yourself. 'Good-morning, Tony,' he said to me. 'How are all the little Wops?' he said."

"All I can say," said Mr. Brown, "is that he's thoroughly dead now— at least, I hope so. As a matter of fact, I never saw a man become so completely dead in such a short space of time. That's what baffles me. Sure you didn't smother him with all those towels?"

"So!" said Tony, explosively. "So! Then I took away his flesh, hey? Poof to you!"

"Don't say 'poof' to me, Tony," reproved Mr. Brown. "You might have hacked it off with your razor, you know."

Tony with eyes ablaze ran round the chair and seized one of Mr. Bland's talon-like hands.

"For why should I shave his hands?" he demanded.

Mr. Bland woke up and looked at Tony in mild surprise.

"Why are you holding my hand, Tony?" he asked.

Tony got rid of Mr. Bland's hand as speedily as if it had been one of Mr. Whittle's loathsome reptiles.

"The dead is back," he told Mr. Brown. "This is against God. Take him away and bury him. He is not good for business."

Mr. Brown was torn between incredulity and professional interest. The latter of the two emotions proved to be the stronger.

"Pardon me," said Mr. Brown, "but are you my old friend, Quintus Bland?"

"I am that," snapped Mr. Bland. "Who did you take me for— Napoleon?"

"You're a trifle long for Napoleon," said Mr. Brown, "but you might easily be any one of thousands of dead persons."

Mr. Bland struggled up in the chair and regarded himself in the mirror.

"I dare say you're right," he observed with surprising mildness for an object so repugnant. "Why not go over to your place and consider the situation? I think I should buy a coffin."

Mr. Brown's establishment was situated next to Tony's barber's shop. It was divided into two separate and distinct units, the funeral parlor lying in the rear of the shop.

"Very well," agreed Mr. Brown, sensing a possible sale. "Come on over." He turned to the dumbfounded Italian. "Tony," he said, "don't stand there boggling at Mr. Bland. Help him out of the chair."

With obvious reluctance Tony righted the chair, and Mr. Bland descended to the floor. The florid-faced gentleman, his robust color momentarily hidden by a coating of lather, gave the skeleton an appalled look. Unlike Mr. Bland, he did not need to be assisted from his chair. He was out of it with surprising agility and making for the door.

"Your face!" cried Tony's assistant. "It is full of soap."

"It is full of horror," replied the man. "Take a look at that face behind you."

The assistant looked over his shoulder at Mr. Bland, then automatically followed his customer through the door. He was fully convinced that Mr. Brown had carried one of his dead bodies over to be shaved.

"Next," announced Tony mechanically to the remaining customer, patiently waiting behind the morning paper. The man lowered the paper and half rose in his chair, then his eyes fell on Mr. Bland, and he remained as if frozen in that difficult posture.

"What sort of a man is that?" he managed to mutter.

"He's all right," Tony assured the man. "He's one of my oldest customers."

"He may be one of your oldest customers," said the man, sinking weakly back in the chair, "but I'll be damned if he's all right. That man's been dead for years."

"Not at all," put in Mr. Bland. "I've merely had a close shave, that's all there is to it."

"If you don't mind," said the man, "I'd rather not speak to you. As soon as I get my strength back I'm going to get out of here."

"Suit yourself," replied Mr. Bland, slipping Tony a five-dollar bill to repay him for his loss of trade. "I'm leaving right now myself."

"Going back to your grave?" asked the man, interested in spite of himself. "Or do you happen to live in a vault?"

"Looking for trouble?" asked Mr. Bland in a nasty tone of voice. "Getting smart, perhaps?"

"Oh, no," hastily disavowed the gentleman. "I've got trouble enough already, and you're all of it."

"Come," said Quintus Bland to Mr. Brown. "Let's go over to your place. I must buy myself a coffin."

This casual remark was a little too much for the waiting customer. Apparently it gave him the strength he required, or at least a part of it.

"Wait," he pleaded, straightening himself unsteadily. "I'm going. Give me three minutes' start."

Mechanically he took his hat from a peg, then slowly left the store, walking like a man in a dream. The mortician turned to the skeleton.

"As much as I'd like to sell you a coffin," he said to Mr. Bland, "I'd hate to be seen on the street with you in your present condition. Isn't there something we can do? You'd be a panic in public, Mr. Bland."

"I have the thing," cried Tony, hurrying to a cabinet. "An artificial beard. It is a clever thing. You hook him over the ears."

"But, Tony," said Mr. Brown, examining the large, white, bushy mop the barber had placed in his hands, "Mr. Bland hasn't got any ears."

"Then hook him over the head," explained Tony. "It works both ways."

"Would you mind hooking this over your head?" asked Mr. Brown, passing the beard to Quintus Bland. "I'll be more used to you in a minute."

With shrinking fingers the skeleton accepted the beard and considered it distastefully.

"Why, Tony," he said, "this is a horrid beard. I've never seen a worse one. Where in the world did you get it?"

"A customer owed me a sum," replied Tony. "So he gave me his beard instead."

"Instead of what?" asked Mr. Brown.

"The sum," said Tony, proudly.

"You lost on the deal, Tony," observed Mr. Bland. "Your customer should have been indebted to you for life. He must have looked a sight behind this beard."

"But consider all the hair," Tony protested, weakly.

"I am," said Mr. Bland, turning to the mirror. "Oh, well, here goes. I can't look much worse than I do already."

He adjusted the beard round his head, then turned on the two men. Both Tony and Mr. Brown took a startled step backward.

"I didn't think anything could look like that," said Tony in a hushed voice.

"What did you think I was going to look like?" Mr. Bland asked, bitterly. "Apollo Belvedere?"

"I have seen that one," replied the Italian. "You are far from him. He has no beard."

"Your hat," suggested Mr. Brown. "Perhaps if you put it on and pulled the brim down—'way down—you might look a little less extraordinary."

"Bah!" muttered Mr. Bland, following this suggestion. "I'm sick of the whole damn' business. The sooner I'm in my coffin the better I'll be pleased."

"So will I," said Tony with feeling.

"Shut up," snapped Mr. Bland. "Tell me how I look."

"I can't," replied Tony, looking helplessly at the mortician. "Mr. Brown, you tell him for me, then tuck him in his coffin, beard and all. He's welcome to it."

"I won't be buried in this beard," said Mr. Bland.

"All right," Mr. Brown soothingly agreed, fearing he might lose a customer. "You don't have to be buried in that beard. Come along with me."

Tony heaved a sigh of relief when he saw the last of Mr. Bland, but not so Officer Donovan when he caught a glimpse of the bearded skeleton for the first time. Donovan, who was directing traffic at a busy corner, for a moment forgot his duty and devoted himself to a thorough scratching of his head.

"Look," he said, seizing a passing pedestrian by the arm and pointing to Mr. Bland. "What do you make of that?"

A little surprised, the pedestrian looked in the direction indicated and immediately became more than surprised. The man was visibly shocked.

"Hanged if I know," he said. "He doesn't look alive, yet he can't be dead. He's the queerest-looking customer I ever saw."

"If the thing wasn't walking so natural-like," declared Donovan, "I'd swear Mr. Brown was dragging a corpse in off the street."

"Maybe he's got one trained," the pedestrian suggested, feebly.

"Who ever heard of a trained corpse?" Donovan retorted, scornfully.

"I don't know," admitted the other, "but who ever heard of a corpse with a beard like that?"

"A corpse can have a beard," Officer Donovan said with confidence. "My uncle was a corpse, and he had a beard something like that."

"Didn't he ever shave?" asked the pedestrian.

"No," replied Donovan, simply. "He was a corpse."

"He wasn't a corpse all his life, was he?" the pedestrian demanded.

"Not all of it," said Donovan. "Just toward the end."

"It wouldn't matter to me," declared the other, "whether I was a corpse or not. If I had a beard like that I'd shave the damn' thing off."

"Maybe that's why this one came back," said Donovan. "He couldn't rest in his grave knowing he had that beard on."

"You mean he came back to get a shave?" asked the other.

"Sure," said Officer Donovan. "He was coming out of Tony's when I saw him first."

"Tony must have refused to shave him," said the pedestrian.

"Would you shave a corpse?" Donovan wanted to know.

"God, no!" exclaimed the pedestrian. "I wouldn't even comb his hair."

At this moment the front mudguard of a quickly arrested automobile struck Officer Donovan from the rear and sent him sprawling on his face.

"I'm so sorry, officer," said the frightened voice of a woman as the outraged policeman came thunderously up to the car. "I've just seen the most terrible sight. For a moment I lost control."

"Did it have a beard on?" asked Donovan.

"Did it have a beard on?" repeated the woman wildly. "Did it have a beard on?" She leaned over the side of the car, her eyes wide with suppressed emotion. "Why, officer, you wouldn't believe me if I told you. You never saw such a beard in all your life."

A persistent hooting of horns and a general confusion of traffic brought Donovan back to an awareness of his duty.

"I'm just after seeing that beard myself, lady," he said. "You'd better drive on."

"Then you're not going to give me a ticket?" asked the woman.

"No, lady," replied Donovan. "You deserve a medal for not having run over me entirely."

The woman started her engine, then once more leaned over the side of the car.

"What did you think of that for a beard?" she asked. "And the rest of it — wasn't it awful?"

"Now don't you begin, lady," Donovan replied wearily. "If I hear any more about that beard and its owner I'll go off my nut and tie this traffic up in knots."

"Somebody should do that to the beard," said the woman as she drove slowly away.

Donovan turned and encountered the wild gaze of the pedestrian.

"Are you still here?" asked the policeman.

"Sure," replied the pedestrian. "Where had we got to about that beard?"

Like a soul in anguish, Officer Donovan shrilled on his whistle, his arms waving wildly. From four directions traffic rolled at him.

"You and your everlasting beard," he flung at the pedestrian.

"It's not my beard," the other protested. "If you hadn't called my attention to it I might never have seen that beard."

"Well," retorted Donovan, "wasn't it something to see?"

"It was too much to see," said the pedestrian. "I don't owe you a thing. The next time you want to show me something pick out a good shaft."

"Do you mean a leg?" asked Donovan. "I do," replied the other.

"Then you ought to be ashamed."

The pedestrian laughed sarcastically.

"I'd a damned sight rather feel ashamed," he said, "than be upset for the rest of the day."

"So would I," agreed Donovan. "That's just the way I feel—all upset."

His subsequent handling of traffic fully proved the truth of his words. By the time he was relieved for his luncheon there had been four minor accidents and one major. In justice to Officer Donovan it should be mentioned that he gave no offender a ticket, ascribing everything that happened to the bearded corpse that had come back to get a shave.

CHAPTER 8.

THE CONVIVIAL CORPSE

In the midst of death and appurtenances pertaining to death the skeleton of Mr. Bland was taking life easy. It was quiet and restful in the decorously subdued atmosphere of Mr. Brown's funeral parlor. It made one feel good to be alive. Seated in a comfortable armchair in front of a large, imposing coffin, Quintus Bland was mildly amused by the thought that he could be just as much at home in the one as in the other. He could sprawl sociably in the armchair or take a turn in that splendid coffin according to his inclinations.

Appreciating the fact that he was dealing with no ordinary, commonplace corpse, Mr. Brown was extending himself to be bright and entertaining. He spoke glowingly of death and interment as if both were ends in themselves greatly to be desired. One of the reasons for the mortician's enthusiasm was a formidable jug of applejack attractively placed on the coffin. Between the jug and the coffin were several thicknesses of last Sunday's newspaper, the thrifty mortician not being so sure as to the quality of the applejack. Both the skeleton and the man who hoped to bury him had copiously partaken of the contents of the jug. Mr. Brown was speaking, and in his present expansive mood he was definitely convinced he meant every word he said.

"It's a fact," he was saying with robust earnestness. "It's God's own truth. It actually hurts me to sell some of these coffins, I've grown so fond of them. Know what I mean?"

"Sort of," hedged Mr. Bland. "You've got some swell-looking coffins here — lovely things."

"Bang up," said the gratified mortician. "Couldn't find a slicker line of coffins even in the city. Take model 1007-A there—that's your coffin, my boy—when I think of you stretched out in that I'm actually burned up with envy. I'd like that coffin myself. I'd nip into it right now if I only felt sick enough."

"If you feel as strongly as that about it," suggested Quintus Bland, "we might get buried together."

"It's an idea," agreed Mr. Brown, taking a hasty gulp from his glass. "There's something in it. We went to school together. Why should we be separated by death?"

"Why, indeed?" said Mr. Bland.

"Death is a splendid institution," continued Mr. Brown. "I don't blame you at all for wanting to go to earth, so to speak." He rose and refilled the glasses. "In death man recaptures the dignity life has taken from him. You'll make a most impressive corpse, my dear Bland."

"Think so?" said Mr. Bland, greatly pleased.

"Know it," replied the mortician. "There's little I don't know about corpses. And when I say a corpse is good that corpse is good, believe me, Charon."

"Believe you who?" asked Mr. Bland.

"Charon," repeated Brown. "A mythical reference. He ferried corpses across the river Styx."

"Guess they have a tunnel nowadays," said Mr. Bland.

"No doubt," replied Mr. Brown. "One-way traffic."

"Tell me this," said Mr. Bland, as if struck by a new problem. "Can a skeleton like me rightly be called a corpse?"

"Sure as you're alive," the mortician hastened to assure him. "You rate a coffin as much as any other stiff. Of course, if you wear that beard I'll have to be careful it doesn't get tangled up in your ribs."

This time it was Mr. Bland who took a hasty gulp from his glass.

"Many wise and comforting things have been said about death," he observed, "but in spite of them all, Brown, we don't seem to like it."

"Prejudice," said Mr. Brown with an explosive snap of his fingers. "Sheer, unenlightened prejudice, my dear Bland. That's what we morticians are up against all the time. We can't sell the idea of death as a thing to do, such as going to Europe or Bermuda or spending the winter in glorious Southern California."

"I know," said Mr. Bland. "But you can come back from these places."

"Ah!" exclaimed Mr. Brown. "My boy, there I have you. People always come back from those places, as you say, but who ever heard of a corpse coming back? Obviously corpses are satisfied to stay where they are—they like it." He paused to replenish the glasses. "Oh, dear me, yes," he continued. "They love it. These people who object to dying haven't a leg to stand on. If more of them popped off in this town I'd go to Bermuda myself."

Too bemused by applejack to notice the inconsistency of this remark, Mr. Bland accepted it at its face value.

"We could both nip into a couple of coffins," he suggested, "and be shipped to Bermuda."

"There's an idea in that," agreed Brown. "The only trouble is, it's mighty hard to go swimming in a coffin."

"Couldn't we float about?" asked Mr. Bland. "With paddles?"

The mortician shook his head.

"No," he said, moodily. "We'd sink like a couple of rocks. And then we'd drown. That wouldn't be any fun."

"But I thought you wanted to be a corpse," said Mr. Bland.

"Not in Bermuda I don't," replied Mr. Brown. "A corpse should stick to his own country and not go barging about in foreign lands. And besides," added Brown, irrelevantly, "I'm very fond of swimming. A coffin makes it harder than a bathing suit or a pair of trunks."

"I guess you're right," Mr. Bland admitted. "Do you wear trunks or a bathing suit?"

"I usually wear trunks," replied Mr. Brown. "There's nothing like sunlight to keep a man alive."

"So do I," said Mr. Bland. "Would it be all right to be buried in a pair of trunks?"

"Sure it would," declared the mortician. "Just the beard and a pair of trunks. Then your wife could sell your best suit or save it for your successor."

"God!" exclaimed Mr. Bland. "You think of everything."

Mr. Brown laughed merrily at the discomfited skeleton.

"Must have my little joke," he said. "Don't mind me. Drink up and have a fresh one."

"That woman would sell my best suit," reflected Mr. Bland, relinquishing his glass. "If I know her at all, she'd sell everything I owned and make my successor buy his own clothes. She's a hard, violent woman, that wife of mine."

"Then she won't miss you so much," the mortician observed consolingly. "That's something for which to be thankful."

"But not much," replied Mr. Bland. "My dog will miss me a lot." He stopped and thought of his dog, remembering that enterprising beast for the first time since he had left the barber's shop. "My dog," he continued. "I had him at Tony's. Did you see anything of a dog called Busy?"

"If you mean," said Mr. Brown, "a square object consisting almost entirely of white wool, then your dog is well named. I caught one glimpse of him, and he was the busiest animal I ever saw."

"What was he busy doing?" asked Mr. Bland.

"He was busy getting out of the store," said Brown. "He had his tail between his legs, and there was a wild look about his eyes."

"Never thought that dog was able to get his tail between his legs," muttered Mr. Bland. "He must have been scared silly."

"He looked silly enough," said the mortician, "but that didn't interfere with his running after he'd taken a look at you."

"Before or after the beard?" asked Quintus Bland.

"Before," replied Mr. Brown. "He didn't wait for the beard."

"Perhaps it's just as well," said Mr. Bland, reflectively. "The shock might have proved too much for the poor animal. He might have gone mad or collapsed."

"I almost did myself," Mr. Brown admitted in a confidential voice. "Even now I don't know how you do it, but I'm not asking any questions. It's your own damn' business. However, there's no getting away from the fact that you should be buried either with or without that beard. And," concluded Mr. Brown with an air of deep satisfaction, "I'm the man to handle the job from soup to nuts. You're in luck. Model 1007-A is the ideal box for you, my boy. How would you like to try it?"

"Suppose you try it first," said Mr. Bland. "Then I'd be able to get some idea."

"Okay," agreed Mr. Brown, rising and putting his empty glass on the vacated chair. "Anything to please a customer. Here goes for a shot at good old 1007-A."

He took the jug from the coffin and with the help of Mr. Bland removed the lid. Then, stepping on a chair, he crawled into model 1007-A and sat in it with a pleased expression on his somewhat flushed face.

"My boy," he declared, "this is the first time I've ever tried a coffin on for a corpse, and let me tell you it's worth all the trouble. This is a magnificent coffin. I couldn't be better pleased if I were being buried in it myself."

Something of the mortician's enthusiasm was communicated to Mr. Bland.

"Lie down in the thing," he said, "and put on the beard. That will give me a good idea of how I will look to Lorna."

"Mark my words," replied the mortician, "you'll look so nice she'll never want to let you go."

"Oh, I've got to be buried," insisted Mr. Bland.

"Certainly you have," replied the other. "If only for my sake. Anyway, you deserve to be buried, and I'm going to see you get what you deserve."

"You're awfully good to me, Brown," said Quintus Bland. "One of the best friends I have, if not the best. Now just lie down in my coffin and try on this beard."

Mr. Brown took the proffered beard, adjusted it over his ears, then stretched himself in the coffin.

"How do I look?" he asked.

"If I look half as well," said Mr. Bland, peering down at his friend, "I'll be more than satisfied. You were made for that coffin, Brown, simply made for it. Climb out and let me have a go at good old 1007-A."

Charlie, Mr. Brown's assistant, had not witnessed the arrival of his employer and Mr. Bland. As he quietly came into the funeral parlor now, however, he was privileged to see them both, but in the dim light of the place he did not at first appreciate the full horror of the scene he was witnessing. Gradually, as his eyes grew accustomed to the modified light, it was borne in on him that he was seeing a strange corpse assisting his boss either in or out of a coffin. And as if to make the whole ghastly affair more difficult of comprehension, his boss had grown a long beard in a remarkably short time. This quaint reversal of procedure Charlie found strangely depressing. Had it not been for his loyalty to the establishment the young man would have withdrawn at once and in great disorder. However, there were a couple of customers waiting, and to lose a possible sale was to Charlie even worse than watching Mr. Brown being prematurely put in a coffin by one of his own corpses. Repressing a natural impulse to rush screaming from the room, Charlie stood in the shadows and awaited further developments. Those were not at all pleasant.

He saw the corpse divest himself of practically all his garments. He saw his newly bearded employer scramble from the coffin to the floor. He saw both his boss and what could be nothing other than a skeleton drink long and deep from a jug, and Charlie wished he could do the same. Finally he saw the skeleton crawl into the coffin where he properly belonged. Although to Charlie's way of thinking the situation in the funeral parlor was still far from normal, a step in the right direction had been taken when the shocking figure of the skeleton had disappeared into model 1007-A, the smartest coffin in the shop. He decided it was comparatively safe to make his mission known. Accordingly he addressed Mr. Brown in a voice that struck even Charlie as being far from normal.

"What sort of a corpse is that, Mr. Brown?" Charlie wanted to know.

Momentarily startled by this unexpected question, Mr. Brown took an extra swig from the bottle, then rallied with reassuring casualness.

"Charlie," he said thickly, but quite naturally, "damned if I know myself, but you need have no fear. Mr. Bland is one of the most entertaining corpses I've ever met, which of course isn't saying a lot. Moreover, he is going to purchase the most expensive coffin in the shop. Charlie, my boy, it is our business to provide corpses with coffins, not to inquire into their conduct."

Yes, sir," replied Charlie. "What I wanted to say was that Mr. and Mrs. Wilks are out there. They want to select a coffin."

"Show them in, my boy, show them in," said Mr. Brown. "The more the merrier, say I. It must be for their uncle. I've had my eyes on the old fellow for some time. I'm delighted he made up his mind to shove off at last."

When Mr. and Mrs. Wilks were ushered into the room, both were visibly shocked by the beard which Mr. Brown had forgotten to remove.

"Why, Mr. Brown," exclaimed Mrs. Wilks, "I didn't know you had grown a beard."

"I haven't, Mrs. Wilks," replied the mortician. "This belongs to one of my most prominent corpses. I'm just wearing it around so that it won't get misplaced."

"What's that?" demanded Wilks, a powerful and aggressive creature. "What are you doing that for?"

"Well, Mr. Wilks," explained Mr. Brown with admirable sang-froid, "there's so much sorrow in this vale of tears that I thought it would be a good idea to make myself look a bit funny. Comic relief, you know."

"You don't see either of us laughing," rumbled Mr. Wilks. "You look anything but funny to me."

"Then I've failed," said the mortician, regret fully. "I'll remove the beard and return it to its rightful owner. He is right over there in his coffin. You must inspect the model. It would be just the thing for your husband or your uncle, Mrs. Wilks, although at the moment your husband doesn't need one. However, to-morrow or the next day — who can tell?"

Supporting himself cleverly between his two clients, he led them unresistingly over to Mr. Bland, lying completely relaxed in his coffin. As if the sight of skeleton dressed only in a pair of orange-striped shorts were not sufficiently arresting, Mr. Brown removed the beard from his own chin and deftly affixed it to that of Mr. Bland, who, as a result of the tickling hairs, sneezed loudly and began to giggle as drunkards occasionally do and always at the wrong time.

"I forgot to mention," said Mr. Brown, quickly, "that this is rather an unusual corpse. Do you think he looks better with or without beard? I'll leave the choice entirely to you."

Slowly Mrs. Wilks sank to the floor, dragging Mr. Brown with her. Finding it impossible to regain his feet without disclosing his condition, Mr. Brown decided to remain where he was.

"Keep your seat, Mrs. Wilks," he said cordially to the lady, patting the thick carpet beside him. "I'll give your husband a drink if you can persuade him to join us."

Rather shamefacedly Mr. Wilks emerged from a closet in which he had taken refuge. In his present state of nerves the man would have joined anything for the solace of a drink. He sank down by his wife and accepted a glass of applejack from Mr. Brown's hand.

"Pass me the jug," said a voice from the coffin, "or I'll snap down there and get it myself."

The three persons seated on the floor glanced up and beheld the bearded skull of Mr. Bland peering down at them over the edge of the coffin.

"Why don't you behave like a decent, self-respecting corpse?" Mr. Brown demanded in a bored voice. "Lie down like a good fellow and stop showing off in front of my customers. It's most annoying."

"Take a look at your customers now," chuckled the skull, one bony finger pointing.

Mr. and Mrs. Wilks, as if endeavoring to recapture the old, lost thrill of their nursery days, were crawling ponderously towards the door on their hands and knees. Upon seeing the efforts of his customers to escape, Mr. Brown emulated their example and began to crawl resolutely after them. Thus, like the Three Bears of happy memory, they lumbered over the carpet. The Rev. T. Whittier Watts, accompanied by a parishioner, stepped quietly into the room and stood regarding this playful little procession with cold, studious eyes, his long cold nose sniffing the while the applejack-tainted air. Finally the Rev. T. Whittier Watts, finding that his presence alone was not sufficient to arrest this exceedingly puerile performance, gave utterance to words in a voice as cold as the rest of his person.

"Mr. Brown," he said, "have you taken leave of your senses?"

"No," replied Brown, thickly, "but Wilks and his wife are about to take leave of my shop, and they haven't picked out their coffin yet. Stand in front of the door and don't let them pass."

"I'll do nothing of the sort," said heaven's gift to a wicked world. "Stand up, sir, and explain your extraordinary conduct."

Totally disregarding the minister, Mr. Brown threw his limbs into high gear and succeeded in decreasing the distance separating him from Mrs. Wilks. With a desperate lunge he threw himself forward and seized the fleeing lady by the leg. The lady uttered a shriek and fell on her face, her free leg waving wildly.

"He's got me by the leg," she managed to inform her husband. "And he's hanging on like grim death."

"Which one?" asked Mr. Wilks, accelerating his pace. "The corpse or Mr. Brown?"

"I don't know," gasped the woman. "I'm afraid to look back."

"So am I," admitted her husband. "But you'd better find out, because if it's the corpse he can have you, leg and all."

"Mrs. Wilks," cried the Rev. Watts, "your skirt is around your neck. Kindly cover your limbs."

"If my skirt is around my neck," declared the floundering woman, "there's lots more to be covered than my limbs."

"Madam, that will do," commanded the Rev. Watts. "This is no place for vulgarity."

"It's no place for man or corpse to be holding me by the leg, either," retorted Mrs. Wilks.

"Mr. Brown," said the minister in his sternest manner, "I order you to remove your hand from that woman's leg."

"Oh," exclaimed Mr. Wilks, "so it's Brown who's after my wife's leg, is it? That's different."

"I'm not after your wife's leg," Mr. Brown disclaimed. "I'm after your wife's business."

"What I" cried Mr. Wilks, twisting his head over one powerful shoulder. "What do you mean by my wife's business?"

"She hasn't selected her coffin yet," said Mr. Brown.

"I'll take any old coffin," moaned Mrs. Wilks, "if you'll only let me out of here."

"Will the three of you get up from the floor," demanded the Rev. Watts, "and stand erect like God-fearing human beings?"

"If he doesn't take his hand from my wife's leg," said Mr. Wilks in an ugly voice, "he'll never stand erect again."

Realizing the utter futility of further effort, Mr. Brown got unsteadily to his feet, philosophically thanking heaven that the situation was not further complicated by the presence of that beard on his chin. He glanced nervously over his shoulder in the direction of model 1007-A. Quiet seemed to reign within the coffin. Mr. Brown fervently hoped that its demoralizing inmate had fallen asleep.

"A pretty way for a mortician to act," Mrs. Wilks was saying indignantly to the Rev. Watts, who did not want to hear her. "Not content with holding my leg, he was actually going after my business, whatever that may be."

"I'm sure he meant no harm." said the Rev. Watts.

"I'm sure he meant no good," the lady retorted with a sniff of feminine scorn.

"What do you mean by that?" came a hollow voice from 1007-A.

All eyes were turned in that direction. Under the concerted scrutiny of so many spectators Mr. Bland snapped back in the coffin with such celerity that all the eyes blinked.

"What's that?" cried the Rev. Watts, his sallow face now paper white. "Am I going mad or did I see a terrible beard on an even more terrible face?"

"You must be going mad," lied Mr. Brown. "I looked and I didn't see a thing."

The minister turned to his companion for further confirmation of his suspicions, but that silent gentleman had beaten both Mr. and Mrs. Wilks to the door by at least three feet and was now increasing the distance as he sped through the outer shop.

Pressing a cold white hand wearily to his temples, the Rev. Watts strove to collect his scattered faculties.

"I have come," he said at last, "to view the remains."

"What remains?" asked Brown, stupidly.

"The remains of Mr. Jessup," said the minister. "You should know at least that much."

"Jessup," repeated the mortician. "Jessup. Don't seem to place that corpse, but I guess he's knocking about somewhere or other."

"Mr. Jessup knocking about?" cried the scandalized man of God. "Is that the way you treat the bodies entrusted to your keeping?"

"Sure," said the drunken mortician, growing a little tired of the Rev. Watts. "We give them the run of the house."

He was about to raise his voice in an impassioned cry for Charlie when a wilder cry than any he could utter issued from coffin 1007-A.

"Calling Mr. Jessup!" came the hollow voice of Mr. Bland, who had arrived at a facetious stage of inebriety. "Paging Mr. Jessup!"

"Charlie," roared Mr. Brown, endeavoring to drown out the sound of Bland's voice. "I say there, Charlie, my boy."

His boy, looking unusually pale and wan, appeared from the outer shop.

"What is it, Mr. Brown?" he asked.

"Ah, there you are, Charlie!" cried the relieved mortician. "What did we do with Jessup? The Rev. Watts here wants to view his remains, but damn me —begging your pardon, sir—if I can remember what we did with the jolly old corpse."

"We shipped a Jessup out to Chicago the first thing this morning," Charlie said, hoping to impress the Rev. Watts favorably by his alertness.

"Dear me!" exclaimed the Rev. Watts, now looking thoroughly startled. "What in the world did you do that for?"

"He insisted on seeing the World's Fair," sang out the coffin. "You know, the Century of Progress."

"Shouldn't Mr. Jessup's remains have gone to the World's Fair?" asked the confused mortician. "I don't mean that, either." Here Mr. Brown raised his voice significantly. "I hope someone," he said, "will learn to mind his own business." Then, addressing the dazed minister, once more he asked, "Shouldn't we have shipped Mr. Jessup to Chicago?"

"No, you shouldn't have shipped Mr. Jessup to Chicago," retorted the minister, who was rapidly losing both his temper and his dignity. "Mr. Jessup was to be buried right here at home. He has never been to Chicago."

"Then it's high time he went," asserted the coffin. "It will do the poor stiff a world of good."

"Who is the godless person speaking from that coffin?" demanded the Rev. Watts in a shaken voice.

"He's a new arrival," answered Mr. Brown. "Guess he hasn't got used to the place yet. He's always gabbing and chattering away just as if he were at a party."

Once more the Rev. Watts pressed a hand to his temple.

"There is something decidedly wrong here," he said in his coldest voice. "And there's something decidedly wrong with you, Mr. Brown. Also, there is something most irregular in the conduct of that coffin."

"Bah!" shrilled the coffin. "One thousand thunders! There's nothing wrong with either of us." The voice broke into a high-pitched, quavering song. "Pals, always pals," it wailed, then stopped abruptly. "It's too good for him," it concluded. "Far too good."

"Who's in that coffin?" demanded the Rev. Watts.

"I'm not sure," said Mr. Brown. "I'm not sure."

"No wonder you shipped poor Jessup to Chicago," the minister observed with a nasty smile. "Not only are you intoxicated yourself, but also you've managed in some way to get one of your inebriated friends into that coffin. I'm going to investigate this and then take steps to see that your license is revoked, Mr. Brown."

Thus speaking, the minister squared his narrow shoulders and walked over to the coffin,

Interested Mr. Brown followed him. Charlie contented himself with waiting in the background. As the Rev. Watts peered down at the skeleton of Mr. Bland, partially concealed behind his formidable beard, one fleshless hand shot up and seized the minister by the lapel of his coat. With a sharp intake of breath the Rev. Watts leaped back and collapsed into a chair.

"Be calm," said the skeleton, sitting up in the coffin. "Pull yourself together. Mr. Brown, give the parson a drink."

Scarcely realizing what he was doing, the Rev. Watts accepted a stiff shot of applejack, which he poured into his shaken and still quivering body.

"Have another?" asked Mr. Brown.

"Pour it out," gasped the Rev. Watts, wiping the tears from his eyes. "I'll take it when I stop burning. What is it, embalming fluid?"

Mr. Brown nodded.

"My own preparation," he said.

"Did it bring that skeleton back from hell?" the minister inquired.

"Listen to me, Watts," the skeleton began, furiously. "You've got away with that stuff about hell altogether too long. I've looked all over for such a place, and damn me if I can find it."

With a hand that trembled, the minister raised the glass to his lips and drained his second drink. Fortified by this, he addressed himself to the skeleton.

"I don't know who you are," he said. "I don't even know what you are, but would you mind telling me how you expect anyone to give you a Christian burial if you keep on talking and singing and popping out of your coffin like a veritable jack-in-the-box?"

"I'm going to bury myself," declared Mr. Bland. "I'm perfectly competent to do so, and it will be much less expensive."

"Perhaps that would be wiser after all," said the minister, holding his glass to Mr. Brown. "I'm sure I could never bury you if you kept interrupting the service and joining in the hymns. Would you mind telling me what you have found on the other side?"

"On the other side of what?" asked Mr. Bland.

"On the other side of the grave," replied the minister.

"I haven't even been buried yet," said Mr. Bland, "but after I'm once planted I'll come back and slip you the dope."

"Don't trouble yourself," the Rev. Watt said, hurriedly. "I'm not as anxious to know as all that." He turned to Mr. Brown. "This embalming fluid is excellent stuff. It's far too good for your patrons. Ha, ha! Must have my little quip even in the face of that god-forsaken-looking object. Just a dash this time."

"Then you don't think I'm drunk?" asked the mortician.

"Far from it," replied the minister. "You're mad. We're both mad. That creature in there cannot be real. It's a figment of our crazed imaginations. I hope the seizure passes, or we'll have to be put away. Oh, look!"

The figment of their imaginations was crawling out of its coffin. When it reached the floor it walked noiselessly to the jug and helped itself to a long drink, then calmly sat down in the other chair.

"Why," asked the Rev. Watts, "are you clad only in your drawers? That's no way to get buried. I can understand the drawers, of course, and I'm gratified you still have some sense of decency left."

"A man is born naked into this world," replied Mr. Bland. "I see no reason why he shouldn't leave it in much the same condition."

"Then why don't you shave that beard off?" the Rev. Watts asked on a note of drunken triumph. "I hope for your mother's sake you weren't born into the world with that."

"If you don't like my beard," said Mr. Bland, "I'll take the damn' thing off."

To the horror of the Rev. Watts the skeleton tugged at his beard and passed it to Mr. Brown, who playfully affixed it to his own chin and stood frowning down at the minister.

"I can't stand it," gasped that gentleman. "Already I've stood too much."

Rising feebly from his chair, he made a zigzag passage for the door. Here he halted and looked back.

"When a mortician and a skeleton start wearing one and the same beard," he said, "it's high time for a mere minister to make himself scarce."

"How about another drink?" asked Mr. Brown.

"Not while you have that beard on," said the Rev. Watts. "Take it off like a good chap and bring me just a dash. My legs are acting in the strangest manner."

A few minutes later Officer Donovan, who was still misdirecting traffic, was the recipient of another shock.

"Holy mackerel," he muttered to himself. "What's come over this burg, anyway? There goes the Rev. Watts, and he's crocked to the eyes."

Although crocked to the eyes, as Donovan had expressed it, the Rev. Watts was feeling better than he had felt in years.

"Want to know what they did with old Jessup?" he asked a passing stranger, clutching the man by the arm. "They shipped old Jessup to the World's Fair, remains and all. Extraordinary piece of carelessness. Has its amusing side, however. Old Jessup at the World's Fair—think of it! What a way to be."

Dismissing the man with a wave of his hand, the Rev. Watts continued on his way. As he lurched round the corner he lifted his hoarse voice in a plaintive song having to do with the continuous loyalty of pals. Those who were privileged to hear the singing of the Rev. Watts were more astonished than entertained.

CHAPTER 9.

1007-A PAYS A SOCIAL CALL

When the wide front door of the Bland residence moved ominously open, Lorna was rising from a solitary luncheon. Solitary, that is, save for the unresponsive presence of a collapsed and deflated Busy who, an hour or so earlier, like a singed bat out of hell, had come streaking up the drive in a high state of nerves.

For a while thereafter the square dog had conducted himself in a suspicious and alarming manner. With mounting anxiety his mistress had watched him alternately staggering and creeping about the house, carefully avoiding dark corners and glancing over his shoulder as if some unseen and unwanted presence were silently stalking his tracks.

Finally Lorna found herself becoming as nervous as the dog. She began to wonder why the animal had returned home unescorted by his drunken and lecherous master. Also, she began to wonder about that fine fellow himself.

She was not long in finding out.

Through the front door four dark-clad gentlemen entered with a certain air of subdued briskness, bearing with them good old model 1007-A.

Following close upon the heels of his cherished coffin appeared a flushed, disheveled, yet happily beaming Mr. Brown. The business in hand was dispatched quickly and quietly, yet not without a somewhat decently festive air. Before Lorna had had time to appreciate fully the inwardness of the events taking place in her home, she found herself in possession of one large and imposing coffin and one obviously drunken Mr. Brown, neither of which she wanted with any great degree of yearning.

Nevertheless she was interested if not gratified.

Hovering curiously in the door of the living-room, Lorna looked first upon the mortician and then upon the coffin. The coffin, she decided, was in far better condition. After industriously mopping his brow with a deep-bordered mourning handkerchief, Mr. Brown turned suddenly upon the lady of the house and held up a protesting hand.

"Now don't be morbid," he told her. "You couldn't get a better coffin if you tried, and besides, I'm sweating like a bull."

"Just how does a bull sweat?" asked Lorna, coolly.

"How should I know?" replied Mr. Brown a little impatiently. "Like anyone else, I suppose. Only on a larger scale."

"I've never seen a bull sweat on any scale at all," observed the woman.

"Then you haven't missed much," said Mr. Brown. "Although it might be worth watching, but don't tax me with it. Maybe bulls are sweatless for all I know, or maybe they sweat like—like —"

"A drunken mortician," suggested Lorna, sweetly.

"Eh, what's that?" he exclaimed. "Who's a drunken mortician?"

"You are," Lorna told him.

"I didn't come here to quarrel," said Mr. Brown with dignity. "So don't go on about it."

"You know," continued Lorna, her voice unpleasantly calm, "no matter how much I may crave and admire that coffin, Mr. Brown, you can't come swooping into my house and forcing the thing on me without any previous warning. I might die from the shock, and that coffin is far too large for me. I'd rattle around in the thing like a pea in a pod."

"Do you always run on like that?" asked Mr. Brown, not insultingly, but from an honest desire to know.

"More or less," said Lorna.

"More," contributed the coffin in a decided but muffled voice. "Never, never less. She always goes on and on and on—endlessly and tiresomely —fiendishly!"

Sleepily the voice droned itself into silence.

"Who said that?" demanded Mr. Brown before Lorna had time to put the same question to him.

"I don't know," she replied, "but whoever it was I'd like to wring his lying neck."

She advanced into the room and held a clenched fist directly over the coffin.

"Why his lying neck, madam?" Brown asked quickly to distract her attention.

"Why not his lying neck?" she snapped. "What else should I wring?"

"Far be it from me to say," said Mr. Brown, "but I might suggest his teeth — people lie through their teeth, you know."

"But people don't always have teeth," she retorted, "and they always have necks."

"Why not wring his hand?" he asked her.

"I don't know who he is," she said.

"You don't know who who is?" inquired Mr. Brown.

"You're very drunk," she assured him.

"Perhaps you're right," he admitted. "Is there anything in the house?"

"It's over there on the table," she said. "Help yourself and pour me one, if you don't mind."

"I don't mind," said Mr. Brown, simply.

"In fact, I'd rather like it."

He poured two drinks, gave one to Lorna. Then both sat down and thoughtfully surveyed the coffin.

"It's a lovely thing," she said at last. "Lovely."

"Exquisite," agreed Brown. "Would you care for one just like it, only smaller?"

"It would make the room too crowded," she said. "And besides, I couldn't afford it unless on partial payments."

"That might be arranged," said Mr. Brown. "You could sell the sofa to begin with."

Lorna considered this, then suggested another drink.

"Tell me," she said when she was given one. "Who is really going to get this coffin?"

"Eh!" Brown exclaimed. "I don't quite understand."

"I mean," she said, "that you've made a mistake, Mr. Brown."

"Of course, I have," he admitted. "I shipped Mr. Jessup to the World's Fair. That was an amusing blunder."

"Who's Mr. Jessup?" Lorna asked.

"I don't quite know myself," said Brown, in some perplexity, "but I'm given to understand he was one of my transient corpses."

"Do any of them stay with you permanently?"

"No corpse stays with me permanently," Brown declared with emphasis. "Not if I know it."

"I guess you'd know it," said Lorna.

"'Most anybody would," said Mr. Brown.

"Is this one going to stay permanently with me?" she asked him.

"That's up to you," he told her.

"Then I say no," she declared. "There are enough queer things in this house already."

"There's nothing queer about a corpse," said Mr. Brown.

"Not when it stays in its proper place," she answered. "But the middle of my best room is no proper place for a corpse. People would begin to talk."

"Let 'em," said Mr. Brown, largely. "Let 'em talk their blasted tongues off. If you want a corpse in your home there's no reason in the world why you shouldn't have your corpse—or a baker's dozen of corpses, if you care for so many."

"But I don't want one corpse in my home," she protested, "let alone a baker's dozen of them. By the way," she added, "just how could you make up a baker's dozen of corpses, Mr. Brown?"

"Quite simply," said Mr. Brown. "Just toss in an extra arm, or leg, or, for full measure, a good torso."

"Gr-r-r," came from the coffin. "How can they do it?"

"Did you hear that?" asked Lorna.

"No," lied Mr. Brown. "Is there a dog in the house?"

"Yes," replied Lorna.

"Then that explains it," said Brown.

"A baker's dozen of dogs wouldn't explain it to me," she declared. "There's something funny about that coffin. Who really owns it?"

"Your husband bought that coffin," said Mr. Brown.

"Then where is my husband?"

"Why, he's in the coffin," Brown told her. "I thought you knew that."

"Why in the world does he want to be in a stuffy old coffin?" asked Lorna.

"Why does anyone want to be in a coffin?" countered Mr. Brown.

"Damned if I know," said Lorna, frankly. "Do you, Mr. Brown?"

"All of my clients want to be in coffins," he replied.

Lorna laughed scornfully.

"They can't help themselves," she answered. "They have to be in coffins."

"Well," said Mr. Brown, "your husband is one of my clients."

"You mean to say," asked Lorna, "that my husband actually wanted to be in that coffin?"

"Couldn't keep him out of it," Brown declared, proudly. "He's crazy about that coffin—admires it quite sincerely."

"It's one thing to admire a coffin," said Lorna, "and quite another to crawl into one. Take me, for example. I admire that coffin, but I'd go to the most extreme lengths to keep myself out of it."

"You could be in far worse places," observed Mr. Brown, defensively.

"Perhaps," she admitted, "but in comparison with that coffin the foulest gutter would be a bed of roses to me."

"Yes?" said Mr. Brown, now thoroughly aroused. "And if you lay long in a foul gutter you'd jolly well need a coffin. What do you think of that?"

"It doesn't make any sense," she answered. "It takes a strong constitution to lie in a foul gutter."

"I never lay in a foul gutter," said Mr. Brown. "What sort of gutters do you lie in?"

"I've never lain in any gutter at all," he answered.

"Then," said Lorna, crushingly, "you don't know life."

"Life is not my business," remarked Mr. Brown. "I deal exclusively with death."

"Not when it comes to drinking," she retorted.

"I have my lighter moments," replied Brown. "For example, madam, I'd like to sell you a crib or a baby carriage."

"With my husband lying dead in that coffin?"

"That coffin," said Mr. Brown, "contains only one husband. There are lots of others knocking about."

"Your calling has corrupted your morals," declared Lorna. "If I thought for one moment you were making improper advances I'd be very much pleased."

"No, you wouldn't," said Mr. Brown. "Not with your husband lurking in that coffin. The lid isn't screwed down."

"Do you mean," she demanded, "my husband isn't quite dead?"

"He's a little more than dead," Mr. Brown assured her. "Your husband is already a skeleton."

"Then it isn't my husband at all," said Lorna. "That's Señor Toledo."

"My God!" cried Mr. Brown. "Have I made another mistake?"

"Let's go and see," she suggested. "Perhaps it is my husband after all."

"I hope to heaven it is," Brown declared, earnestly.

"Thanks for your kind wishes," was Lorna's tart reply. "Just for that I do hope it's Señor Toledo and that he died without a cent to pay for your old coffin."

"If it is that Toledo person," retorted Mr. Brown, "I'll yank him out of that coffin a darned sight faster than he ever got in it, mark my words."

"And I'd have you run in for body-snatching," Lorna calmly stated.

"How can you snatch a body," Mr. Brown wanted to know, "when this one consists entirely of bones "

"That, said Lorna, "strikes me as taking an even unfairer advantage of the dead. A skeleton must be about the easiest type of body to snatch. The judge would want to know why you didn't pick on a body your size."

"Will you two please stop bickering about snatching my body?" demanded the coffin, and this time the voice though thick was by no means muffled.

Both Lorna and Mr. Brown looked up from their glasses to encounter a rare and awesome resurrection. Quintus Bland, clad in a flowing beard, was sitting up in his coffin and peering at them dimly out of sleep-laden eyes.

"Want a drink," announced Quintus Bland.

"I thought you said you put a skeleton in that coffin," said Lorna, turning on the dazed Mr. Brown.

"I didn't say I put one in," protested that worthy mortician. "I said a skeleton crawled in unaided, and I stand by that statement."

"Was he wearing that astonishing beard at the time?" she demanded.

"Am I not a skeleton any more?" Bland mildly inquired.

"I should say not," replied Lorna. "You're as naked as a coot, aside from that offensive bush."

"That being the case," reflected Mr. Bland aloud, "the beard should be a couple of feet longer, estimating conservatively."

"Get out of that coffin at once," snapped Lorna, "and remove that silly beard."

"That," observed her husband, "is an indecent suggestion."

"Indecent suggestions are the only kind you like or understand."

"I like them when it is the other party who does the suggesting," he replied, "or when it's mutual. If you, my love, will remove your frock I will gladly yank off my beard. The only thing that will get me out of this exceedingly comfortable coffin is the refusal of a drink."

Gratified by this glowing testimonial to 1007-A, Mr. Brown arose and presented Mr. Bland with the entire bottle.

"You look even better in it the way you are," said Brown, "than when you were a skeleton."

"That's saying a lot," replied Bland, eagerly plucking the bottle from the mortician's hand. "I've had a most refreshing little nap in this fascinating crib. If my wife were not so snooty, I'd take up the matter of removing our antiquated nuptial couch and substituting twin coffins instead."

"There's an idea in that," observed Mr. Brown. "Only it might be bad for my furniture business."

"I fully appreciate the point," said Mr. Bland. "People can hardly be buried in their beds, whereas they can be in their coffins. I withdraw the suggestion, old boy. At this stage in our so-called national recovery we must stimulate sales rather than retard them."

"Exactly," agreed Mr. Brown. "More people should go to bed, and many more should die."

"I suggest that both of you die," said Lorna. "Your loss would be a gain to the nation."

"Silence, woman!" commanded Mr. Bland, peering fiercely at her over his terrible beard. "If economists practiced what they preached, there would be damned few economists, and I, for one, would be just as well pleased."

"Listen," said Lorna. "You've got me licked. I can't talk to you if you're going to keep wearing that homicidal-looking beard."

"Madam," Bland told her calmly, "this beard and coffin are indispensable to my happiness."

"They are most detrimental to mine," said Lorna. "That, together with the knowledge that I have an occasional skeleton for a husband."

"Would you prefer a skeleton to a dirty dog?" asked Mr. Bland, significantly.

"Both are equally objectionable," said Lorna.

"Yes, but if Señor Toledo had not gallantly saved you from your folly," Bland retorted, "you'd have been in a pretty fix, my dear young wench."

"You did it for your own selfish interests," Lorna replied. "You saved me for yourself."

"At the risk of breaking every bone in my body," supplied Mr. Bland. "Which reminds me, has your dear Phil fully recovered from his fright?"

"Why wash your dirty linen in public?" Lorna asked, evasively.

"As you can see," said Mr. Bland, "I haven't a scrap of linen about me, either clean or dirty. An old dish-rag would do me a world of good."

"What did you do with your clothes?"

"My apprentice embalmer," said Mr. Brown, "was trying them on a client when we left. A conscientious young man."

"I did have a pair of drawers," Bland wistfully observed, "but they must have got jolted off during the drive."

"I don't know what we're going to do about all this," lamented Lorna. "Here I find myself conversing with a drunken mortician and a naked and falsely bearded husband seated in a huge coffin in the middle of my best room. You can see for yourself it's unnatural. Suppose somebody should call?"

And that was precisely what somebody did at that inauspicious moment. Somebody called—two, in fact. They called to give Lorna a pleasant little surprise and were all brimming over with well-being and merriment. The surprise they gave was returned in full measure, but it was far from pleasant.

Finding the front door off the lock, Mr. and Mrs. Tucker, Lorna's brother- in-law and sister, crept into the house and continued creeping until they arrived at the door of the living-room. Here they stopped creeping. Had they possessed the power they probably would have crept backwards and as silently left the house. But the scene that confronted them robbed them of all powers for the moment. However, it could not stop Mrs. Tucker's set greeting. Not knowing what she was saying, she cried out in a dead voice: "Hello, everybody!"

"Who's that?" shouted Quintus Bland.

"How do I know?" said Mr. Brown.

"Dear God," quavered Lorna.

Then the scene became one of frenzied action.

CHAPTER 10.

THE BODY IS VIEWED WITHOUT FAVOR

It was Brown who shot fire through the frozen tableau. As drunk as he was, his brain and body functioned with startling rapidity. Like a seasoned football player he flung himself upon the body of a shocked and protesting Bland and bore him down into the depths of 1007-A. Even then Mr. Bland did not abandon the battle or, better still, the bottle. For a brief moment it was flourished aloft like the sword of a fallen chieftain, then it was deftly snatched from view by an extremely busy mortician. The next moment an amazing change came over the man. His still flushed face grew calm and assumed an expression of sorrow controlled by resignation. He clasped his hands in front of him in an attitude of silent prayer. He bowed his head slightly in humility and sorrow. In this posture he stood by the coffin and gazed down at its shocking contents with spellbound reverence.

What he actually contemplated was the entirely naked figure of a long, lank Quintus Bland, stretched out at full length with his horrid beard far off center and completely concealing his mouth. While the eyes of Mr. Bland glared up malevolently at Mr. Brown, the beard puffed and bellowed wickedly as the hot breath of its wearer surged indignantly through its strands.

Looking down on this weird yet formidable figure, Mr. Brown could not help thinking how much more colorful his life would be if the corpses he did business with had only one-tenth of the spunk and animation of the unlovely body now stretched out before him. Also, the distressing thought occurred to him that if that alarmingly active beard crept up a little higher Mr. Bland stood in imminent danger of becoming a corpse in reality through the simple process of suffocation.

While Mr. Brown was occupied with his varied reflections, Lorna was doing her bit in another direction. Flying to her sister, the stunned Mrs. Tucker, she fell so heavily on that lady's neck that both of them nearly collapsed to the floor. Lorna's breath alone would have floored a much stronger woman than the one now staggering under her sudden assault.

Meanwhile Mr. Tucker, a man of an observant eye and an inquiring disposition, having rallied from the first shock, was about to advance into the room to investigate the situation. Surely, he decided, if any situation deserved investigation, this one did.

Lorna was quick to sense his intentions. Immediately she took steps. She gave her sister a violent push backwards, thus further removing her from the coffin and its inmate, then hurled herself into the arms of her brother-in-law. The man had no other choice than to catch hold of her. Otherwise she would have crashed to his feet.

For a moment, at least, the advance of the Tuckers was checked. Lorna needed time to parley with them. In the back of her mind she wondered if the drunken mortician possessed sufficient sense to throw something over the naked reaches of her equally drunken husband. If not, she hoped he had flipped Mr. Bland over on his stomach. An unconventional posture for a corpse, perhaps, but one which would cover a multitude of sins, including that desperate beard. She could tell the Tuckers that it was being done in Hollywood, or that it had been her husband's last request.

"Lorna," he had said, "bury me on my stomach. I've always slept that way."

Such mad thoughts flashed through her distracted mind before she regained the ability to express herself in words. When she did they came in great quantities.

To her surprising expressions of sorrow Dolly, who had always been dumb, could find no adequate reply. Also, she was too deeply engrossed in adjusting the disarranged garments which her emotional sister had half dragged off her body. Not so Mr. Tucker. He was smelling rats in ever-increasing numbers.

"I say, old girl," he said, "this is a terrible shock. Is it—is it —?

"Yes, Frank," Lorna broke in, "it's Quintie. Little Quintie—the dirty old dog."

Frank considered this information while delicately sniffing a familiar odor on the air.

"Was it sudden, old girl?" he asked.

"Was it sudden?" repeated Lorna, enthusiastically, snapping her fingers. "Like that. Just like a snowball in hell. The mortician is adjusting him now. What a man!"

"Adjusting him?" said Frank. "Looked more to me as if he were wrestling with him when we came in."

"No, Frank, you're wrong," declared Lorna. "Quintie was a punk wrestler."

Deep in 1007-A, Quintie was chewing his beard in rage while Mr. Brown pressed two reverent hands heavily down on his chest.

"Are you burying him with a bottle?" asked Frank. "I could have sworn I saw him holding one in his hand."

"We were thinking of it, Frank dear," said Lorna. "He was such a lovable sot. Seldom did he have a bottle out of his hand or two inches from his mouth. And what a mouth! Just like a split watermelon."

At this, Mr. Bland's mouth did split just like a watermelon as he fairly devoured his beard. From the depth of the coffin issued low, gurgling sounds, horrible to hear.

"That's the mortician," said Lorna, quickly "He's intoning a prayer for the drunk, or the dead, it doesn't matter which. Both are helpless. If the mortician couldn't intone he couldn't mort. He doesn't do it so well, does he? I think he's a little mad."

Upon hearing this, Mr. Brown felt inclined to allow the demented occupant of 1007-A to escape with his beard and his nakedness. "After all," thought Brown, "this is none of my affair." However, he still pressed down for the simple reason that he was not so sure that he himself would not be the first object of Mr. Bland's attack.

"What's that fellow doing?" Frank Tucker suddenly asked. "Looks like he's kneading the body of good old Blandie."

Dolly Tucker gave a little scream at this. She was still too shocked to speak.

"Needing him?" asked Lorna, puzzled. "Oh, yes, he needs the body. He needs it for his business. Money in the pocket, you know."

"But, Lorna, dear," said Dolly, made vocal by weariness from having stood so long in the hall, "won't you even allow us to view the remains and then sit quietly down somewhere? You act and talk so strangely. I'm sure you need a little comfort and consolation."

"I'd rather have a drink," replied Lorna. "That's all I've lived on since the world's worst photographer passed out."

Part of the statement was true. Lorna was so deep in her cups and so angry with her husband that she had deliberately set out to torture him. She was succeeding far beyond her fondest expectations. Her only regret was that she could not peer down into 1007-A and enjoy his reactions. What right had he to bring a great, hulking coffin into her house and reveal himself naked in that beard? If he thought he was funny, well, she would be funny, too.

On his part Frank Tucker now knew that something was definitely wrong with the whole queer business. The one thing that gave him pause was the presence of that huge and obviously expensive coffin. The situation amused as well as puzzled him. And he knew that the wild ravings of his sister-in-law sprang more from a bottle than from a grief-stricken heart.

In the living-room Mr. Brown had developed a new and improved line of strategy. Instead of holding Mr. Bland down by brute force, he was now letting a bottle do it for him.

"Will you stay here quietly and take off that beard if I give you a bottle?" he had asked Mr. Bland.

"I'll lie here quietly," that gentleman had replied, "but I won't take off the beard."

"Why won't you take off the beard?" Mr. Brown had whispered.

"I don't know myself," Mr. Bland had whispered back. "I've an odd feeling the thing has taken root and become a part of my chin. Anyway, most of it is in my mouth, and I can't get it out."

"Very well, then," Mr. Brown had replied passionately. "Keep your damned beard, but for God's sake don't pop up."

Mr. Bland had kept his beard and had not popped up. Now he was incapable of popping, except of popping the bottle through the beard whenever he found the strength. All signs pointed to a speedy return to slumber.

With so much freedom on his tired hands Mr. Brown, having found the residence of the bottles, was doing a little popping on his own account. This he did by stealth in an obscure corner of the room.

Lorna had at last allowed Dolly and Frank to sit down. They were now in the dining-room, where they were having a little of something wet, wetness being Lorna's one and only idea of hospitality. Beyond this her mind could not penetrate. It made entertaining simpler and happier.

"When are you going to bury him?" Dolly was asking.

Lorna gulped.

"At the full of the moon," she said.

"My God!" exclaimed Frank. "The moon won't be full for two weeks."

"Well, replied Lorna, "you know how time flies. I was never one for rushing things myself."

Fanny, the passionate maid, appeared with Busy.

"Oh, Fanny," said Lorna, "did the dog howl just before?"

"Before what, madam?" asked the puzzled Fanny.

"Don't be dull, girl," said Lorna. "Before his master passed out?"

"Why, no, madam," replied the startled Fanny, who had been absent from the house during most of the afternoon.

"Then he's no sort of dog at all, said Lorna. "All decent dogs howl just before and frequently during. And Fanny, keep him away from the body. He might try to play with it. I wouldn't mind if the beast wasn't so rough. It's a bother to have to keep doing a body over and over again. Mr. Brown, the mortician, is a charming man, but they tell me he does get impatient with his bodies. He might give this body the gate."

Fanny looked completely dazed. For once her arrogant pride of sex seemed to desert her.

"When did the master die, Mrs. Bland?" she managed to get out.

"About an hour after he had chased you downstairs," Lorna maliciously informed the maid. "Remember, Fanny? He was all naked and howling. Perhaps that's why that square dog didn't howl. He probably thought there'd been enough howling in the house for one day. The doctor said the poor man died from thwarted passion, and you know what that means. But I don't hold it against you, Fanny. You had your housework to do and you very creditably thought of duty first. However, I hope it teaches you a lesson, my girl. I hope it does. Never keep a man waiting. He might die on your hands. And then where would you be? I ask you. You'd be without a man, and that is just no place. We must have our men, my girl, in spite of the fact that they're all scum, including Frank Tucker. Oh, my heart is breaking. That's all, Fanny. I'll be seeing you. Where are you going, Dolly?"

Dolly turned on her sister indignantly.

"I'm going in to poor Quintus," she said. "Someone should be with him for the sake of decency. And then I'm going home. Lorna, I hate to say it, but you're either out of your mind or you're a very, very wicked woman. Come, Frank. I won't permit her to call you names."

Frank rose and looked down at Lorna, who solemnly winked up at him. Frank grinned and followed his wife from the room, as husbands have been doing ever since doors were invented.

"You can have the last word," Lorna called after Dolly. "Mine would raise the roof. But mark me well, sister. If you're going to look at Quintus for the sake of decency, I shudder to think of what you'd look at for the sake of fun."

"Now, I wonder, Frank," said Dolly, "just what she meant by that?"

Dolly soon found out.

Mr. Brown had continued his popping until he could pop no longer. He now sat slumbering gently beside the glistening flank of his well-loved 1007-A. Within the coffin its temporary resident had popped himself into even deeper oblivion. Momentarily he was, to all intents and purposes, as nearly dead as a man can well afford to be. Fortunately, before his final collapse, Mr. Brown had exhibited the decency if not the good taste to find Mr. Bland's drawers and to help him to put them on.

Upon the entrance of Frank and Dolly Tucker, Mr. Brown awoke and made a feeble attempt to rise. This effort failing, he made the best of a bad situation and waved a welcoming hand to his visitors.

"May we view the body now?" asked Dolly in a hushed voice.

"Whose body?" asked Mr. Brown.

"Why, the deceased's, of course," replied Dolly.

"Well, I'm nearly dead myself," Mr. Brown affably informed her. "I didn't know. One body to me is about as bad as another."

In spite of himself Frank Tucker could not suppress a low laugh. Dolly was shocked. She was even a little frightened.

"Frank," she murmured. "I'm ashamed. You're as bad as Lorna."

"Sorry, dear," he said. "It's nerves. Death always makes me giddy."

Turning icily from her husband, Dolly made another try at Mr. Brown, who by this time had managed to get himself back to sleep.

"Mr. Brown," she began.

"What's that? What's that," he said in a startled voice. "Has the prisoner escaped?"

"I don't know what you're talking about," Dolly replied, desperately.

"Doubt if I do myself," said Brown. "Please state your business, madam. Do you want a baby carriage?"

"No, Mr. Brown," said Dolly with sweet patience. "Have you finished with Mr. Bland?"

"My God, yes," Mr. Brown replied with more vigor than he had yet shown. "He's nearly ruined me. It's been the toughest job I've ever tackled."

"Then may we look at him?" continued Dolly, striving to hide her horror of the man.

"If you want a good laugh, yes," said Brown. "I can't stand the sight of him myself."

Once more Mr. Brown drifted off to sleep. With a shudder Dolly turned away and approached the coffin. Taking her husband's arm and assuming a sort of hushed, tense expression, she gazed down upon Mr. Bland. Then her expression stiffened and solidified. She looked as if she would never lose it. A small, fluttering cry escaped her lips.

"The beard makes up for a lot," murmured Frank. "Have you noticed it?"

"But, Frank," breathed Dolly, "it's growing all wrong. It's—it's —it's a frightful beard. That man should be a butcher instead of a mortician."

"Do you smell anything, Dolly?" asked Frank.

"Whisky," gasped Dolly—"He reeks of it."

"And he still has some left," said Frank, pointing to a bottle clutched in the hand of the corpse.

"I just won't permit that," declared Dolly. "Even if it isn't any of my business."

"His beard still seems to have a spark of life left in it," observed her husband. "Notice how it sways gently as if fanned by a light breeze."

"Do you think —" said Dolly as she reached for the bottle. "Can it be —" she continued, taking a firm grip on the bottle itself.

While she was thus engaged, Frank Tucker placed his forefinger experimentally on the tip of Mr. Bland's nose. This action, together with the threatened loss of his property, produced a startling manifestation in the corpse. With a loud sneeze he blew his beard down to his chin. At the same moment he half rose in his coffin.

"What the hell!" said Mr. Bland.

It was the most awful moment in Dolly's life. With a shriek that frightened Mr. Bland still further out of the coffin, and Mr. Brown completely out of his chair, Dolly fled from the room and from the house. She was followed reluctantly by her husband, as husbands often, if not always, do.

"Would you mind telling me," said Mr. Bland, addressing himself to a startled Brown, "just what the hell all this is about?"

"I'm not sure," said Brown, "but I think you've just had callers."

"Thank God they're gone," Lorna remarked, coolly, strolling into the room with a glass in her hand.

"That's the only point upon which we agree, you little viper," retorted her husband.

"Go on, be a skeleton for us, Quintie," she amiably jeered back. "We need some fun."

Even Mr. Brown disapproved a little of some of Mr. Bland's subsequent remarks to his wife.

CHAPTER 11.

A DIRTY MAN DIGS HIS GRAVE

Had Quintus Bland been a horse or even a rabbit, it would have been an easy matter to lure him from his coffin through the trifling inducement of carrots. And it would have been a better thing for Mr. Bland, because carrots are good for one's health, whereas, we are told, whisky is not. On the other hand, it has never been successfully established that carrots elevate the soul. Incontrovertibly whisky does, assuming the subject has a soul to elevate. One cannot eat a carrot, then almost immediately burst into loud song, or dance with rugged abandon. Yet if one but consumes an equal displacement of whisky one can achieve both of these feats even though one has never attempted them before.

The suggestion of carrots to Mr. Bland, reclining in 1007-A, and clad in the tightest of raiment, would have been revolting. It might have driven the man mad or broken his heart. The mere hope of a drink of whisky caused him to scramble out of what threatened to become his permanent habitation with even greater alacrity than he had shown on entering it. This came to pass only after he was convinced that he possessed within himself the last drop in his bottle.

It was not a pretty sight nor an edifying one to see Quintus Bland draping his long naked body over the side of the coffin, yet it did show perseverance.

"I'm not sure that you did him a favor, Mr. Brown, when you dragged on those drawers," observed a critical Lorna as she and the mortician sat watching Mr. Bland's heroic efforts. "No," she continued, "I'm sure you didn't. There might have been something primitively appealing had you left him entirely naked, but those drawers deprive the man of his last shred of dignity. Regard how they hang askew."

"Will you please go to hell?" Mr. Bland mildly asked his wife as soon as his feet touched the floor. "But before going be so good as to give me a drink."

"Not," she told him, "until you've removed that lovely little beard. It's dangling from your left ear. If you strapped it about your waist you'd look like a Scotch highlander."

"Must I go through all this for the sake of a mere drink?" inquired Mr. Bland.

"Men have gone through more," said Lorna and gave him a drink.

He drank the drink, returned the glass, and wanted to know if that was all. Deep in her eyes as Lorna looked up at her husband was a veiled glow of affection. She handed him a fresh bottle.

"Fanny," she said, "has telephoned for a carload."

Mr. Brown swayed over to the coffin and peered into its depth. Then he extracted an empty bottle therefrom and returned to his chair. He appeared to be in a thoughtful mood.

"What I'd like to settle," he said after a moment's reflection, "is just this: is that your coffin or is it my coffin?"

"An interesting point," said Mr. Bland. "Tell me, Brown, is the coffin greatly damaged?"

"Somewhat crushed," Mr. Brown admitted. "Sort of thumbed and fingered here and there, and then it is stained with whisky in spots, but fairly speaking, it is still a top-notch article."

"I loved it," said Mr. Bland, wistfully.

"Couldn't it be sold as a second-hand coffin?" asked Lorna.

"Who ever heard of a second-hand coffin?" Mr. Brown wanted to know.

"That's just the point," replied Lorna. "If nobody has ever heard of a second-hand coffin, that fact might make it easier to sell one."

"Even to me," declared Mr. Brown, "the idea is unpleasant. Imagine. A second-hand coffin. Gracious."

"Perhaps you're right," Lorna admitted. "It would be hard to find a second-hand body to fill it."

"All bodies are second-hand after they've once been used," observed Mr. Bland. "Just like automobiles."

"That's ridiculous," protested Lorna. "My body is better to-day than it ever was."

"Did you ever try to sell it?" asked Mr. Brown, crudely.

"I'd like to kick a hole in your damned old coffin," Lorna retorted, viciously.

"I defy you to kick a hole in that coffin," said Mr. Brown, quite blandly. "The thing is practically bullet-proof, and besides that, who said it was my coffin?"

"Well, it isn't our coffin," declared Lorna. "I wouldn't let Quintus get buried in it, as much as I'd like to see the last of him."

"Have you definitely decided not to die?" the mortician asked, turning to Mr. Bland.

"Sorry, old man," said Mr. Bland. "I think it would be better if I didn't."

"Then don't let's think about it for the present," Mr. Brown suggested, wearily. "The problem bewilders me."

"Right is right," put in Lorna, for no particular reason.

"I find that vague," said Brown. "Let's change the subject."

Fanny changed it for them. She entered the room on tiptoe, then uttered a little scream upon seeing Mr. Bland. Since the removal of his beard he had taken a fancy to a Paisley shawl which he was now wearing toga fashion like some lean and debauched Roman emperor.

"I thought he was in that," said Fanny, motioning to the coffin.

"He was," Mr. Brown replied, calmly, "but he's back again."

"Should he remove the shawl, Fanny?" Lorna asked, darkly. "Has he got too much on?"

"Goodness, no, Mrs. Bland," replied the passionate maid. "I've seen enough of him."

"I should say so," agreed Lorna. "You couldn't have seen any more of a man unless you encountered a freak with three legs, or a double stomach, or an extra toe here and there."

"I don't like that kind, Mrs. Bland," confessed Fanny with the utmost simplicity.

"I'm glad you're not greedy," observed Mrs. Bland. "Did you come in here to view the old familiar body, or what?"

"I might have taken a squint at it," the maid admitted, "but that's not why I came."

"Are we supposed to guess," asked Mr. Bland, "or would you like to tell us?"

Fanny regarded her master with a pair of smouldering eyes which fairly tore off the Paisley shawl and flung it in a corner, then she turned back to Lorna.

"The stuff has come, Mrs. Bland," she said. "I thought you might be needing it for your little celebration, but now I see you've no occasion to celebrate."

"All women are wenches," observed Mr. Bland, tossing his remark somewhere in the general direction of 1007-A.

"All this bickering is making me feel decidedly uncomfortable," Mr. Brown complained. "Why not send this lush young filly for another bottle? She's doing me no good as she is."

"Fanny," said Lorna, "bring the gentleman a bottle. We must handle our leading mortician with kid gloves. Personally, I wouldn't touch him with tongs."

Alarming chemical changes were taking place beneath the Paisley shawl. Fanny, glancing in that direction, unleashed a series of short, sharp shrieks. They ended abruptly in speech.

"He's back!" she cried. "The skeleton—Señor Toledo. Oh, look! How did he do it? I'll go for the bottles."

"Bring 'em all in," Mr. Brown shouted after the speeding maid, then turning to look at the horror lurking beneath the Paisley shawl, he said severely: "For God's sake, man, why don't you ring a bell or blow a horn before you do a thing like that?"

"It's positively indecent the way that man sneaks into a skeleton," complained

Lorna. "If I were going to be a skeleton I'd writhe and gnash and make noises of a distinctly unpopular nature. Now I do need a drink."

"Oh, damn," said Mr. Bland. "Oh, damn, damn, damn. How I hate it all. And just as we were getting on so well together."

There was a note of real tragedy in his voice. Lorna glanced at him quickly and for no reason at all felt a catch at her throat.

"If we can stand you, old comrade," she said, "you should make an effort to stand yourself."

"But can't you see," he explained in a low voice. "I'm so damned different from you all, so cut off and useless."

"Oh, look," said Lorna, pointing. "Enter totteringly: the world's most passionate maid, bearing an armful of pretty bottles."

"Give me a pretty bottle," muttered the Paisley shawl.

When Mr. Bland rose to find the corkscrew the effect was immense. The shawl dropped from him, and he stood in all his bony structure, clad only in his drawers. Fanny hastily put down the bottles, so poignant were her emotions. Mr. Brown was fascinated beyond speech. He merely stared at Mr. Bland and gulped. The wife of the skeleton was prey to mingled emotions. On the whole she decided she would rather not look at him for a moment.

"If you have any pity in your ribs," she said at last, "you'll remove those drawers without further delay."

"They're coming off unassisted," Mr. Bland informed her. "They invariably do when I am in this condition."

"And I for one don't blame them," observed Mr. Brown with feeling.

"But suppose I should suddenly turn back?" asked Mr. Bland.

"Then we'll turn ours," said Lorna. "Any sight is preferable to a skeleton in drawers. Just be yourself for a while. We've all been through such a lot."

"Is eating an exploded theory in this house?" asked Mr. Brown. "If we keep drinking on empty stomachs we will soon be unable to drink at all, and that would be just too bad."

"Oh, yes," said Lorna, vaguely, "we occasionally glimpse food. That is to say, we used to before this binge started years and years ago. When did it start, anyway?"

"When you brought home a badly painted picture of a cow," Mr. Bland told his wife. "Before that cow we were fairly respectable, or seemed to be on the surface."

"And now you haven't any surface," said Mr. Brown, "and I'm no longer respectable. Let's eat."

"Oh, yes," said Lorna, returning suddenly from a fit of abstraction. "Fanny, please tell cook to prepare a few solids. It doesn't matter much what they are as long as they're composed of food."

"Is Fanny a servant in this house," asked Mr. Brown when the passionate maid had departed, "or is she a sort of unofficial observer? At one time you treat her like a servant, at another like a hated rival."

"She's a misplaced harlot, if you want my opinion," declared Lorna, "but I've a yen for the wench. She's so refreshingly depraved she keeps me from growing stale. A respectable servant in this house would soon give notice. Cook drinks and steals and tells dirty stories. Whenever I get lonely I go out to the kitchen and she tells me a new one. She gets them from the iceman, the milkman, and such like. When she has stolen so much of our silver we can't set the table she gradually gives it back, or rather lends it to us for a while. Name of Blunt. Our occasional gardener is a self-confessed hop-head. Sometimes his hands shake so violently he can dig and weed in half the time it would take a normal man. When he's full of snow he's no good at all. Spends his time leaping hedges and playing he's a butterfly. Want to know his name?"

"What shall I do with these drawers?" asked Mr. Bland, holding the unlovely article up before his wife.

"What's that?" said Lorna, snapping out of her lyrical outburst.

"Drawers," replied Mr. Bland.

"I didn't say they weren't," said Lorna. "Do you want me to put them on?"

"No. What shall I do with them?"

Lorna thought deeply.

"I've got it," she said at last. "Get the beard and wrap it up in the drawers, then take the little bundle and tuck it away somewhere where it will be handy. One can never tell when one will need a beard or a pair of drawers. Personally, I never wear either."

Mr. Bland looked at Mr. Brown. Both men nodded comprehendingly. The lady of the house was bottle dizzy. It was a good way to be. Both drank deeply, then silence settled over the room. Fanny came in with the solids, which were dispatched in a somewhat impromptu and casual manner.

"Does coffee make you sober?" Lorna wanted to know.

"Nothing makes you sober," said Mr. Brown, "after you've drunk as much as we have."

"Then I'll drink mine," she declared. "What hour is it?

"It's been late for a long time," said Mr. Brown.

"How late?

"Varying stages."

"Can't I pin you down?"

"It's eleven now," said Mr. Brown, struggling with his watch.

"Do you come with the coffin?" Lorna inquired. "I mean, if we decide to keep the coffin do we have to take you with it?"

"No," replied Mr. Brown. "But I'll come and visit it often."

Suddenly the skeleton of Bland rose with an air of tragic resolution.

"I've had enough of this," came hollowly from the skull. "I might as well be dead. I'm going out and bury myself in the backyard."

"Great!" cried Lorna. "A swell idea. Let's all go out to the backyard and dig a big grave."

"I know a lot about graves," said Mr. Brown.

"I'll be head digger."

"Then come along," commanded Mr. Bland. "The sooner I'm underground the better it will be for all concerned. Things can't go on like this. Snap out the lights and bring some bottles. There are picks, shovels, crowbars, spades, clippers, a lawn mower, and a very nice garden hose, not to mention various other useful and instructive implements, in the tool shed."

"Can't very well dig a grave with a garden hose," said the experienced Mr. Brown.

"I'm aware of that," Mr. Bland replied. "I was merely thinking of all the things I'm going to leave behind me."

"We can chuck a few in with you," Lorna suggested, happily.

"Why not on me?" asked Mr. Bland.

"Don't worry," Lorna assured him. "We'll dig you a swell grave. Funny thing, I never thought of digging a grave before. Think of all the graves I've left undug. Never be able to catch up now, but I'll do my best with this one. I'll dig and I'll dig and I'll —

"For the love of God," cried Mr. Bland, "don't go on about it. Isn't there any pity in you? Aren't you at all sorry I'm going underground?"

"Naturally, my little subway," said Lorna, taking a swig from the nearest bottle. "Terribly. But the thrill of digging a grave at night is almost adequate compensation for the loss of a husband who is two-thirds gone already."

The skeleton of Mr. Bland stalked with dignity from the room.

By the light of a lantern they opened operations. Mr. Brown stepped back and measured Mr. Bland with a sharp, appraising eye, humming softly the while.

"About six foot one and a half," he murmured. "Better make it about seven. Give him plenty of room."

"Oh, I must have plenty of room," said Mr. Bland. "If there's anything I detest it's a skimpy grave."

"Are we going to bury him head down or feet-first?" Lorna wanted to be told.

"What do you mean?" asked Mr. Bland, shrinking a little from her.

"Well," she explained. "I was thinking of digging a sort of hole so we wouldn't spoil so much garden."

"God! Did you hear that?" exclaimed Mr. Bland, turning to the mortician. "Even if I am a skeleton I deserve some consideration. Think of it! Head down."

"It was just an idea," said Lorna.

"A shocking idea," said her husband. "Horrible."

After half an hour's steady digging considerable work had been done and considerable liquor consumed. Lorna insisted the grave was quite deep enough.

"You wouldn't want Busy to be scratching me up every other day, would you?" Mr. Bland demanded.

"No," admitted Lorna—"Although I wouldn't mind seeing you, or parts of you, from time to time, knocking about the lawn."

"Damn me if I'm going to talk to you any more," said Mr. Bland. "Every time you speak you say something more repulsive."

"I don't mean to," replied Lorna.

"That's just the trouble. That makes it worse."

"Well, we could put a lot of stones on top. How would that do?"

"Rotten. I want a regular grave or no grave at all."

"Okay," said Lorna. "One more drink, then we'll all set to work."

"I would like the subject to lie down in there, if he would be so good," came the highly professional voice of Mr. Brown. "It would be just as well to see that the dimensions are correct before we proceed further."

"A good idea," declared Lorna. I'd like to try on that grave myself, I can throw in that old piece of canvas to keep my dress clean."

That was the first sight that smote Officer Kelley's eyes as he sneaked round a corner of the house and stood watching in the shadows. And it was almost the last sight, for Kelley, in spite of his stout heart, did not hold with graves and skeletons and burials by night.

"Mother of God," he murmured, piously crossing himself. "A skeleton, no less. Now, are they putting him in the ground or taking the poor soul out, I wonder?"

He momentarily turned away to see that a retreat was open. When he turned back again he received even a greater shock. A young and beautiful woman was lying in the grave, while the skeleton, bottle in hand, was standing in a nonchalant attitude, conversing with the town's leading mortician.

"I was never born to look on sights the likes of this," moaned Kelley under what little breath he had. "First the skeleton gets into the grave, then the photographer's wife—'twill be the undertaker's turn next. A bad black game it is they're playing this night."

"It's nice down here," said Lorna. "I love it."

"Golly," muttered Kelley. "She loves it, no less."

"When I go down," said Mr. Bland, "I'm going to take you with me."

Kelley began to sweat frankly and freely. He was facing a terrific problem. If the photographer's wife wanted to get herself buried alive with a long, lanky skeleton, did he, Kelley, have any right to stop her? On the other hand, if he let that black-hearted undertaker cover up the woman, he, Kelley, would be allowing murder to be done before his very eyes. Of one thing alone Officer Kelley was sure: the sooner that skeleton was buried the better he would feel.

Then things started to happen. The skeleton, still holding the bottle, climbed down into the grave. He gave the photographer's wife a drink, then took one himself.

"For the last time," Kelley heard the skeleton say, and every bead of sweat on Kelley's body paused on its way to listen. "One more drink, Brown," continued the skeleton, then let the clods fly."

This was too much for Kelley. With a cry more of horror than command he lumbered towards the grave.

"No more funny business," he shouted. "In the name of the law."

In the tail end of one of those well-known split seconds the backyard became the scene of kaleidoscopic activity. The sudden appearance of Officer Kelley together with the great, unfriendly noises he made completely unnerved Mr. Bland. He sprang from the grave, and with him sprang his wife, no less impressed by Officer Kelley and the things he was going to do, for Kelley, when once in action, was a man of vocal as well as physical fury.

No sooner had the four feet of the two Blands touched the brink of the grave than they started in to show Officer Kelley what feet could do when thoroughly alarmed. Finding himself confronting either one of two disagreeable prospects—solitude or Officer Kelley—mortician Brown dropped his spade and made all possible speed to overtake, if not pass, the flying couple ahead. In the rear, but not far enough to satisfy Mr. Brown, plunged the bellowing Kelley himself.

"If he keeps up making that noise," thought the speeding Brown, "he'll soon drop in his tracks."

With faith rather than confidence the mortician followed the Blands. They rounded a corner on even terms and continued along the side of the house. In the heart of Mr. Bland beat a frantic prayer to the gods of all dead and active religions that he should not fall. Fear for the safety of his brittle structure caused him to exert caution, which enabled Mr. Brown to overtake him.

"He may have a gun," panted Mr. Bland.

"He damn' well has," wheezed Brown.

The three flying grave diggers rounded another corner and sped across the front lawn.

"This is no place to be," Mr. Bland explained.

"For neither of us," said Mr. Brown.

As they rounded the next turn, they almost ran into Lorna.

"Where have you been?" she said. "I've been waiting for you."

"Well, wait no longer," gasped her husband. "There's a man with a gun behind us."

"Bullets would pass clean through your ribs," said Mr. Brown, enviously.

"I wish I were sure of that," replied Mr. Bland. "If a bullet hits my pelvis I'll shatter like a flower pot."

On through the night zoomed the slow-footed Kelley.

"Think of me chasing a skeleton," he thought, proudly. "If the damn' fool only knew it I'd fall over backwards if he even so much as turned about."

In the meantime those he sought had returned to their original point of departure.

"Don't think I can make another lap," Mr. Brown informed them.

"Damned if I'm going to be circling my own house the whole night long," declared Mr. Bland.

"Let's all jump in the grave," suggested Lorna. "He might not think of looking there."

At that critical moment the slanting door to the cellar miraculously opened.

"In here," came the voice of Fanny. "Quickly!"

And in there they went so very, very quietly that they failed to close the door behind them.

When Kelley had completed the circuit, he looked about him in mystification; then, spying the open door, he, too, descended into utter darkness.

For a full minute the room was filled with the sound of heavy breathing, but no movement was made, owing to the fact that both pursuer and pursued were incapable of making any. Nor did it at all appeal to Officer Kelley to pass the remainder of the night in a dark cellar with an active if timid skeleton. The thing might suddenly show a change of front and start in searching for him with those long, bony arms. In spite of this gloomy outlook Kelley was reluctant to give up the pursuit. He had worked too hard in his circuit of the house to abandon the field now.

While the officer was having his bad time in the darkness, Fanny, with great presence of mind, guided Lorna and Mr. Brown to the stairs leading up to the kitchen.

"Hide in the living-room," she whispered. "He'll be afraid of the coffin."

"Like hell," mumbled Mr. Brown. "If a skeleton doesn't faze him he'll probably cut his initials in the sides of 1007-A."

When Fanny returned to fetch the skeleton, her groping hands encountered bare flesh. With a supreme effort Mr. Bland stifled a shocked scream. Not so Fanny. Hers fled through the cellar and did terrible things to Officer Kelley's spine.

"Oh, my," said Fanny. "Are you all naked?"

"What's that?" demanded Kelley, outraged in spite of his fear. "I was never naked."

"How do you do it?" called Fanny. "Are your clothes sewed on?"

"You brazen-mouthed baggage," Kelley retorted. "I'd like to run you in."

A third voice was heard.

"If you don't take your hands away," said Mr. Bland, "I'll give myself up to the officer."

"What's that?" demanded Kelley. "Who's talking now?"

"It is I, the skeleton, who speaks," said Mr. Bland.

"Then don't give yourself up to me," said Kelley. "I don't want any part of you."

"How did you get that way?" Fanny asked Mr. Bland.

"What way?" he parried.

"You know—the way you are."

"What way is he, lady?" Kelley wanted to know.

"Oh, you're fired!" came the explosive voice of Mr. Bland. "Don't do that again."

"I'm going to run in the lot of you," said Kelley suddenly, but without enthusiasm.

"You can begin with me," said Mr. Bland.

"Go back to your grave," urged Kelley. "That's where you belong."

For some minutes he had been fingering his flashlight, wondering whether or not it would be wise to use it. He was frankly afraid of what he might see. Now he decided to take a chance. Its beam revealed a naked man, struggling to escape from a strange woman.

"For shame," cried Officer Kelley. "Where did the both of you come from?"

"Does it matter?" cried Mr. Bland in desperation. "Can't you see I'm busy? Turn off that damned light."

Officer Kelley did so for the good of his own soul. The moment the light went out Mr. Bland made a dash for the kitchen stairs, Fanny crowding him for first place. He quickly achieved the top and ran through the kitchen, snatching up a dish towel on the way. It was dark in the living-room, and Bland was glad of that. He crept in quietly and concealed his new-found nakedness behind a large chair. Fanny tried to follow him, but he gave her a ruthless push. So Fanny crept somewhere else. Silence reigned in the room, yet there was a feeling of other hidden, breathless figures crouching in odd corners.

Presently in crept Kelley according to that stout officer's idea of creeping, which was, in reality, a ponderous shuffling of weary and heavy feet.

It was then an incident occurred that horrified not only Kelley but also everyone else in that silently crowded room. As he turned the beam of the torch upon the coffin, a pallid, inhuman head popped up over its side and two terrible eyes blazed in the darkness. The gasps and groans that filled the room served only to heighten the officer's demoralization.

Dropping the torch with a cry of stark anguish, Kelley staggered stiffly from the room and slid through the front door with as much determination as Dolly Tucker had displayed several hours before him. No sooner had Kelley made his final exit then the thing in the coffin rose up still higher, then dropped with a thud to the floor.

"God! What is it?" cried Lorna. "I'm going into convulsions."

"Now I lay me down to sleep," came the pious voice of Fanny from a corner.

"All we can do is wait," mournfully said Mr. Brown. "Which one of us does it want, I wonder?"

"All," quoth Lorna, hopelessly.

Then came a sudden volley of short, sharp barks, followed by a series of playful bounds and pounces.

"Damn," said Mr. Bland. "The poor fish has got my towel." He rose and switched on the lights. "Will somebody kindly pass me my Paisley shawl? I've got my body back."

This announcement broke the tension. Lorna, Fanny, and Mr. Brown arose and stretched their cramped limbs. Lorna looked about her.

"If cook were only here," she said, "we'd have a full cast. Get us a drink, Fanny."

"What a hell of a place for a dog to sleep," Mr. Bland complained.

Busy was rushing from one to the other, giving each a frantic greeting.

"One dirty dog after another," Lorna told her husband. "They sleep in the same kennel."

"Now you'll have to buy that coffin," said Mr. Brown. "I might have overlooked his master, but I'll be damned if I will his dog, especially when the block-headed monster scares me nearly silly."

"We'll take that up later," replied Mr. Bland. "I've too much on my mind and too little on my body."

Lorna gave him the Paisley shawl. Fanny passed the drinks. Everyone felt much improved but too jaded to become convivial. Lorna was considering her husband through enigmatic eyes.

"You're the most volatile creature I've ever met," she said to Mr. Bland, "but now that you've got your body back we'd better hurry to bed." She paused to look at Fanny, then turned to Mr. Brown. "You," she went on, "can go to sleep on the sofa."

"Go to sleep on the sofa," Mr. Brown repeated, bitterly. "I'm going to die on the sofa. Nothing less will satisfy me."

"And you, Fanny," said Lorna. "Where are you going to sleep?"

"Alone," said the desolate Fanny. "Unless —"

Her mad eyes strayed appraisingly to Mr. Brown.

"Don't look at me that way," said that gentleman. "I tell you I'm going to die."

"Why don't you?" Fanny asked him. "You're long overdue."

CHAPTER 12.

THE SQUARE DOG IS STRICKEN

Busy had slept badly, and he was worried about it. He had always been such a sound sleeper. When all other pursuits failed and time hung heavy on his paws, even in the face of hunger and disparagement he had hitherto been able to depend on sleep. But last night had been a bad one. As a matter of fact, the square dog had so little of importance on his mind he was becoming neurotic about it, which is one of the troubles with so many modern dogs. They have neither to think nor shift for themselves.

Consumed with self-pity he bleakly sniffed his way about the house in the early-morning hours. Nothing smelled right, and when nothing smells right to a dog he is out of luck indeed. He found himself wondering how he was ever going to get through the long day confronting him. What a night it had been! He felt that if he did not bite something or somebody almost immediately his nerves would snap.

After he had been so rudely awakened from his slumber in the snug coffin the game had been up. No dog could sleep in the same room with that man Brown whistling and rasping in the darkness. Every time the mortician snored, which was steadily, Busy had thought he was being either called or vilified. Of course, there was no putting up with that. In one corner after another the dog had searched for sleep only to find them empty. He had even tried his own private quarters in the kitchen, but to no avail.

He wondered now if it would do any good to go in and bite the mortician. Busy decided against the idea. It would take a lion to disturb that horrid man. In his heart Busy envied him his repose.

He padded upstairs in search of absolutely nothing. There were the stairs — one might just as well go up them. Somebody had to go up those stairs. He would do it. An open window in the hall gave on to a balcony that ran the breadth of the house. Busy lugged himself through this window and regarded the day with a dubious eye. It did not smell right. Too bad he couldn't bite it. Any other dog was welcome to this day. He did not want it.

Glancing along the balcony, he remarked that the French windows of the master's and mistress's room were open. He would go in there and barge about, knock something over if he could—wake them both up. He felt he would risk almost anything to relieve the depressing solitude. After all, a dog had to have some companionship. He wondered if they thought he was a bird in a gilded cage, a mere thing with no needs or life of his own.

All of which goes to show that Busy, usually the best of dogs, could become a very bad one merely through the loss of sleep.

He padded through the French windows, then squatted squarely down and stared fixedly at his master. There would be a really nice man if he only understood more about dogs. Busy transferred his gaze to Lorna. That one would never suffer from lack of sleep. She was burrowed in like a squirrel. One small hand hung limply over the side of the bed. Busy could not resist sniffing it a little. It was a good sniff, the first agreeable sniff of the day, but then, his mistress always smelled pleasantly. He tried the hand delicately with the tip of his tongue. Automatically the hand moved and made a feeble attempt to pat the dog's square head. Well, that was a little something, at any rate, some slight recognition.

Then Busy discovered something that aroused his worst instincts. The door to his master's sacredly private dark room was half open. Never had he been allowed in that room, and it seemed unfair. He would go in there now and find out what it was all about. Certainly it must be a matter of food. People were always barring his path to food. They conspired to keep him hungry.

The moment Busy entered the dark room his nose was assailed by a symphony of smells it had never dealt with before. The multitude of smells in that room gave the dog a momentary glimpse of a larger and busier life. Here was a new world of smells from which his master had selfishly excluded him. Might as well make the most of his present opportunity. It might never come again.

Springing to a long bench, the square dog began a methodical sniffing of the individual bottles, lingering long over some and with-drawing with repugnance from others. Two flat, moplike paws were pressed against the shelf on which the bottles stood, and in his eagerness to get in as much sniffing as possible before retribution fell, Busy allowed one of these paws to brush a bottle to the floor. There was a small noise of shattering glass, and then the room was filled with the most difficult smell the dog had ever tried to study.

Busy caught his breath and kept his eyes on the door. Soon it would be all over with him, and he did not much care. As time passed and nobody came, Busy began to take heart. He was glad now that his master and his mistress could sleep so deeply. Probably he could knock all those bottles off the shelf and still not disturb their slumbers. He felt almost inclined to try it, but decided instead to investigate this mystifying smell. Accordingly, he jumped to the floor and approached an experienced nose to the fluid. For a long time he sniffed, then thrust out his tongue. Not nice. It tasted like a sneeze. Busy tried again just to make certain, then he decided to get himself the hell out of there. If his master kept such stuff in that room it was no place for a dog.

Mr. Bland had heard the noise made by the smashed bottle. He had opened one eye and kept it open. Further than that he had not acted. Now he saw the square dog issue from the dark room and disappear through the French windows.

"You dirty, white, square-headed bum," Mr. Bland inelegantly muttered, then closed his eye in sleep.

Some hours later, while they were dressing, Lorna decided to take her husband to the doctor. His case needed investigation. When he had fully awakened he had shaken his own hand to discover whether he was a skeleton or a man in the flesh. He had been happy to find he was still in the flesh. Perhaps he might remain so permanently. He did not have much hope, however. When Lorna suggested the doctor, Mr. Bland had at first rebelled. Eventually he had capitulated, as, eventually, all husbands do.

It was a bright, fair day, one of those portions of weather that bring householders out of their snug little houses in snug little suburban towns. Husbands do things to their lawns, and wives do things to their baby carriages. People get themselves on to the streets, where they do nothing at all save block the way for others who have something to do. Taken all in all, it is an exhibition of man at his worst—a futile and fatuous reaction of a community to sunlight and blue sky.

Into this brave day Lorna introduced her husband. On a leash he was leading Busy, the leash being a precaution against numerous delays caused by the dog's insistence on investigating the neighbors' pets, premises, and other private property.

Behind them in the house Mr. Brown still lay slumbering. They had left a note for him strongly suggesting that for his own sake he should go back to work and that for theirs he should take his coffin with him. They asked him to call again, but not accompanied by good old 1007-A.

As they walked along the street Mr. Bland became faintly conscious of a slight tapping sound behind him, as if someone were doing silly things with a cane. However, at first the sounds were not sufficiently arresting to capture his entire attention. He was much more interested in Lorna, who seemed to be in one of her less harsh and caustic moods. This, perhaps, was due to the fact that she was happily telling him what he in turn should tell the doctor.

"Listen, Quint," she was saying, "make no bones about it."

"I hope not," replied her husband. "I've had enough of that."

"Don't be funny," said Lorna, briefly. "It doesn't become you. As I was saying, don't be delicate about it. Just walk up to this doctor person and tell him the whole story. That's why I'm taking you to a new doctor instead of to old Freeman. He won't know a thing about you, so he may believe your story. Old Freeman, knowing you as he does, would naturally put you down for a liar."

"How you do love to go into everything," observed Mr. Bland. "Do you hear some damn' fool following us with a cane?"

"I've been hearing it for some minutes," replied Lorna, "and it's making me nervous."

"I wish he would get ahead of us," said Mr. Bland, glancing back over his shoulder. Then suddenly he stopped. "Oh, look," he spluttered. "For goodness' sakes. Dear, dear, what a pity. Lorna, this is too bad."

"What's the matter?" asked Lorna, not wishing to look around. "Is the poor man blind?"

"Hell, no," said Mr. Bland. "I've got my own flesh back, but my dog's lost his."

What!" gasped Lorna. "Mean to tell me—Oh, this is quite impossible."

"I just wish you'd take a look."

"I'm afraid I'll be forced to," she said, turning round and confronting the dog.

Now the skeleton of a dog is an altogether different proposition from that of a man. Strangely enough, it is even less palatable and far more conspicuous. When thinking of skeletons the average person, for no definite reason, almost invariably visualizes a human skeleton instead of that of a horse or a cow or a dog. For this reason the human skeleton if not altogether acceptable is at least a familiar concept. About the skeleton of a dog there is something exceptionally unalluring, especially when that skeleton is jauntily animated. There is a suggestion of great speed and mobility and of a wide striking radius. In a pinch one might run or hide from a human skeleton, but not from a dog's. It would either overtake one or smell one out.

Busy in the bone was one of those things no normal person would ever want to see again. When Mr. Bland and Lorna stopped he stopped, too, and sat down with a pronounced tap.

"He'll chip himself to splinters," said Lorna, "if he carries on like that."

"The poor sap was in my dark room early this morning," said Mr. Bland, "and he knocked over a bottle of that formula I had brought from the office. That's what did it."

Suddenly the once square dog was seized with a desire to scratch. One of his hind legs got into action and rattled across his ribs like a stick across fence palings. This was too much for even the dog. He uttered a sharp yelp and looked up at his owners; then, lifting a front paw, he studied it searchingly.

"I never thought I'd live to be present on such a ghastly occasion," murmured Lorna. "Come on, we can't stand here like this. We'll have to make the best of a bad situation."

She took her husband's arm, and they continued on down the street, Busy tapping behind them.

"I can't stand that," said Lorna at last. "You'll have to make him walk on the grass."

So Busy was made to walk on the grass bordering either side of the street. A near-sighted gentleman coming down his front walk almost stepped on the dog.

"Great Scott!" he exclaimed. "What in hell is that?"

Both Lorna and Mr. Bland pretended they had not heard and continued on their way. The gentleman took out his glasses and fixed them firmly on his nose. Then, bending far over, he followed the skeleton of Busy. Disliking such a prolonged scrutiny from a stranger, the dog cocked his head on his vertebrae and made a bad sound at him.

"Great God!" exclaimed the gentleman this time, considering the substitution of the Deity permissible under the circumstances. "The thing can also make sounds. Decidedly unpleasant sounds." The gentleman was either a complete fool or else bereft of fear, for he thrust out a gloved hand and actually touched the dog on the tip of his tail. This time Busy's teeth clicked like a trap.

"God bless and keep me!" muttered the gentleman, invoking divine protection. "What a thing it is. My goodness! What a thing it is."

Leaving Busy to his own devices, the gentleman overtook Mr. Bland and tapped him politely on the shoulder.

"Pardon the intrusion," apologized the gentleman, "but do you know there's something following you?"

"Yes," said Mr. Bland, imperturbably, "Yes, I do. It's my dog."

"Your dog!" repeated the gentleman, vastly surprised. "What sort of a dog is it, may I ask?"

"Oh, just the usual sort of dog," Mr. Bland told him.

The gentleman removed his glasses and wiped them meticulously. Then he looked back at the skeleton of Busy.

"I find it a most unusual sort of a dog," he said at last. "It hasn't got any skin on and no hair at all. Dogs usually have one or the other, most times both."

"This dog has been intensively inbred," said Mr. Bland, wishing the gentleman would go away.

"Have you seen your dog recently?" asked the gentleman.

"Not within the last ten minutes," said Mr. Bland. "Why do you ask?"

"Well," replied the gentleman, "I don't want to alarm you, but I'm afraid you'll find most of your dog gone. I mean to say, what's left of it isn't a dog, properly speaking. It's merely the framework of a dog. Look for yourself."

Against his will, Mr. Bland looked back at Busy, then uttered a short laugh.

"Why, that isn't the dog I meant," he said. "That's just a toy."

"We bought it last year in Germany," put in Lorna. "They're clever that way."

"I should say so," said the gentleman. "I looked through this one's ribs and I couldn't see a cog of clockwork."

"You wind him up by the tail," explained Lorna.

"You do!" exclaimed the gentleman. "Fancy that. I just touched it on the tip of its tail and your toy fairly snapped at me."

"That's one of its amusing tricks," said Mr. Bland.

"Amusing for whom?" asked the gentleman. "I was greatly startled, but your toy seemed to enjoy it." He glanced back, then once more tapped Mr. Bland on the shoulder. "I thought you might like to know," he said in a low voice. "There are lots of people following us."

Lorna could not resist casting a glance over her shoulder.

"About half of the village," she muttered, "including a cop. What are we going to do with the damn' dog?"

"Carry it in your arms."

"My arms!" she exclaimed. "Carry that horror in my arms? Don't be silly."

"We'll both be silly if this keeps up," said Mr. Bland. "One more person added to that throng and it will look like a parade."

"Then pick him up and carry him in your own arms," suggested Lorna.

"For some reason I feel disinclined," said Mr. Bland. "Maybe this gentleman would carry him. He seems to be almost frantically interested."

"Want to carry the funny toy?" Lorna asked him as if addressing a child.

"Dear me, no," said the man. "I'm sorry to admit it, but I'm afraid of that funny toy."

At this moment the funny toy in question suddenly faced about and in no uncertain terms began to curse at the interested spectators behind him.

"That toy barks just like a dog," the gentleman informed them. "If I shut my eyes I'd think it was a dog."

"Damn," muttered Mr. Bland. "It's tragic enough being a skeleton one's self without one's dog getting that way."

The policeman detached himself from the crowd and hurried up to the smaller group. Before he arrived Mr. Bland carefully picked up Busy and held him in his arms.

"Be still," he whispered. "Be a dead dog, Busy." At this command the scaffolding of Busy obediently collapsed.

"That toy absolutely mystifies me," said the near-sighted gentleman. "If I didn't know it was impossible I'd say the thing was alive. Dear me, here's a policeman. Fancy that. I think I know this fellow. Morning, Officer Burke. Want to see a funny toy?"

"I want to see what this gentleman is holding in his arms," said Officer Burke, looking closely at the relaxed skeleton of Busy. "It's causing a public disturbance."

"Sorry, officer," said Mr. Bland. "I'm taking it to be stuffed."

"Stuffed?" said Officer Burke. "Stuffed where?

"Now, officer, that's difficult," admitted Mr. Bland. "You know, just all over, the way they do. And anyway, what does it matter?"

Officer Burke seemed to think it important.

"Stuffed," he repeated, as if trying to convince himself he had heard correctly. "What are you going to stuff it with?"

"God, officer, how should I know? What do they stuff things with?" asked the exasperated Mr. Bland. "I'm not a taxidermist."

"Meaning that I am?" said the officer threateningly. "Better be careful who you call names."

"No harm intended," replied Mr. Bland. "A taxidermist is quite all right, you know."

"Yeah," sneered Officer Burke. "Well, you can be a taxi whatever you call it. I don't like the word. And another thing, that skeleton can't be stuffed. There ain't any place for stuffing."

"All right," said Mr. Bland. "If it will make you any happier I'll give up the whole idea. I won't get it stuffed. What do we do next?"

"That skeleton of a beast," said Officer Burke, "was jogging along the streets and barking at people, and you can't tell me anything different. I saw it with my own eyes."

"It's a toy, officer," explained the near-sighted gentleman. "This lady bought it in Germany."

"Yes, officer," said Lorna, sweetly. "It's just a little toy. You wind it up by its tail."

At this point in the discussion Busy grew tired of being a dead dog and made that fact known by an expansive yawn. Then he stuck out his head and took a sniff of Officer Burke, after which he began to wriggle vigorously to be put down.

"I can't hold him," cried Mr. Bland.

"For God's sake do," said Officer Burke. "That damn' thing is alive."

"What?" asked the near-sighted gentleman. "Then it isn't a German toy after all."

"Put the dog down," Lorna commanded. "He might twist himself in two."

As Mr. Bland placed the wriggling skeleton of Busy on its feet, Officer Burke drew his revolver. Both Lorna and Mr. Bland threw themselves in front of the gun. A brief struggle ensued, which was interrupted by the mild voice of the near-sighted gentleman.

"Oh, look," he said. "Now, that is strange."

The three contestants paused to look. Seated on the pavement was a whole and complete Busy. From the crowd behind came exclamations of awe and wonderment. Officer Burke blinked stupidly, which was the only way Officer Burke could blink.

"Come," said Lorna to her husband. "They certainly do have the most peculiar policemen in this town. Come along, Busy. That nice man was going to shoot you."

They strolled off down the street, leaving the near-sighted gentleman and Officer Burke in a state of mental turmoil. Finally the policeman found it essential to express himself in action. Luckily for him there was a job close at hand. As he looked at the crowd his anger mounted. Then, when his rage had been satisfactorily worked up, he charged down upon the peaceful but naturally curious citizens of that community.

"Clear out of this," he shouted, "or I'll back up the wagon."

CHAPTER 13.

DR. MACQUIRK IS CONVINCED

Like Busy, Dr. MacQuirk had had a bad night. He had lost a lot of sleep. Naturally, this offended his Scotch sense of thrift, which was offended by losing anything. Also, Dr. MacQuirk was, under the best conditions, a high- strung and nervous man. Loss of sleep increased these natural tendencies to such an extent that, had his patients known it, they would have avoided him to-day as they would have avoided a man on the border line of madness.

Nevertheless, Dr. MacQuirk was a profound believer in the power of mind over matter. Emotional exhibitions of any nature rubbed him the wrong way. His set of introductory injunctions at almost any consultation were designed, according to his own lights, to create an atmosphere of perfect calm.

"Come in, madam," he would say, "and pull yourself together. There is nothing to fear. Everything is going to be quite all right. Just be calm and relax. Don't let yourself go. Let's have no excitement, please."

Dr. MacQuirk was usually too upset himself to notice that this little speech frequently served only to enrage his patients, especially those of a placid, nerveless disposition who needed far less pulling together than did the good doctor himself.

This morning he arrived at his office late, a circumstance which did not increase his good nature. His waiting-room was crowded with patients, who by this time were far from cheerful themselves.

"Why can't they come in and leave their fees in a plate on the table?" MacQuirk irritably inquired of himself. "In turn they could select a handful of pills I would set out in a big bowl. I don't want to see them and they certainly shouldn't see me this morning. How I hate them all."

When Lorna, Busy, and Mr. Bland arrived, after an already trying experience, the waiting-room was not so crowded, but there were still enough members of both sexes present to make Lorna feel decidedly uncomfortable.

Sobered somewhat by his recent experience, Busy sat down on one side of her and Mr. Bland on the other. Busy considered his hairy body with every indication of relief and satisfaction. Mr. Bland self-consciously considered his boots. Lorna considered her husband and his dog with a prayer in her heart that they would remain in their present state of flesh.

"Here I sit," she thought a little wildly, "between man and beast, and for the life of me I don't know which one is going to turn to a skeleton first."

She was surprised to find herself feeling a little sorry for them both, especially for her husband. He looked so miserable and utterly out of place in a doctor's waiting-room. He was much too long and rangy to be sitting on that small chair like a morbid Abraham Lincoln. He probably felt lonely and shamed in his heart. She wanted to say something comforting to him, something slightly affectionate, but discovered with a sense of inadequacy that she did not know how to talk that way. She wondered how other wives gushed over their husbands. Most of the wives she knew were usually gushing over other women's husbands. She, Lorna, was unable to gush over anything. She was a hard-bitten little woman who thrived on battle and opposition. Yet she knew that somewhere within her was a capacity to love this long man, although she would never give him the satisfaction of knowing it. He was much too disagreeable himself.

A nurse appeared and suggested that Mr. Bland should follow her. Busy promptly decided that he should follow Mr. Bland. This was the first contretemps, and it created no little disturbance in the waiting-room. In the midst of the struggle a mental case called out excitedly: "Spinach! Spinach! Spinach!"

For a moment the struggle ceased. Even Busy looked at the mental case in some perplexity. Apparently having forgotten all about spinach, the mental case was now reading a hunters' and anglers' magazine with stony indifference to her surroundings.

"What does she want with spinach?" Mr. Bland asked the nurse.

"She doesn't want anything with spinach," said the nurse. "She was kept waiting so long for an order of spinach in a restaurant last year that she had a nervous breakdown. She's much better now."

"Thank God for that," returned Mr. Bland. "She's made me feel much worse."

With a backward look at Lorna, who was still struggling with Busy, Mr. Bland followed the nurse into the presence of Dr. MacQuirk. For a moment the two men regarded each other with all the hostility of ancient enemies.

"Sit down, Mr. Bland," said MacQuirk at last, "and for heaven's sake let's have no more nonsense. There's nothing to get excited about, absolutely nothing."

"Am I excited?" asked Mr. Bland, who had a disposition to place implicit trust in doctors.

"Don't you know whether or not you're excited?" demanded the doctor. "If not you're in a bad way, a very bad way indeed. Do you sleep well?"

"Always," said Mr. Bland.

"I don't," muttered MacQuirk, enviously regarding his lanky patient. "Why don't you sit down? I'm getting a pain in my neck trying to look up at you."

"Sorry," said Mr. Bland, looking about for a chair.

His selection was an unfortunate one, but perfectly logical, for it looked like the most comfortable chair in the room. As he folded himself into it he was startled by a piercing cry from Dr. MacQuirk.

"E-e-e-e-yah!" mouthed the doctor. "Not there, man, not there! You're not ready for that yet. I just bought that operating chair. It cost a lot of money."

"Sorry," said Mr. Bland again as he heaved himself out of the chair and found another one.

"You should be," pronounced the doctor. "What did you come here for, may I ask?"

"I wanted a thorough physical examination," said Mr. Bland. "Recently I've been turning to a skeleton every now and then."

"Losing weight, eh?" muttered the doctor, far from appreciating the full purport of Mr. Bland's information. "And you don't know when you're excited. No wonder you're losing weight. You're probably seething with excitement all the time and imagine you're resting. That's bad."

"You don't understand," Mr. Bland pursued, patiently.

"Don't tell me I don't understand," MacQuirk threw back, explosively. "It's my business to understand. That's why I'm a doctor. Are you setting up your judgment against mine?"

"No, Doctor," said Mr. Bland. "I merely meant that I actually turn to a skeleton. My flesh disappears and, to all intents and purposes, I'm composed entirely of bone."

For a moment or so there was silence in the room while the doctor considered his patient out of brooding, bloodshot eyes. At last he spoke.

"How would you like to go to a nice, quiet place for a while?" he asked. "You'll be very comfortable and everybody will be kind to you. And," added the doctor with the failure of a bright smile, "you can play skeletons there just as much as you like."

Quintus Bland swallowed hard. The consultation was proving even more difficult than he had expected. He hardly blamed the doctor. No one would believe without proof the incredible statement he had made. It was essential, However, that he should convince this irascible physician.

"Doctor," he said, "still you don't get me. I'm not suffering from a delusion. I'm just as sane as you are. My condition can be traced to a perfectly definite cause—a chemical formula which I have inadvertently assimilated into my system. Should the same thing occur to you, your reactions would be the same as mine. Why, even my dog has begun to change to a skeleton."

"The madder they are the more convincingly they talk," murmured Dr. MacQuirk as if to himself. "I don't think your dog could accompany you to this nice, quiet place, Mr. Bland, but he might come to see you, and then you could romp around on the lawn and play skeleton together. How would that be?"

"Doctor," pleaded Mr. Bland, "I realize it's difficult to believe, but I assure you most earnestly that what I have told you is the plain, unvarnished truth. Both myself and my dog actually change to skeletons. It has just occurred to my dog, but for several days past I have been subject to these seizures. My wife will confirm my statement. She is waiting outside with my dog."

"I suppose she becomes a skeleton, too, occasionally?" observed the doctor. "Tell me, Mr. Bland, am I a skeleton?"

"No," shouted Mr. Bland, suddenly losing his temper, "but I wish to God you were and buried in your grave. You're not a skeleton. You're a pig-headed torturer."

"Now, now, Mr. Bland," said the doctor, soothingly. "Mustn't go on like that. We're old friends. Don't you remember me? I'm the doctor, and you are in my consulting-room. Everything is going to be all right. There's nothing to get excited about."

White-lipped, Mr. Bland rose and faced the doctor. MacQuirk was already standing, watching his patient with a wary eye. One hand was in his desk drawer, in which there was a gun. He was thoroughly convinced he was dealing with a dangerous maniac, and he was taking no chances.

"Doctor," said Quintus Bland with the calm of desperation, "are you going to examine me or not? Are you going to take a blood test and endeavor to find out what can be done? If not I'll walk right out of this room and find a more enlightened physician."

MacQuirk was convinced that Mr. Bland should not be allowed at large. It was his professional duty to place the man under restraint. He was a danger to the community as well as to himself. A man who claimed to own a skeleton dog was very far gone indeed.

"Of course I'm going to examine you," he replied in as hearty a voice as he was able to assume. "There never has been any question of that. Now, if you'll just remove your clothes and get yourself on to that table we'll see what can be done about it."

The moment Mr. Bland was stretched on the table, MacQuirk threw himself upon him.

"Miss Malloy!" he shouted. "Come here and clamp him down. Quick! The man is dangerous."

Like a white flash the nurse joined forces with the doctor. Mr. Bland felt himself being strapped and clamped to the table. The attack had been so unexpected that the advantage lay all with the doctor. In spite of this Mr. Bland succeeded in giving him a vigorous kick in the stomach before his legs were expertly captured and strapped to the table. It was not until he was entirely helpless that he raised his voice in a loud cry for Lorna. The cry was immediately answered. Like a small blonde whirlwind Lorna entered the room with the square dog at her heels. Without waiting to ask questions she spun the nurse about and gave her a terrific punch on the nose. Although trained to handle rough patients, Miss Malloy was not equal to the speed displayed by the infuriated wife of the captive Mr. Bland. Before she could get into action Lorna had seized the nurse's skirt and pulled it over her head. Then she tripped the unfortunate woman and stepped on her prostrate body.

In the meantime Busy had permanently affixed himself to the lapel of the doctor's coat while the doctor was trying to jab the dog with a hypodermic needle originally intended for Mr. Bland.

Leaving the nurse to work out her own salvation, Lorna slapped the doctor's glasses into a thousand pieces, then hit him over the head with the nearest object at hand. It proved to be a bottle, and the doctor sank to the floor. So far it had been a wordless battle, but now Lorna became vocal. She had snatched the doctor's revolver from the desk drawer. With this weapon in her hand she felt that further effort on her part was unnecessary.

"Now," she said in a deadly cold voice, "get up from that floor, both of you, and tell me the big idea. If I don't like your explanation I'm going to telephone for the police and have you locked up. Snap to it, damn you! You'll be sorry you ever laid a hand on my husband."

Dazed, battered, and bloody, the doctor and his nurse eventually succeeded in rising from the floor. They found themselves confronted by a small woman with a large gun. At this moment the mental case thrust her head through the door.

"Spinach! Spinach! Spinach!" she shouted, and everybody jumped.

Busy took a quick run, then left the floor in the general direction of the doctor. He struck the man on the chest and knocked him flat again. Then he stood over the fallen physician while he selected a fresh spot to bite. From the dog's point of view the day had vastly improved.

"Will you please call your dog off?" the doctor pleaded in a feeble voice. "I didn't sleep well last night."

"For his sake, not yours," said Lorna, "you cowardly little quack."

The appellation of "quack" momentarily fired the battered physician with a faint spark of courage.

"Madam," he said from the floor, "you're going to pay dearly for this."

"Shut up, you," snapped Lorna, knocking a row of bottles from a shelf with the long, blue. barrel of the revolver. "Come here, Busy, and let that would-be assassin get up. I haven't finished with him yet."

As the bottles crashed to the floor, screams came from the ante-room, the loudest of which issued from the mental case, who was still calling for spinach.

"Why doesn't somebody give her a plate of spinach?" came the calm voice of Mr. Bland.

Lorna turned to regard her husband, then whirled back just in time to swipe the nurse across the cheek with the heavy revolver. With a cry of horror the nurse staggered back and abandoned the battle. Nevertheless she was consumed with hatred for her small blonde victor, who was eyeing her coldly.

"Listen," she said to the nurse, "you look like the wrath of God already, but if you want to look even worse I'm perfectly willing to help you. Take a look at yourself in the mirror, then let me know."

"Godamighty!" came the startled voice of Mr. Bland. "I'm a skeleton again! That damn-fool doctor wouldn't believe me. Give him a chance to see for himself."

"Are you still strapped down?" asked Lorna. "I'm more tangled up now," he told her. "It's like being in a spider's web."

Lorna swung on the doctor, who was holding a handkerchief over his eyes.

"Take that handkerchief away," she commanded, "and release that skeleton."

"I can hardly see without my glasses," said the doctor, brokenly. "There's an extra pair in my desk. May I get them?"

Before Lorna could answer, the nurse uttered a piercing scream. She had turned away from the mirror and seen the writhing skeleton of Mr. Bland.

"Doctor!" she cried. "Doctor! There's a skeleton where the man used to be. And it's squirming all over the table. Please, Doctor, do something about it."

"There's more life in that skeleton than in me," said the doctor. "I can barely move. This has been a very discouraging morning. Madam, may I get my glasses?"

"If you're as bad as all that," replied Lorna, "I'll get them for you."

She found the glasses in the middle drawer and handed them to the doctor. With trembling hands he placed them on his damaged nose. Then he turned to look at the table.

"Good God!" he said. "Do you expect me to unstrap that?"

"Yes," replied Lorna. "And without further delay."

"Then you may as well shoot me," said the doctor, decisively. "I won't go near a living skeleton who has it in for me already."

"Very well," retorted Lorna. "I'll shoot you. The law is on my side."

She raised the revolver and levelled it at the doctor. He held up a restraining hand, too filled with horror to speak. This woman was more dangerous, more bitterly determined, than all the devils in hell. She would shoot him in his tracks without the slightest compunction. He would have to give in. With drooping shoulders he approached the writhing skeleton. Mr. Bland increased his writhing just to make the situation more difficult for the doctor. While the trembling physician was unstrapping him Mr. Bland amused himself by stroking the doctor's arm and cheek with his long, bony fingers. Once he gently tweaked the man's nose and chattered agreeably in his face. For a moment MacQuirk had to steady himself against the table, so great was his fear and revulsion.

"Don't do that," he pleaded. "If you only knew how awful you are. Take the word of a doctor."

"Like hell I will," said Mr. Bland. "How would you like to go to a nice, quiet place?"

"Nothing would please me more," replied the doctor. "I slept very poorly last night, and after this experience I fear I'll never sleep again."

When Mr. Bland was released he swung his legs from the table, then eased himself to the floor.

"Come on," said Lorna. "Let's go."

As she placed her hand on the knob of the door she was arrested by a cry of protest from Dr. MacQuirk.

"My God," he pleaded, "don't go out like that. You might kill some of my patients or drive them mad. Imagine what they'd think. They see a man come in and a skeleton go out. Naturally, they'll assume I stripped him clean of his flesh. The news would spread and my practice would be ruined."

"Very well, then," said Lorna. "I don't want to be too hard on you. What are we going to do about it? We've got to get home."

"We might do this," said MacQuirk after a moment's thought. "If Mr. Bland will agree to play the part of a dead skeleton I'll carry him out to a taxi and pay your way home. That is," he added, hastily, "if you don't live too far away."

"Scotch to the last," said the skeleton. "How do I know you won't drop me on the pavement?"

"I'll shoot him dead if he does," declared Lorna in an effortless voice that carried conviction.

When the taxi arrived, MacQuirk shudderingly lifted Mr. Bland in his arms.

"Now just relax quietly," he said. "Make no effort of your own. No, don't put your arms round my neck. That would look too silly, and besides I couldn't stand it. And try not to breathe so hard. I'm not going to drop you. Just strike an attitude and hold it. Ready?"

"Right, Doc. Shoot," said Mr. Bland.

Miss Malloy opened the door, and the doctor with his odd burden passed through, followed by Lorna, holding the gun under her jacket. Busy padded after her, ready for immediate action should teeth be needed. Although he had only a vague idea of what was going on, he was definitely certain that Dr. MacQuirk was a low-grade man who required close watching.

When the waiting patients saw the doctor with an oversized skeleton in his arms their expressions were a study in horror and incredulity.

"Hello! Hello!" said the doctor by way of a cheery greeting. "I'll be right with you. Just getting rid of some old junk."

"I don't blame you for wanting to get rid of it," declared a wan-looking lady, "but I question your good taste in selecting this particular moment."

"Frankly speaking," said a smartly dressed, middle-aged gentleman, "I believe the doctor's a murderer. If you remember, the gentleman who went in there was lean and lanky just like that skeleton."

"There was a terrible rumpus going on," put in a young prospective mother. "That I know. It sounded like a murder."

"Let me assure you," protested Dr. MacQuirk, "there has been no murder."

"Then produce your patient," challenged the middle-aged gentleman.

"He left by another door."

"There isn't any other door," said the wan lady. "I know because I've looked."

"I'll explain everything in half a minute," the doctor flung back over his shoulder as he staggered from the room.

"No monkey business, Doc," said Lorna. "I've got the gun levelled on your spine."

"Don't make my task any harder," MacQuirk panted, beads of sweat standing out on his fore-head. "If we all pull ourselves together everything will be all right."

Just for something to do, Mr. Bland leaned over and chattered into Dr. Mac-Quirk's left ear. The doctor almost dropped him, so profoundly was he moved.

"That," he declared, emphatically, "was about the worst sound I've ever heard. If you value your life and limb don't do it again."

Out into the sunlight emerged this quaint little procession. Several passers-by stopped to witness the spectacle. By the time they had reached the taxi a tidy crowd had gathered. Suddenly Mr. Bland's weight took a decided upward turn, and the doctor, to his infinite mortification, found himself holding a naked man in his arms. For a moment he swayed on the side-walk, struggling gamely to support his burden.

"Put me down, you damn' fool!" shouted Mr. Bland. "Don't hold me up to the crowd as if I were an offering."

"All right," muttered the doctor. "All right. There's nothing to get excited about."

"Oh, no," snarled Mr. Bland. "Nothing at all. Would you suggest I dance naked on the pavement for the edification of the crowd?"

Before Dr. MacQuirk could be any more encouraging he sank with a deep sigh and a naked Bland to the side-walk. The crowd was mute with stupefaction for a moment, then out of the silence a woman's voice was heard.

"Close your eyes this minute, Betty," cried the voice. "That man is all naked."

"You don't have to tell me, Mom," Betty replied. "I could tell that at a glance. He's not so hot."

"Well," quoth a lazy voice from the crowd, "considering he was a skeleton a moment ago I think he's done very well."

"He's scarcely more than a skeleton now," observed a feminine voice. "And I thought my husband was thin."

"Mind your own business," Mr. Bland shouted, furiously. "If you had any sense of decency you'd get to hell out of here."

Busy was barking passionately and making frantic lunges at whatever parts of the doctor he could find.

"Mr. Bland! Mr. Bland!" sobbed Mac-Quirk. "Your knee is in my stomach, and your dog's got hold of my leg."

"Are you crying?" asked Mr. Bland.

"A little," admitted the doctor. "I told you I had a bad night."

"Well, I slept like a top," said Mr. Bland, "but I could cry like a baby myself."

The crowd parted, and Officer Burke once more appeared on the scene. For a full minute he stood looking down at the tangled bodies on the side-walk, then, after scratching his head, he brought himself to ask a question.

"What's the meaning of all this?" Officer Burke demanded.

"Officer," said Mr. Bland, "it hasn't any meaning. The whole thing is perfectly ridiculous."

"This man is a patient," put in the doctor with great presence of mind. "A serious nervous case. I'm trying to get him back to my office."

"What's he doing naked out here?" asked Burke.

"I was giving him a physical examination," said the doctor.

"Right out in public?" exclaimed the officer. "You oughter know better than that. I've a good mind to back up the wagon."

"You and your old wagon," Mr. Bland grumbled. "I bet you haven't got a wagon."

Before the officer could think up an answer to this, Lorna inadvertently fired the revolver and Busy turned to a skeleton.

"It's all right, officer," said Lorna, quietly. "It's the doctor's gat. We were going to shoot my husband if he started to run away."

It is doubtful if Burke had ever been so hopelessly confused. There were too many situations with which he had to deal. There was the naked maniac on the pavement. There was the irresponsible lady with a revolver. And there was the animated skeleton of a dog barking furiously in the face of the laws of God and man. Finally there was the watching crowd. With this Officer Burke could deal. Abandoning the other problems to their own solution, he once more charged down on the spectators.

"Clear out of here," he shouted, "every mother's son of you, or I'll back up the wagon."

While this diversion was in progress Mr. Bland rose from the pavement. He picked up the winded physician and draped him over his shoulder for the sake of protection. MacQuirk did not cover much of Mr. Bland, but he did serve the purpose of making his wearer feel a little less naked.

"Let's go back and get my clothes," said Mr. Bland to Lorna. "That damn-fool dog has lost his flesh again."

"Don't I know!" replied Lorna. "Between you and that dog my life isn't worth living. There's always a skeleton."

"Put me down, Mr. Bland," pleaded the doctor. "This is most undignified. What will my patients think?"

"Sorry, old chap," said Mr. Bland, "but I simply must wear you. What little protection you afford is absolutely essential. Figure it out for yourself."

"Say, lady," said the taxicab driver, "is anybody going to use me?"

"What's the matter with you?" snapped Lorna. "Aren't you having a good time?"

"I am that, lady," conceded the driver, "but I ain't getting paid for it."

"Oh," said Lorna, "the doctor will settle up later."

"Don't listen to her," shouted MacQuirk as he was borne into the house.

If the doctor's first appearance had caused a sensation, his reappearance created a panic.

"First, the doctor goes out carrying a skeleton," summed up the well- dressed, middle-aged gentleman, "and then a naked man comes in carrying the doctor. An odd sort of business."

"And we're supposed to be here for our nerves," complained the wan lady. "I think I'm going to have an attack."

"Let me out!" another patient suddenly cried in a strangled voice. "Look! Look! The living skeleton of a little something."

Still barking under his breath like a thunder-storm on the ebb, the skeleton of Busy followed Lorna across the room and disappeared into the doctor's office.

"Hey, Doc," called Mr. Bland, pointing to what was left of his dog. "Are you convinced now?"

From his own operating table MacQuirk raised a weary head.

"Thoroughly," he said. "Miss Malloy, please go out and dismiss my patients. Tell them I've had a sudden attack of frenzy—tell them anything. It doesn't matter. I'll never get over this."

"They're all gone already," announced the nurse when she returned. "All except the mental case. She still wants some spinach."

"Well, what are we going to do?" MacQuirk asked, distractedly. "I haven't any spinach to give her. And if I did give her some spinach I would be establishing a dangerous precedent. First thing you know, mental cases would be dropping in, demanding a square meal."

"Have you," asked Bland, "by any chance a drink to give us?"

"Why didn't I think of it before?" replied the doctor. "Of course, of course, most certainly. A drink is the very thing. Miss Malloy, if you please. You know where the stuff is. Didn't sleep a wink last night."

By the time Lorna and Mr. Bland were ready to leave, the square dog had regained his body and the exhausted physician a sunnier outlook on life.

CHAPTER 14.

THE TRAVELING BEARD

The express train was swarming with commuters. And Mr. Bland was one of them. Some were reading papers, others playing cards, and some were impatiently awaiting their opportunity to explain the N.R.A. to others who were explaining it to them.

Quintus Bland was far from happy. He had no confidence in himself. Although he had retained his flesh for nearly twenty-four hours he had no definite assurance it would not fade away at any moment.

He would hate to become a skeleton among so many well-dressed and well-fed gentlemen. They would never understand. They were too firmly rooted in convention—too all-fired orthodox. They might have their own failings, but they were the failings of the average man. They might sin and commit crimes, but they would do so according to well-established lines. And yet, thought Mr. Bland, here was a trainload of problems, each individual intent on solving his own. After all, there was something admirable in the way these men accepted their destiny, which seemed to be largely that of catching trains, taking other men's orders, keeping their automobiles in shape and their homes intact. And above all they had to maintain a certain prosperous front. In spite of failure and reverses they had to meet the commuting standard and keep their troubles to themselves. A smug lot, perhaps, but partly so because of the insecurity of their own economic futures. They had to keep up the pretense. At home their wives were doing the same thing, while in the privacy of their own houses they scanned newspaper advertisements of alluring wearing apparel with broodingly envious eyes that held but little hope.

The tragedy of this train, Mr. Bland continued to reflect, was that most of its inmates were in a position to glimpse without grasping the full possibilities of a good, fat, materialistic life, the only one their training and traditions had equipped them to understand. They lived on the fringe of security, desperately clinging to prospects, and often their wives grew old and bitter with those prospects unfulfilled. They themselves never grew old, for that is against the laws of commuting which say that a man must always be brisk and snappy until suddenly he dies and another commuter takes up his fallen cards or moves into his seat. Mr. Bland found himself wondering if it would not be a better thing to be so hopelessly poor that all this strain and pretense would become unnecessary and a man would be able to be his natural slovenly self, always about two-thirds binged.

These thoughts passed through his mind as the familiar landscape passed by his eyes. Seated by the window, he protected himself from observation with a newspaper which he did not read. The gentleman seated beside him he knew only slightly, but the gentleman had no intention of letting matters rest at that. He was one of those exceedingly trying persons who believed that the more people you knew the better off you were. He had a ruddy face, a thick body, and virtually no mind at all. He could talk for a long time in a loud voice in the face of polite indifference or hostile opposition. His success in the advertising world was assured. Already he sat at the speakers' table whenever the Advertising Club stepped out. He was one of those elbowing individuals whose faces stand out with shocking vividness whenever a flashlight picture is taken of groups. And he had a disconcerting habit of thrusting his head round Mr. Bland's newspaper to see what he was reading and then telling him about it with the addition of his own personal views on the subject.

This morning he was a little baffled, for Mr. Bland had not had the enterprise to turn past the women's page before he had abandoned reading entirely. The thick man, whose name was Blutter, was puzzled by his silent neighbor's preoccupation with matters exclusively pertaining to the home, the table, and the adornment of the feminine body.

"Interesting page, that," he said at a venture. "It has always been my claim that the average American husband is far more interested in his home than is the average American wife."

"He doesn't have to live in it so much," retorted Mr. Bland, his lips closely approaching a snarl.

"Perhaps there's a little something in that," Mr. Blutter strode confidently on in his speech, "but I still maintain — and I have an insight into things through years of advertising experience — that the average American husband is far more competent to deal with domestic problems than the average American wife. In fact, I know he is."

"Then that's all settled," said Bland with dangerous mildness. "You appear to be pretty well sold on the average American husband. You must be one yourself."

Mr. Blutter did not get within jumping distance of this remark.

"Yes and no," he stated. "I am essentially a creative man, being, as I am, in the advertising profession, but in every other respect I dare say I represent the point of view of the average American husband."

"You must be no end of a comfort to your wife," observed Mr. Bland. "After she's had a long day of petty frustration about the house, no doubt you come home and set things straight with one large, inclusive gesture."

This observation was too sharply barbed to escape the notice of Mr. Blutter, as dumb as that gentleman was.

"As an average American husband," he retorted with some heat, "I'm not ashamed to say that I enter directly into all matters pertaining to the home and its management. Mrs. Blutter, I am proud to say, finds my co-operation not unhelpful."

"I'm either too drunk to eat," announced Mr. Bland, "or the cook is too drunk to cook. We seldom eat at our house, and when we do, the meal, such as it is, almost always ends up in a row. As a matter of fact, my wife and myself only maintain a home in order to have a quiet place in which to fight. We're both fond of the lower diversions of life and spend most of our time either acquiring or getting rid of a hang-over."

Mr. Blutter's eyes bulged behind his glasses.

"You're a whole pack of cards, Mr. Bland, he said with an uncertain laugh. "I'll bet you run an A-1 plant, you and the missus. I knew a chap like you once. Name of Dobbs. Always comical. Never took life seriously, but at heart one of the finest fellows you'd want to meet. Mighty good company, but of course he couldn't last. Not in the advertising world, he couldn't. You have to have get up and go there and keep your eyes open."

"On what?" Mr. Bland asked, innocently.

"Your clients' interests," replied Mr. Blutter. "What about the buying public?" pursued Mr. Bland.

"The what?" said Mr. Blutter, as though the buying public were a new idea to him. "Oh, yes, the buying public. It's my business to educate it to purchase the right products."

The word Mr. Bland employed at this point has recently become quite the vogue in the best circles of society, although for years it has been unmelodiously shouted through the streets by the commoner run of man. It popped so explosively now from Mr. Bland's lips that the good Blutter was at first startled and then offended.

"To who?" he asked with faint truculence.

"To you," said Mr. Bland.

"Then right back at you," retorted the advertising ace, feeling he had held his own in a difficult exchange.

Quintus Bland grunted and retired behind his paper. A man like Blutter was bad for his soul. He hoped that for the good of the advertising profession there were not many Blutters in it. Not much good hoping a silly thing like that. All professions were overcrowded with Blutters. Blutters ran the world and retarded its progress. There were Blutter statesmen and Blutter generals and, doubtless, Blutter safe-crackers. Blutter was a frame of mind throughout all walks of life.

Idly, as he watched the flying billboards, Mr. Bland began to compose an aimless bit of doggerel in which the words "splutter," "clutter," and "gutter" were employed to rhyme insultingly with that of Blutter.

In the meantime that individual had closed his eyes, the better to concentrate on the problems of the day. They were not quite insuperable. A big client was coming to town, and it would be his, Blutter's, duty to entertain him. Speakeasies, a show, more speakeasies—perhaps girls. Mentally Mr. Blutter smacked his lips. It would be a relief to give Mrs. Blutter the gate for a change, especially when acting in the line of duty. The average American husband would lose his flair for business if he did not step out occasionally. And the less the average American wife knew about such steppings the better for domestic relations. It was not so much cheating as toning a fellow up.

In spite of the fascination of his anticipatory debauch, Mr. Blutter was not completely satisfied with himself. That word Mr. Bland had flung at him still rankled in his mind. He, Blutter, had failed to impress sufficiently this long, crude, scoffing creature at his side. He would retain his good nature and try again.

Accordingly Blutter reopened his eyes and thrust his head round the barrier of Mr. Bland's paper. Then with startling suddenness Blutter's head sprang back as if it had been rudely pushed. For a moment he sat in dazed silence, his eyes still blinking from what they had seen. Then he made another try, this time more circumspectly. He had been right the first time. The man sitting beside him had the face of a grinning skull. And even as he looked, the fleshless face turned slowly toward him and two vacant eyeholes peered inquiringly into his.

"Who are you looking at?" croaked the skull.

"I—I—I confess I don't know," stammered Mr. Blutter. "There was a gentleman sitting there named Bland, but he must have slipped out."

"Slipped out?" repeated the skull, disapprovingly. "Slipped out on what?"

"You know," Blutter faltered. "He just went away."

Suddenly the skull thrust itself into Blutter's horrified face.

"Rats!" snapped the skull with an ominous click of its teeth. "Rats, I repeat. No more loose talking. Who am I?"

By this time Blutter's eyes had discovered the hands of the skull. The sight of those fleshless fingers clawing the morning newspaper struck terror to his heart.

"I don't know who you are," he said in a strained voice, "but I think I'd better be going."

"You'll stay right where you are," replied the skull, once more approaching itself to Mr. Blutter's face.

"Don't!" gasped Mr. Blutter. "I think I'm going to die. Do you want to kill me?"

"Yes," said the skull, "I want to kill you, and I will, too, if you even so much as budge."

"Tickets!" came the voice of the conductor from a few seats down the aisle.

The skull promptly retired behind its newspaper, and when it next emerged it had amazingly grown a beard.

"What do you think of the beard, you rat?" demanded the skull. "How did I do it?"

Mr. Blutter had thrust a handkerchief into his mouth to keep himself from screaming. He now removed this self-inflicted gag and struggled to make his trembling lips form coherent words.

"I don't know how you did it," he managed to say at last, "but won't you take it off? I don't want to be seen talking to a person with such a beard."

"What's wrong with the beard, rat?" the skull rasped, dangerously. "Feel it! Stroke it!"

"Oh, no," babbled Mr. Blutter. "Oh, no, indeed. You don't know what you're asking."

"Feel it! Stroke it!" said the skull, inflexibly.

The arrival of the conductor saved Mr. Blutter from losing what little mind he had. Automatically the conductor accepted the two commutation tickets and punched them. It was not until he was returning them to their individual owners that he noticed anything wrong. It was the bearded skull's hand that first attracted his decidedly unfavorable attention. The beard was the next point of interest. Over this he lingered a moment with rapidly mounting astonishment, but it was not until he looked at the face itself that he received the full shock of the object he was scrutinizing.

"Who are you?" demanded the conductor. "You're not Mr. Bland."

"No," mumbled a cracked voice through the beard. "I'm Mr. Bland's grandfather. He said you wouldn't mind."

"Never knew he had a grandfather," said the conductor.

"Why should you?" asked the beard. "My grandson has lots of things he never told you about."

"What happened to your hands?" the conductor wanted to know.

"My hands?" repeated the beard. "Oh, those. I started biting my fingernails when I was a baby, and I just kept on going."

"Mean to say you bit your hands off?" incredulously demanded the conductor.

"Nibbled," Mr. Bland corrected. "Nibbled. It took years and years to do it. Now there's nothing left to nibble, so I've broken myself of the habit. I'm a very old man, you know."

"Well, you'd better tell your grandson," said the conductor, "that he ought to buy you a pair of gloves. Your hands are a sight."

"He did," mumbled Mr. Bland. "He bought me a pair of gloves, but I ate holes in the fingers. There was fur inside. I boggled a bit at the fur, but finally I got used to it. Never got to like it much. Too old, I reckon. Did you ever try fur?"

The conductor gulped, then shook his head. This horrid old man was positively making him sick.

"Don't," said Mr. Bland, briefly. "It gets in the teeth."

The conductor gagged slightly and passed to the next seat, but his mind was not on his work. His thoughts kept reverting to Mr. Bland's grandfather and his unattractive ways. He was about the oldest old man the conductor had ever seen. He looked more dead than alive. However, if he could eat fur and get away with it he must have a strong constitution.

Being a natural-born gossiper, the conductor did not delay long in telling some of his more favored passengers all about the strange old grandfather of Mr. Bland and of how he had nibbled off his hands and then started in on fur-lined gloves. Soon Mr. Bland was the center of no little attention. Heads were turned in his direction, and low conversations ensued. Mr. Bland was not happy about this, but Mr. Blutter was still less happy. He was looking around for a means of escape when he felt five bony talons burn into the flesh of his thigh. Involuntarily he uttered an inarticulate cry. This attracted even more attention.

"No, you don't," grated Mr. Bland. "You're going to stay here and keep me company, and when the train reaches the station you're going to help me along the platform. See this?"

Under the cover of the seat ahead Mr. Bland pulled up the right sleeve of his coat and displayed the bare bone of his arm.

"Oh!" gasped Mr. Blutter, fairly cringing in his seat. "Oh! I can't last much longer. Please don't show me any more awful things."

"I'm like that all over," Mr. Bland informed him with a note of pride. "Would you like to see my ribs? You can look right through them."

"I don't want to look," said Mr. Blutter.

"Then how's this?" continued Mr. Bland, giving his beard a slight twist. "Do you like it better on the side or in the middle?"

"Off," said Mr. Blutter.

"Can't take it off," Mr. Bland observed, reflectively, "because then I wouldn't be my own grandfather, and if I'm not my own grandfather who the hell am I?"

"That's what I'd like to know."

"I'm an average American husband," announced Mr. Bland. "A part of the buying public, and you're my very old and very dear friend. How about stroking my beard?"

"Please pull it back," said Blutter. "Beards don't grow like that even on a face like yours."

"Very well," Mr. Bland agreed, amiably. "Back goes the beard. And just in time, too. Here we are."

Mr. Blutter's relief in putting that trip behind him was short-lived. This was due to the fact that Mr. Bland's trousers slipped over his pelvis about half-way down the platform, and he, the redoubtable Blutter, had to assist in securing them while all the world looked on. What Mr. Blutter saw of Mr. Bland during this feverish and complicated procedure improved his morale very little.

"I'll hold 'em up," Mr. Bland told him, "while you twist the belt."

"What will I twist around?" Mr. Blutter chattered.

"I've a bit of a spine back there. Twist it around that."

"If I wasn't so damned scared of you," said Blutter in a burst of frankness, "I'd like to twist your spine off."

"You can have a twist if you like," Mr. Bland replied, generously. "I can grow another one."

With his trousers securely in place, Mr. Bland took his unwilling companion's arm and continued on down the platform, shuffling noisily as he went.

"Can't you lift your feet a little?" complained the freely sweating Blutter. "We're conspicuous enough as it is without you making all that noise."

"No," said Mr. Bland. "My shoes would come off. If you think the rest of me is horrid you should take a look at my feet."

At the telephone booths Mr. Blutter was released from his terrific ordeal, but not before he had experienced the harrowing sensation of shaking hands with a skeleton.

"Good-bye, old chap," said Mr. Bland. "Be a good average American husband, and some bright day I'll drop round to call on you and the—er— missus. I think that's the acceptable term for the average American wife, or is it 'the little lady'?"

Without stopping to answer, Blutter sped like an arrow from the bow the instant his hand was released from the blood-chilling grasp of that fleshless hand.

Mr. Bland watched the retreating figure of Mr. Blutter, then mentally took stock of the situation.

"I'm in one hell of a fine fix," he said to himself. "Here I stand with an obviously false beard, no flesh at all, and a pair of treacherous trousers. What am I going to do? I'll get picked up sure as shooting if I try to barge along on my own. Wonder what Lorna's doing."

Feeling much more miserable than he was willing to let himself know, he turned toward a telephone booth, the queer, awkward figure of what recently was a man, now entirely cut off from the flesh-and-blood people milling busily round him.

CHAPTER 15.

THE WHITTLES REAPPEAR

It was an inspiration on Mr. Bland's part to think of Claude Whittle. Both Whittle and his wife were cast in an imperturbable mould. They could take an animated skeleton in their stride without batting an eyelid. More than that, they could bring themselves to associate with that same skeleton on terms of unstrained equality. Sound people in a tight fix. Mr. Bland was certain that if any man's fix was tight, his was that fix. Accordingly he dialed Mr. Whittle's hotel and was soon connected with that gentleman himself.

"Hello, Whittle," he said when a mild voice at the other end of the line had announced that its owner was there. "This is Quintus Bland."

"What a name that first half is," said the mild voice, plaintively. "You can't imagine how silly it sounds just coming out of nowhere, although when I saw you last you were nearly next to nothing yourself. It's raining."

"Listen," said Mr. Bland, "are you sure you've finished about my name and your zippy little weather reports? I'm paying for this call and you're using it all up."

"People so seldom telephone me," Mr. Whittle explained, "I'm actually telephone hungry—starved, I might say. Famished. Where's your body now?"

"That's just the trouble. I haven't any body."

"But you did have some body? Is that it? I'm no detective. Never was."

"Don't you ever stop drinking?" Mr. Bland demanded. "I'll try again. Listen well. I did have a body only a few minutes ago, but the damned thing has done a bunk on me and left me stranded in the D.L. & W. station with a long white beard and no place to go."

"Whose beard is it?" asked Mr. Whittle.

"Does that mean a lot to you?" Mr. Bland replied, impatiently.

"No," admitted the mild voice, reflectively, "but it's sort of interesting. You have a beard, you say, and it's white. That means you have a white beard when one really gets down to brass tacks. What more do you want —another beard?"

"God, no!" exclaimed Mr. Bland, slipping another coin in the slot at the urgent behest of the operator. "I've got enough beard to last one a lifetime if I'm careful. I want you to come over here and get me."

"You or the beard?" asked Mr. Whittle. "Me in the beard," said Mr. Bland.

"Will you wear the beard for me?" the mild voice asked with increased animation.

"What do you think I'm going to do with it, wave it like a flag?"

"You could," said Mr. Whittle after a short pause. "That is, if it's long enough, and the way I figure it, a beard doesn't have to be so long to be waved like a flag. I'm to look for a skeleton in a white beard, is that it?"

"You're to be prepared for a skeleton in a white beard," Mr. Bland told him.

"Oh, I won't mind greatly," said Mr. Whittle. "You're not as bad as loathsome reptiles, at any rate. If I could stand you in a pillowcase I guess I won't baulk at a beard. Where will you be?"

"In one of those private washrooms."

"Oh, I know those places," said Mr. Whittle. "Went to sleep in one of them once and they thought I'd committed suicide."

"You were drunk," said Mr. Bland.

"Yes," said Mr. Whittle, sorrowfully, "I was drunk."

"You won't be long, will you?" asked Mr. Bland, a note of real anxiety creeping into his voice. "And you won't forget all about me?"

"Certainly not," protested Whittle. "Pauline will remind me. She's collected my clothes already. There's something morbid about that woman the way she falls for the abnormal. She wants to know if your beard flows."

"Freely," said Mr. Bland, "and without stint."

"I can hardly wait," came the mild voice of Mr. Whittle. "How will I know which one you are in?"

"Just call my name softly," replied Mr. Bland, "and I'll snap right out."

"Well, don't snap out too fast," said Mr. Whittle. "I'm willing, but my heart is weak, and your beard might get caught in the door. I won't say "I'll be seeing you,' because the last person who said that to me I called an exceptionally vile name. Shall I ring off now?"

"Why not?" said Mr. Bland.

"All right, I'll do it," the voice of Whittle replied, "but isn't it funny, me looking for a skeleton with a white beard in a gentleman's private washroom. Don't you think so, or do you know of something funnier?"

"I'll tell you when I see you," said Mr. Bland. "Get started."

"Don't forget," came the voice of Whittle, faintly. "I'm going now. Good-bye."

Mr. Bland returned the receiver to the hook and got himself into a private washroom as unobtrusively as possible, warning the Negro attendant not to disturb him until called for. When the Negro looked at the size of his tip, each tooth in his head fairly gleamed its gratitude.

"Thank you, boss," he said. "Thank you kindly. You can stay a solid month, and if you want your meals brought in, I'm your man."

Mr. Bland entered the small room and, knowing the casual ways of the Whittles, sat down and prepared himself to wait for an indefinite period. However, on this occasion Claude Whittle did not tarry long on the way. About an hour after Mr. Bland had heard his voice over the wire he heard it again outside the door to his room.

"George," Mr. Whittle was saying to the attendant, "I'm looking for a white beard feebly supported by a tall, thin gentleman. Have you seen anything like it?"

"Sure have, boss," replied the attendant. "He's right in there, suh, and he can stay just as long as he wants."

"Good!" cried Mr. Whittle; then, slightly elevating his voice: "Señor Toledo, how long do you want to stay in there?"

"Señor Toledo doesn't want to stay in here another minute longer," replied Mr. Bland. "Señor Toledo comes."

Unlatching the door, he stepped out and faced Mr. Whittle. Perhaps it would be more accurate to say he outfaced that gentleman, for after one swift look at Mr. Bland and his beard, Mr. Whittle's eyes fell.

"Well?" said Mr. Bland, feeling somewhat self-conscious. "What do you think of me?"

"Don't let's take that up at this moment," replied Mr. Whittle. "Give me a little time to analyze my emotions. I will say this, however, you're not an anticlimax. Pauline has a taxi waiting."

The door to the taxi swung open at the approach of Mr. Bland and his escort. A woman's low voice came from the semi-darkness of its interior.

"Is he wearing any drawers?" Pauline wanted to know.

"How about yourself?" snapped Mr. Bland as he jack-knifed himself through the low door.

"What do you think I am?" asked Pauline Whittle, indignantly. "A prude?"

"Do you know what she's trying to get at?" inquired Mr. Whittle in his mild, patient manner.

"I hope she isn't trying to get at anything," replied Mr. Bland.

"Come, come," said Mr. Whittle.

"I asked merely because I want to have a clear understanding of the situation," Pauline explained. "If his trousers fall off in the lobby it would be well to have a second line of defence."

"My drawers are no defence at all," said Mr. Bland. "They're a second source of anxiety. If my trousers fall off in the lobby my drawers will accompany them. They have always been too large."

"I say, lady," said the taxi driver, thrusting his head through the partition window, "is there anything criminal in this?"

"There is," replied Pauline. "Now do you feel at home?"

"It's all right by me," said the driver, "but that's a damn' poor disguise. The dumbest flattie on the force could spot him a mile off."

"We're not going to let him play with flatties," said Pauline. "He's keeping under cover. Snap to it and drive on. You're carrying the oldest gunman in the world. He's likely to knock you over just in the spirit of fun."

"Okay, lady," said the driver. "Tell the old murderer I'm on his side."

The Whittles lived in a large and ostentatious uptown hotel. About it there was no suggestion of home atmosphere. For this reason the Whittles liked it, never having been able to get through their heads what home life was all about. It was frankly a pagan temple, this huge structure dominating the Gay White Way. It offered every modern convenience except a morgue. Its Turkish baths and dormitories did much to keep gangsters both clean and sober. In luxurious suites of rooms beautiful women lived not such beautiful lives. And almost everybody had a good time until he was either shot down or kicked out. So far the Whittles had managed to avoid both of these unpleasant occurrences.

When the trio emerged from the taxi its bearded member was discovered wearing Mr. Whittle's raincoat. It was much too short for him, but that slight detail made little difference. Mr. Bland could look no worse than he did regardless of what he wore.

"Pull your coat collar up and your hat brim down," Pauline commanded, "and hang on to your pants and beard."

"Trousers," muttered Mr. Bland. "I keep on telling you."

The desk clerk's name was Booker, and his eyes were harassed and weary from looking into so many different types of faces. Booker believed there was not a face in all the world of which he had not seen the counterpart. He promptly revised his opinion when he looked into Mr. Bland's. Confronted by this somewhat synthetic gentleman, Booker for once lost his air of cynical detachment. He held his left hand up before his eyes and told off the fingers with his right. Once more he looked at the bearded face as if still unconvinced. Then he repeated the performance, only this time he held up his right hand and counted its fingers with the left.

"Why are you doing that?" asked Mr. Bland. "You're making me very nervous."

"You've already made me that," said Booker. "I was trying to discover if I was losing my eyesight. I almost wish I were."

"This gentleman is a friend of ours," Pauline Whittle explained. "He wants a large room with a bath."

"I should say," replied Booker, "the gentleman wanted a doctor, or a barber, or better still, a hearse."

"Nonsense," snapped Mrs. Whittle. "Señor Toledo is a distinguished Spanish magician."

"Then Señor Toledo should play some tricks on himself," said the clerk. "He'll have a hard time holding an audience if he doesn't do something about his appearance."

Annoyed, Mr. Bland held two fleshless fingers directly beneath Booker's nose, then snapped them suddenly. The resulting noise was not unlike the explosion of a small firecracker.

"Bah to you," said Mr. Bland. "Do I get a room or don't I?"

"I guess you get a room all right," replied Booker, "but I hope to heaven you stay in it until you've decided to change your make-up. It might go big in Spain, but it's a little too strong for Broadway."

"I'll knock them cold," said Mr. Bland.

"You will that," agreed the clerk. "I'm chilly as hell myself— pardon my language, Mrs. Whittle."

"Don't show off," replied Pauline, "or pretend you have any gentlemanly instincts left, if you ever had any to begin with."

Mr. Booker grinned and, summoning a bellboy, handed him the key to 1707.

"Take Señor Toledo to his room," said Booker, "and see that he stays there—I mean, see that he's made comfortable."

As they were turning away from the desk, Mr. Bland was politely accosted by a small, suave individual with piercing eyes and a black goatee.

"Pardon me," said this gentleman, deftly extracting a visiting card from Mr. Bland's beard, "but did I hear this lady say you were Señor Toledo, a distinguished Spanish magician?"

"You did," announced Pauline, aggressively. "What are you going to do about it?"

"Simply this, madam," said the stranger, suddenly wiggling his chin like a rabbit and flipping his goatee into oblivion. "I am the Great Girasol, the mysterious jewel of all magicians. What did you think of that?"

"Great Scott!" exclaimed the simple-minded Mr. Whittle. "The little beggar fairly tossed his beard away."

"Yeah," put in Pauline, nastily. "Well, just keep your eyes on our entry. Come on, Señor Toledo, show this rank amateur some real hot stuff."

By this time they found themselves in the center of a circle of spectators, all intent on extracting the last ounce of amusement from whatever was taking place, which is a good old New York custom. Mr. Bland glanced nervously about him, then looked at the inflexible Pauline. Previously he had suspected, but now he felt convinced, that both she and her husband had been drinking.

"Do you mean," he asked, uneasily, "right out here in front of all these people?"

"Why not?" she retorted. "Girasol started it. Show the little geezer up, or I'll leave you flat."

For a moment Mr. Bland pondered. He knew that as he stood he was the most remarkable man in the world, yet he felt disinclined to demonstrate that fact before so many spectators. Nevertheless he could not allow this challenge to pass. Pauline had already announced to the world that he was Señor Toledo, a distinguished Spanish magician. He could not let her down. He took another look at the mysterious jewel of all magicians, then quickly made up his mind. Girasol was strutting like a game cock, a smug smile on his vividly red lips.

"All right," said Mr. Bland. "For the honor of dear old Spain."

He stepped back a pace, then gave his skull a violent snap. When he looked up, the white beard was resting beneath his left ear.

"What do you think of that?" he demanded. "Girasol did better," said a voice in the crowd. "He made his beard disappear."

"That's all very well," another voice argued, "but look at the difference in the sizes of the beards. Girasol's beard you could put in a thimble. You'd have to get a truck to lug that other brush away."

Pauline was somewhat disappointed in Mr. Bland's effort, but she did not show it.

"Swell work, Toledo," she said. "That's got the little guy guessing."

The Great Girasol held up a hand for silence.

"Observe," he said in a magnificently deep voice, then quite casually tossed his left arm away. "Match that if you can."

Before the cries of horror and approval of the spectators had died away, Mr. Bland, now thoroughly aroused, got into action. Once more he snapped his head, but this time with such violence that his hat flew off with the beard nesting in it. Then he raised his head and presented a grinning skull to the crowd.

"God!" exclaimed a professional gambler. "If they keep it up at this rate they'll be getting rid of themselves entirely."

Girasol looked at Mr. Bland's skull, then blinked several times. Here, indeed, was a new one on him. He was game, however, and did not show his perturbation.

"What did you think of that?" asked Mr. Bland, feeling a little better about himself.

"Good," admitted Girasol, "but not good enough. Watch this!"

He extended his right arm in the air and snatched back his left, which he fitted into place, then with a wriggle of his chin he somehow succeeded in recapturing his black goatee.

"Thank Gord," said a well-kept blonde. "If he'd started in flinging his legs away I'd of gone clean batty."

"Get in there, Toledo," Pauline urged. "Get in the game and show them what you're made of."

"Shall I?" asked Mr. Bland.

"Sure," said Mr. Whittle. "Give the Great Girasol the shock of his life."

Without another word Mr. Bland busily stripped himself to the waist, then slowly turned around like a mannequin displaying the latest Paris model.

"What do you think of that?" he asked the Great Girasol.

Girasol was sweating. He mopped his fore-head and made a heroic effort to pull himself together. The spectators gazed at Mr. Bland with a mixture of admiration and revulsion in their dilated eyes.

"Don't know why I'm standing here," came the voice of the well-kept blonde. "That Spanish lad has aged me ten years already."

"You can see clean through his ribs," whispered the gambler, "and out the other side. What manner of man is he?"

The Great Girasol, realizing the tide had set against him, made a supreme effort.

"Attend!" he cried. "The Great Girasol will make Señor Toledo look sick."

"He looks every bit of that already," said a well-known racketeer. "He looks damn' well near dead."

Sitting down on the floor, Girasol created the perfect illusion of a man tossing his legs into space.

"What do you think of that?" he cried, turning triumphantly on the partial skeleton.

"I knew it," said the well-kept blonde. "That little guy's been itching to chuck his legs away, and now he's gone and done it. Next thing you know the kid from Spain will be pitching his skull in our laps."

Pauline, tense with excitement, took Mr. Bland aside.

"Girasol has shot his bolt," she whispered. "Now you must shoot yours. Take off your pants and give them everything."

"Trousers," murmured Mr. Bland. "I keep on telling and telling you. Men wear trousers and women wear pants."

"I don't wear either," said Pauline, "but that's another matter."

With a brief nod Mr. Bland stepped forward and tauntingly confronted his rival, then bowed to the spectators.

"Girasol," he said, looking down at the dapper magician, "you'd better get your legs back and be prepared to run. Clap your eyes on this."

Quickly releasing his belt, he stepped out of his trousers; then, kicking off his shoes, he stretched himself to his full height and extended two long, bony arms in the direction of the seated Girasol. That jewel of mystery did not remain long seated. With a startled cry he unfolded his missing legs and sprang to his feet.

"Toledo isn't a magician!" he cried. "He's the son of the devil himself."

And with this parting denunciation the Great Girasol turned on his heel and took both himself and his magic off.

"I don't know but what he's right," observed the well-kept blonde. "I must get myself a facial to get rid of my horror-stricken expression."

Having driven his opponent from the field, Mr. Bland was calmly dressing again.

"Don't trouble about that now, Señor," said Pauline, swiftly gathering up Mr. Bland's abandoned garments. "You can dress in your room."

"I'd like to have my beard," said Mr. Bland. "I don't feel quite so naked with it on."

"Oh, he's got to have his beard," declared Mr. Whittle.

"Take your old beard," said Pauline, "and stick it on your chin."

CHAPTER 16.

CONVERSATION IN A CAGE

If he is really out to get it, a skeleton has little difficulty in obtaining as much privacy as he wants. The problem with which he is confronted is the establishment of desirable social contacts. Mr. Bland was fortunate in having the loyal if somewhat inebriated friendship of Mr. and Mrs. Whittle. These two hard-boiled exponents of the lower pursuits of life were a host in themselves. To know the Whittles was much like associating with a three-ring circus on the loose. Although very little occurred that surprised this well-matched couple, it was interested in almost everything. And when the Whittles' interest was aroused, some sort of trouble usually resulted. If Mr. Bland had hoped to obtain quietude and contentment when he called on them for sanctuary, he was doomed to disappointment. The Whittles were opposed to quietude and constitutionally incapable of contentment. Both of them were now jubilant over the defeat of the Great Girasol at the hands of Mr. Bland. As they followed the boy to the elevators they were making elaborate plans for their protege's stage début, entirely disregarding his voluble opposition.

"I didn't like it at all," said Mr. Bland, "the way you made me exhibit myself in public. Suppose I should have regained my flesh when I stood there before all those people?"

"Why, that would have made your act even more piquant," replied Pauline. "I wish you could figure out a way of controlling the comings and goings of your body."

"Nothing would please me more," Mr. Bland assured her.

The elevator was crowded. When the skeleton walked in, it tried to be less crowded, but the operator was quick with the door. At that, one gentleman did succeed in getting himself out with the exception of his left foot, and even though he found himself in great danger and lying in a most undignified position on his face, he felt he had materially improved his position. When his foot was released he took it away to the nearest speakeasy, where he drank himself into a state of happy forgetfulness.

Within the ascending cage a state of panic reigned. In their eagerness to remove themselves as far as possible from the immediate vicinity of the skeleton, men and women climbed impartially on one another's shoulders. In the presence of an animated skeleton chivalry strikes a man as being nothing less than folly. Before the elevator had lifted itself six feet from its base, Mr. Bland found himself isolated in a corner with only his beard for company. This state of isolation did not long endure. Strong men, in endeavoring to achieve a point of vantage, catapulted defenseless women against him. The cries and screams that followed caused the operator to stop the elevator between floors. This did not help matters any, because everyone had planned to get off at the first opportunity, and now there was none. They were literally up against a blank wall with a skeleton in their midst.

In vain did Pauline and Mr. Whittle endeavor to bring comfort to the occupants of the cage by assuring them they were traveling with Señor Toledo, a distinguished Spanish magician. This information brought scant comfort to them so long as Señor Toledo remained in his present wasted condition.

"If he's such a distinguished magician," a gentleman inquired, "why doesn't he make things a little easier for us all by taking on a little flesh?"

"Yes," came the positive voice of a woman. "Who asked him to play nasty tricks in a public elevator? When he gets in his own room he can practise being a skeleton to his heart's content. We don't want to see him do it."

And as if in answer to these questions, Mr. Bland momentarily regained his flesh. He was first apprised of this fact by a startled exclamation from one of the ladies pressed against him.

"Gracious!" he heard her say. "There's a naked man in this lift."

"How do you know?" her friend wanted to know.

"Don't be silly," replied the first lady.

It was now Mr. Bland's turn to become panic-stricken.

"Go 'way!" he cried. "Can't you see I'm naked?"

"Well," began the lady. "I —"

"Will you two be still?" cut in Mr. Bland. "You must be bereft of shame."

He deftly yanked the skirt off the loquacious lady and wrapped it about himself.

"Oh," cried the lady to the occupants of the elevator. "The naked man has stolen my skirt, and now I'm nearly as naked as he is. What shall I do?"

"Hide behind the naked man," someone suggested.

"Like the deuce," said the naked man in an injured voice. "If she'd only kept her mouth shut no one would have been any the wiser."

"It doesn't make me feel any wiser to look at a naked man," a woman declared, stoutly.

"I'd have known," said another woman who had been forced against Mr. Bland. "At first I couldn't believe what I was—well, I just couldn't believe it, that's all," she ended up, lamely.

"What the hell sort of a hotel is this anyway," came the voice of a gentleman in complaining accents, "allowing skeletons and naked men to go riding about in elevators?"

"What I want to know is," said a fresh voice, "are we going to stay here all day with this naked man?"

"I'd rather stay in here with a naked man," proclaimed a feminine voice with disarming frankness, "than with a grinning skeleton. What's become of him?"

"He must have turned into the naked man," someone replied.

"If that's the case," said another voice, "Señor Toledo should travel with a bathrobe."

The elevator got under way, then halted again at the first floor. It is a striking commentary on the relative popularity of a naked man and a skeleton that only a few passengers got off at this floor. Panic in the cage had now given place to curiosity, and there was none more curious than Pauline Whittle.

"Do you know," she said to Mr. Bland when the crowd had somewhat thinned, "this is the first time I've seen you in the flesh? You make a perfect picture standing beside that pretty girl in those perfectly ridiculous little panties."

"He won't give me back my skirt," said the girl.

"Don't worry, my dear," replied Pauline. "You look much better with it off."

"If you'll tell me the number of your room," said Mr. Bland, "I'll bring you your skirt. You can see for yourself it wouldn't do at all to give it up now."

"Isn't he long," observed Mr. Whittle, "and lean and knobby? Don't know but what I prefer the skeleton. I'd got sort of used to that."

"I like him as he is," declared Pauline.

"You would," said Mr. Whittle.

"I wish you'd both keep your opinions to yourselves," said Mr. Bland.

"Never change back," Pauline urged him. "And never get dressed. Men look so dull with their clothes on."

"You're an incorrigible voluptuary," Mr. Whittle told her. "A sex-ridden hag."

"God gave me sex whether I wanted it or not," Pauline replied. "I say make the best of it, or the most of it, or the worst of it, according to your lights. It isn't a subject for adult consideration. Sex is simply a fact — about the only pleasant fact of life."

"How long are you going on about it?" Mr. Whittle asked her.

"I seldom talk about sex," she replied. "I let it speak for itself."

"And in no uncertain terms," said Mr. Whittle.

"Here's your skirt," said Mr. Bland to the girl in the ridiculous little panties as the elevator stopped at last at the seventeenth floor. "Thanks a lot for letting me use it, but now I don't need it any more."

The girl uttered a little cry and snatched at her skirt.

"Why, you're a skeleton again," she said.

"Unfortunately," Mr. Bland replied, stepping from the cage.

And so he was.

"There goes a beautiful friendship," said Pauline Whittle, following the skeleton out of the elevator, "not to mention some other rather entertaining possibilities."

"Am I not present," asked her husband, "that you should go on thus?"

"You should know whether you're here or not," Pauline told him.

"I know where I am, all right," said Mr. Whittle, "but I wasn't sure whether you did or not."

"I've always been above board," declared Pauline.

"And below par," added her husband.

"Little boy," said the skeleton to the page, "please lead me to my room. These people are unnecessarily tiresome."

As they progressed down the corridor, a door suddenly opened and a thuggish, bloated face appeared in the opening. Two bloodshot eyes were fixed on Mr. Bland with such burning intensity that he stopped in his tracks and turned to confront the owner of such a malevolent gaze. Mistaking the skeleton's intentions, the man whipped out a revolver and sprang into the hall.

"Ha!" he mouthed. "So you've come back to torment me. Well, I sent you to the grave once and I'll send you there again."

"There must be some mistake," said Mr. Bland, politely. "I'm not dead and I've never been buried."

"No?" sneered the man. "Then where did you get that beard?"

"I got it from a friend," Mr. Bland told him. "It's not really mine."

"You lie!" the man shouted. "You grew it in the grave. That's the only place you could grow a beard like that."

"Don't you like it?" asked Mr. Bland, hoping to keep the man's attention from straying back to the gun.

"You know I don't," said the man, excitedly. "I hate it. And when I've finished with you they can suck up your powdered bones in a vacuum cleaner."

"Gur-r-r," said Mr. Bland. "How graphically you put it."

"Look out!" warned Mr. Whittle.

And then the shooting started.

CHAPTER 17.

FROM BED TO BED

The first report of the revolver galvanized all legs present into desperate action. And with each subsequent explosion those legs got busier and busier.

The Whittles, led by the bellboy, fled in one direction; Mr. Bland with the man behind him sprinted in the other. And Mr. Bland did very well. He tried to do even better. The prospect of being blown to powder to make life easier for a vacuum cleaner added many inches to his stride.

As Mr. Bland bounded past the floor telephone operator, that courageous young woman promptly plugged in on the desk clerk. He had just relieved Mr. Booker, so the operator's information was all news to him.

"There's a skeleton up here," said the girl. "He's running through the halls."

"What's that to you?" snapped the clerk. "A guest in this hotel has a perfect right to be as thin as he wants."

"This one's a real skeleton," said the girl, unemotionally.

"Well," replied the clerk, "you're not so fat yourself."

"And a man is shooting at him," went on the girl, disregarding any implied dissatisfaction with her figure.

"Who's doing the shooting?" the clerk wanted to know.

"That person in 1782," replied the girl.

"Up to his old tricks, eh?" said the desk clerk. "Well, you can tell him for the management that if he pulls another murder in this hotel we'll throw him out on his ear."

"He's in no mood to listen," replied the operator.

"He's nothing but a drunken gangster," said the clerk, a little irritably.

"That's quite a lot to be," said the girl and pulled out the plug.

In the meantime Mr. Bland was weaving his frantic way down the long, heavily carpeted corridor. Bullets were either speeding past him or through him. He could not be sure what the bullets were doing, but from the speed he was making he felt satisfied he was still alive. He pranced round a corner and ran into a volley of shrieks issuing from a door on his right. Some woman was in mortal terror of her life. Forgetting his own peril, Mr. Bland flung open the door and sprang into the room, slamming the door behind him.

A brutal-looking man was busily choking a scantily clad woman. Mr. Bland noticed she was wearing cerise-colored garters. He was not sure he liked them, then decided they looked excitingly meretricious. The rest of the woman was in keeping with her garters. She could still be a useful and active member of society if she were not choked too much.

Upon the entrance of Mr. Bland the man gave the woman a rest and looked over one shoulder to see who had so rudely interrupted his pleasant occupation. When he got it through his head that he was looking at a heavily panting skeleton he froze in his position, one great hand still open, as if waiting for a throat to fill it. When the girl saw the skeleton she closed her eyes and thrust her neck back into the extended hand.

"Go on and choke me," she said in a flat voice. "Finish me off quickly before that thing has a chance to drag me down to hell."

For the moment the man had lost his taste for any further murderous activity. He backed away from the girl, allowing her body to fall on the bed. Mr. Bland moved away from the door. If the brutal man wanted to go, there was nothing to be gained in preventing him. Mr. Bland would be only too glad to see the last of him.

The man made a rush for the door and seized the knob, pausing for a moment to glare back at the girl on the bed.

"I see how it is," he cried. "I see everything."

Mr. Bland looked more closely at the girl.

"Don't leave me alone with that," she pleaded.

"Acting!" cried the man. "Always acting! Not content with snatching them from the cradle, you also snatch them from the grave. I'm going to get a gun and blow you both to bits."

"That makes two marksmen," thought Mr. Bland as the door closed on the brutal man's exit.

He turned and considered the girl lying half crouched on the bed.

"I'm not going to hurt you," he told her.

"What else can you do?" she asked, sitting up quite unexpectedly and fluffing out her hair, which was, Mr. Bland noted, almost the color of her garters.

"Are you suggesting games?" he asked her. "Anything that's friendly," the girl replied. "I'm tired of being choked."

At that moment the voice of the drunken gambler sounded in the hall.

"Where are you?" it shouted. "Hey, skeleton, come on out and take your medicine. Back to the grave for you."

A loud report immediately followed this uncongenial suggestion, and a bullet buried itself in the door. Mr. Bland had no desire either to take any medicine or to go back to the grave. He dived into the girl's bed and pulled the covers up over his skull.

"Your beard is sticking out," she told him.

"Tuck it in, won't you?" he asked her. "There's a man outside with a gun."

"It would take a lot more than gunplay," said the girl, "to get me to tuck that beard in bed."

"What's wrong with the beard?" Mr. Bland demanded.

"It isn't human, if you want to know," she answered.

"A beard isn't supposed to be human," he told her. "It's merely a decoration."

"Come on out," cried the voice of the gangster. "Hey, skeleton, come on out. I hear you whispering in there."

A second shot lodged in the heavy door.

This was a little too strong for the girl. She tumbled into the bed and pulled up the covers on her side.

"Just because you saved my life," she whispered, "don't think you've a right to get gay."

"Gay," muttered Mr. Bland. "My dear young lady, I'm feeling far from that."

"Don't blame you," whispered the girl. "I couldn't be gay either if a man was looking for me with a gun. Think it's all right, me being in bed with a skeleton?"

"It's all right with me," said Mr. Bland. "As a matter of fact, I'm glad you're here. Being shot at by strangers is one of the loneliest feelings in the world."

"Did anybody ever choke you?" asked the girl.

"Not yet," said Mr. Bland.

"Well, that isn't any fun, either," she told him.

"This seems to be a very violent sort of hotel," observed Mr. Bland.

"It is," agreed the girl. "You can get away with murder here as long as you pay your bill."

"I hope that man owes a lot," said Mr. Bland.

The door banged open, and the drunken gangster stood on the threshold.

"Hey, skeleton," he called; then, seeing a girl in the bed, he addressed himself to her: "Have you seen a dirty skeleton?" he asked her.

Mr. Bland did not like this description of himself one little bit. Lorna called him a dirty man, and this drunken gangster called him a dirty skeleton. Something should be done about it, but all he could do at the moment was to lie quite still and hope against hope his beard would remain undetected.

"No," replied the girl, "but I saw a dusty skeleton once in a sideshow."

The drunken gangster shook his head in a dull way. His lips fumbled for the words before they formed and spoke them.

"This was a dirty damned skeleton," he said with stupid gravity, "this skeleton I'm looking for. Thought he'd come back to torture me, but I showed him different. I put him in his grave once and I'll put him there again. The damn' thing's wearing a beard. I don't care if he wears a dozen, understand?"

Mr. Bland thought this over. He fervently wished he had a dozen beards. A dozen beards like the one he had on would make a fur coat, not a long one, perhaps, but adequate for the purposes of concealment. The girl beside him was speaking. Her voice sounded coolly annoyed. As Mr. Bland listened he reflected that women were at their best when they had something to conceal. They generally came up to scratch. Man with his arrogance and physical superiority had forged a weapon against himself and placed it in the mouth of a woman.

"Why are you confiding all this in me?" asked the girl. "I'm not your big sister. If you'd stop stuffing my door with bullets I'd try to get a little sleep."

"I won't be able to sleep," said the man, "until I've put that skeleton —that dirty skeleton—into a can of tooth powder."

"That man is a sheer genius," thought Mr. Bland. "He can think of the most amusing things to do with me. I'd hate like hell to be cooped up in a can of tooth powder. A vacuum cleaner would give me a better run for my money."

The man turned to the door, then turned back again and made a sudden lunge across the room to the bed. Mr. Bland had just sufficient time to snatch off his beard and thrust it under a pillow before the bedclothes were dragged from his body.

"Jeeze!" said the gangster. "He's as naked as a babe."

The familiar comparison sounded quaint on the gunman's lips.

"What!" exclaimed the girl in genuine surprise. "Why, so he is. I don't think I ever saw a nakeder man."

"Don't look!" cried Mr. Bland.

Frantically he ploughed up the bedclothes like a dog digging sand. Both modesty and caution prompted him to cover himself as speedily as possible. He had been changing form so frequently since arriving at the hotel that he was afraid he might return to a skeleton at any moment.

"Why don't you go skeleton-shooting?" he demanded, indignantly. "You're wasting three people's time here, and that's too much for any one man."

"Jeeze, mister," said the gunman, apologetically, "I'm sorry, honestly I am. Thought you might be that dirty skeleton."

"Are you thoroughly convinced I'm not?"

"Sure," said the man. "I could tell you wasn't a skeleton."

"So could I," said the girl in an ominous voice.

"But if you see that skeleton," went on the gangster, "just give me a shout. I'll be sneaking along the halls. You can tell him by his beard. You won't like it."

"Why should I?" said Mr. Bland. "On the spur of the moment I can't think of any beard that claims my admiration."

Holding his automatic ready for immediate action, the gangster placed a finger to his lips, winked frightfully, and left the room.

"I wouldn't be in your spot for all of Radio city," said the girl as soon as the man had gone.

"What do you mean?" asked Mr. Bland a little nervously.

"That's easy," replied the girl, sitting up in bed. "If you stay the way you are, my boy friend will shoot you, and if you change back to a skeleton, that drunken thug will fill you full of lead."

"His present plans are much more elaborate than that," said Mr. Bland, moodily. "You heard what he said about a can of tooth powder. His heart is set on putting me in one."

"That's what you get for diving into my bed under false pretenses," declared the girl. "I don't know what manner of man you are, or how you pull your stuff, but I do know that a skeleton is the last thing in the world a lady in bed wants to see."

"I'd better be going now before your boy friend comes back with his gun," said Mr. Bland.

As he half rose in the bed, the girl flung two cool arms round his neck.

"This," she whispered, "is for saving my life."

And she gave him a long and experienced kiss.

How long it might have lasted will never be known, for it was rudely interrupted by a ferocious cry from the door.

"By God, what a woman!" came the furious voice of the boy friend. "First a grinning skeleton and then a naked man."

Under such unfavorable circumstances all the laws of decency were so much unnecessary ballast. Mr. Bland snatched his beard and sprang from the bed. He could never recall how he got himself out of the room, but he had a vivid recollection of dashing down a long corridor while bullets overtook and passed him. This time he was pursued by both the boy friend and the gangster, the latter apparently willing to shoot at any moving object.

Although Mr. Bland could outrun his pursuers, he could not hope to equal the speed of their bullets. With a pang of alarm he realized it would be a matter of only a short time before one or more of these missiles laid him low. Putting a corner between himself and his two unreasonable enemies, Mr. Bland turned sharply to the left and disappeared down an off jutting hallway. It was not such a good move. The passage was a short one and offered no outlet. Mr. Bland was forced to choose between one of two doors. The first one was uncompromisingly locked. The second one gave to his hand. In went Mr. Bland and into another bed, this one also attractively filled by a woman, as were most of the beds in that hotel.

"Heavens! What a rush you're in," said a sleepy voice. "Didn't you stop to lock the door?"

"I'll lock it in a minute," Mr. Bland panted.

"It isn't very tidy to fling yourself into bed with your clothes on," continued the sleepy voice, "shoes and all."

"I haven't any clothes," muttered Mr. Bland. "Not a stitch."

"Haven't you?" said the woman beside him, reaching out a hand. "Why, I should say you haven't. Don't see how you did it."

Mr. Bland shrank back in the bed.

"You mustn't do that," he said, reprovingly.

"Why not, I'd like to know?" the woman demanded.

This time she reached out two hands and rolled over on her side. They both screamed at the same time and almost in the same key.

"I told you you shouldn't do it," said Mr. Bland.

"I thought you were a different man," replied the woman.

"Oh, dear," said Mr. Bland. "Don't tell me you're expecting a different man."

"I certainly am," the woman told him. "He will be here at any minute. That's why I left the door unlocked."

"Does he carry a gun, too?" asked Mr. Bland.

"Does he carry a gun?" said the woman with a hard laugh. "My man isn't a lizzie. He carries two guns."

"One would be more than enough," Mr. Bland replied in a heavy voice. "There are two guns already after me. I might just as well lie here and get shot in comfort."

"But you can't lie here," the woman protested. "He's likely to kill us both."

"A gun for each," said Mr. Bland with a shudder.

"And then it isn't nice," continued the woman, as if the idea had just occurred to her. "A lady shouldn't allow naked strangers to come bounding into her bed. What did you do with your clothes?"

"Another lady has them," said Mr. Bland in a hopeless voice. "At least I think she has. The last time I saw her she was running with them along the corridor."

"Gord," breathed the woman. "You're a terrible sort of man. Mean to say you got undressed in the hall?"

"No," said Mr. Bland. "In the lobby."

"In the lobby!" exclaimed the woman. "Did the lady get undressed there, too?"

"No," said Mr. Bland. "Just me. I was doing tricks."

"Getting undressed in that lobby is a trick in itself," observed the woman. "Wonder the management let you."

"I was a skeleton then," said Mr. Bland.

"You're hardly more than one now," the woman told him.

"I mean I was a real skeleton," explained Mr. Bland. "All bones and no flesh at all. I've been changing to a skeleton on and off all day."

This last piece of information was a little more than the woman could bear. She slipped out of the bed and from a safe distance stood nervously watching Mr. Bland, who was now wearing his beard. The woman gasped and put a hand to her eyes.

"Please don't play any more tricks in here," she said. "Go on back to the lobby and have a good time."

"I haven't had a good time in years," Mr. Bland told her.

The door opened quietly and a tall, powerful, competent-looking man entered the room. With purposeful deliberation he drew two automatics and levelled them at Mr. Bland.

"So you haven't had a good time in years," said the man in a mocking voice. "Well, I'm sorry to interrupt, but you're not going to have one now. You're going to have the worst time you ever had in your life."

"I've been having it all morning," answered Mr. Bland in a small dull voice.

"You can't shoot him," said the woman, throwing her arms about the man. "Look at his long white beard. He's old enough to be my grandfather."

"I don't want to look at his beard," replied the man, struggling to free himself from the woman's arms. "He might be old enough to be your grandfather, but he still has young ideas. Let me at him."

Tired as he was, Mr. Bland sprang from the bed. While the man and the woman were struggling, he succeeded in opening the door and getting into the hall. This time as he fled through the corridors he was pursued by three heavily armed men, the other two suddenly appearing the moment the two-gun stranger opened fire on the fleeing Bland.

"The management of this hotel is very lax," he reflected as he endeavored to equalize the discrepancy in numbers by running three times faster. "Very lax indeed. It's all very well to let guests have a good time occasionally, but there's no sense in allowing three murderers to chase a man through the halls."

His reflections were cut short by the sudden appearance of a woman at the far end of the corridor. As well as Mr. Bland could make out she was partially clad in a bath towel. She was so excited that apparently she forgot the sparse state of her attire, for she quickly snatched off the towel and waved it frantically at Mr. Bland.

"That," thought Mr. Bland, "must be about the only woman in this hotel who hasn't any so-called boy friend. She seems to want to see me."

When he reached the woman he discovered she was Pauline Whittle.

"My God!" he panted. "Don't wave that towel at me. Throw it around you somewhere. I can tell who you are."

"The hell with all that," she retorted, seizing him by the hand. "This is no time to stand on ceremony. Quick!"

She pulled him through the door, and together they raced for the bed. Mr. Bland was too exhausted to cover himself up. Pauline performed that office, then flung herself in his arms.

"I'm so frightened," she murmured, lazily.

"You don't act it," said Mr. Bland. "Where's your husband?"

"He's gone out to look for you," she told him. "Save me from those bad, bad men."

"Listen, Pauline," said Mr. Bland, "this is the third bed I've been in this morning, and each time I get in a bed another man appears with a gun. I'm getting sick and tired of it. I can't get rid of them. They keep chasing me about the halls and popping off their guns at me. If this keeps up there'll be so many gunmen wanting to take a shot at me they'll have to make appointments."

"Were there women in the other beds?" Pauline wanted to know.

"Is that all that interests you," demanded Mr. Bland, "with three murderers waiting outside that door ready to blow me to bits?"

"Did you try to get in bed with them?"

"No," said Mr. Bland. "I got in bed with their women."

"Did the women mind?" Pauline asked.

"They were much more adaptable," said Mr. Bland with some dignity, "than their boy friends."

"I'm adaptable, too," Pauline told him. "Why don't you take off your beard?"

"I won't," said Mr. Bland. "You're more than adaptable. You're damn' well depraved."

At this moment Mr. Whittle walked into the room and stood regarding the couple in the bed.

"There are a lot of rough-looking men standing outside the door," he announced, "and all of them are holding great big guns in their hands."

"Have you a gun by any chance?" Mr. Bland asked, uneasily.

"No," replied Mr. Whittle. "I couldn't hurt a fly, but if Pauline doesn't get out of that bed I'll beat her within an inch of her life."

"That," said Mr. Bland with a feeling of deep relief, "is what I call the reasonable attitude to take."

Outside the door the waiting gunmen were conversing in low voices.

"He's the damnedest man for women I ever saw," proclaimed the strangler. "I chase him out of my Jane's bed, and by God, he runs smack into the arms of a naked woman waiting for him in the hall."

"After first having got in bed with my girl," said the man with two guns.

"With all of us shooting at him," observed the man in search of a skeleton, "you'd think he'd cut it out for a while."

When Mr. Whittle appeared among them and busily entered his room the three gunmen fastened their eyes expectantly on the closed door.

"If that guy doesn't shoot him down," said the strangler, "we'll get him when he rushes out."

But Mr. Bland never appeared, and eventually the gunmen abandoned their vigil.

"I know what it is," said the strangler in tones of deep disgust. "I learned all about it in France, during the war. Them Frenchies call it a *ménagerie à trois.*"

And that was just about what it became after the Whittles and Mr. Bland had finished the second bottle.

CHAPTER 18.

THE FURIOUS BATH

Pauline Whittle was sleeping the sleep of a weary wanton. She was weary of her husband and weary of Mr. Bland; also, so far as strong drink was concerned, she hail reached the point of saturation. She was now lying handsomely if a little untidily on the bed with a flame-colored *négligé* tossed over her. Although much of her long, slender body was exposed, the conventions had been satisfied because the fair Pauline was technically covered. An attempt had been made.

In two comfortably upholstered chairs, Mr. Bland and Mr. Whittle were sitting by a large window, surveying in Jovian aloofness the myriad lights throbbing through Central Park like a swarm of golden bees. These two worthy gentlemen were carrying on a conversation which neither of them ever remembered. From time to time they addressed themselves to their glasses. Mr. Bland was still in the flesh.

"Bland," said Mr. Whittle with ponderous deliberation, I will admit you had a difficult morning, not to say a dangerous one, but I'll be damned if I can see how that entitles you to remain here alone with my wife when both of you are quite without clothing."

"But I'm sleepy," protested Mr. Bland.

"Granted," said Mr. Whittle, "but that woman over there on the bed, once the mood is on her, could arouse a graven image. Why, man alive, if she woke up and found you sleeping here she'd burn your feet with the curling iron until you were willing to keep her company."

"I'd do my best," said Mr. Bland.

"That woman over there on the bed —"

"Why don't you call her Pauline," Mr. Bland interrupted, "and save yourself six words?"

"Eh?" said Mr. Whittle. "Oh, that. I don't know hardly. Sometimes I just can't bring myself to call her by her Christian name. But, as I was saying, that woman over there on the bed doesn't want you to do your best. She wants you to do your worst. At heart she is, perhaps, not altogether vile. At heart, I dare say, she is no worse than any other woman, but the fact remains she's a woman, and therefore not safe. I don't want to expose you to the risk of betraying me, your best and oldest friend."

"That's awfully good of you, old chap," said Mr. Bland, deeply impressed. "Are you my oldest friend?"

"Absolutely."

"Then," said Mr. Bland, "let's drink to the traditional friendship existing between the famous house of Whittle and the illustrious house of Bland."

"That's exceptionally handsome of you," declared Mr. Whittle, reaching for the bottle. "How lovely it is in the park. Did you ever dance in the dew?"

As drunk as he was, Mr. Bland took exception to this question. He peered at Mr. Whittle suspiciously from beneath his heavy eyebrows.

"Do I look like one who would go dancing about in the dew?" he asked in a cold voice.

"No," replied Mr. Whittle, "but all sorts of persons go dancing about in the dew. You'd be surprised."

"I'd be disgusted," said Mr. Bland. "Can you do tricks with string?"

It was now Mr. Whittle's turn to be annoyed.

"Don't be insulting," he said. "I once knew a man who did tricks with string and he came to a very poor end—oh, a very poor end."

"What happened to him?"

"He was hanged by the neck until dead. That was his last string trick —and his best."

"I believe you made that up," said Mr. Bland. "It's much too pat. However, had you once known a man who did do tricks with string, which, mind you, I very much doubt, he should have been hanged by the neck and then drawn and quartered."

"Then we are in complete accord," remarked Mr. Whittle, happily. "What would you rather do, dislike a person thoroughly or like him only a little?"

"An interesting question," observed Mr. Bland. "Speaking quite frankly, I derive more downright satisfaction in disliking a person thoroughly."

"So do I," said Mr. Whittle. "The happiest friendships always exist between persons who have a lot of hates in common. Only trouble with me is I hate almost everybody except you and Pauline and this lovely bottle. I can't quite hate Pauline. I pity her too much."

"I find it very stimulating," remarked Mr. Bland, "to sit on the veranda on a bright, sunny day and think how insufferable my neighbors are, what wretched children they have, and what low-spirited dogs they own. At the country club and on the train I find myself doing the same thing— quite cheerfully detesting most of the people around me. I very rarely stop to think of how admirable a certain person is. That's far too depressing. It lowers one's self-esteem. I owe a debt of gratitude to the people I dislike."

"How true," agreed Mr. Whittle, "and how beautifully expressed. You should have sold things. I'm sure I'd have bought some."

"Without knowing what they were?" asked Mr. Bland.

"Certainly," declared Mr. Whittle. "Even if you didn't know what they were yourself."

"I wonder what they would have been," Mr. Bland wondered.

"You mean the things you might have sold me?" inquired Mr. Whittle.

"Yes," said Mr. Bland. "Those things."

"Well," reflected Mr. Whittle, "if I didn't know what they were you might have tempted me with neckties. Would you have liked to sell them, do you think?"

"I never sold any," said Mr. Bland, "but they are rather cheerful. I feel myself losing the thread of this conversation." He paused and looked out over the park. "It is a lovely night," he continued. "I wish I were in a swan boat with Lorna—Lorna's my wife, you know."

"Good God!" exclaimed Mr. Whittle in an agitated voice. "I haven't thought of swan boats for years. They've gone completely out of my life, and once they meant so much. I must go out and look at a swan boat some morning, or better still, later in the day."

"You should," declared Mr. Bland, "and so should I. Call me up next week and we'll look at some swan boats together."

"I certainly will," promised Mr. Whittle. "Swan boats are singularly festive things. Would you like to take a Turkish bath?"

"In what?" asked Mr. Bland.

"In an extra pair of slippers and a bathrobe," replied Mr. Whittle. "And then there's a special elevator."

Mr. Bland rose with a sigh and got himself into the slippers and bathrobe provided by Mr. Whittle. Into the pocket of the bathrobe he thrust the long white beard.

"What about the drink?" he inquired.

"I'll carry a flask along," said his host.

"We'll take a couple of hot shots before we go. It would never do to be seen in a Turkish bath sober."

"I hope I retain my body," said Mr. Bland. "It would be one hell of a note to lose it in a Turkish bath."

"Probably do you a world of good," the optimistic Whittle told him. "Especially the steam room. Might sweat all of that chemical stuff out of your system."

"If it does," said Mr. Bland, "I'll bring my dog, Busy, to a Turkish bath. He spilled a bottle of the fluid and now the poor damn' fool keeps changing to a skeleton dog at the most embarrassing moments."

"No!" exclaimed Mr. Whittle. "Does he really? Who are the moments embarrassing for, you or the dog?"

"For me," replied Mr. Bland. "It's not pleasant to have a skeleton dog tapping along at your heels. Especially if you're likely to turn into a skeleton yourself. Busy has no sense of shame. I suspect he rather enjoys it."

"I don't think I'd fancy seeing him," observed Mr. Whittle with a little shiver.

"You'd hate to see him when he scratches," said Mr. Bland. "His nails scrape across his ribs and he sort of rattles all over. It's ghastly."

"Oh, I say," protested Mr. Whittle. "Don't go into detail about that dog. I might have a severe attack of loathsome reptiles at any minute, and I'd hate to have a skeleton dog scratching himself among them. Let's talk of other things. Let's drink."

"Just the same," said Mr. Bland, "it is sort of odd to see a fleshless dog scratching non-existent fleas."

Mr. Whittle hastily gulped down a drink.

"Did you ever think of going to New Guinea?" he asked Mr. Bland.

"No," the other replied. "Frankly, I never did."

"Neither have I," said Mr. Whittle. "Let's think about it. I'll even be willing to think about New Rochelle if you'll only stop telling me about that damned disgusting dog of yours."

After another stiff drink they left Pauline still sleeping well but immodestly, and quietly let themselves out of the room. In the hall Mr. Bland looked about him nervously for signs of lurking gunmen.

"You know," he said to Mr. Whittle, "this is the first time I've traversed these corridors without being shot at. I'd gained the impression that the only way to get about this hotel was on a dead run."

"Lots of people sneak along very quietly," Mr. Whittle told him.

"I don't doubt it," said Mr. Bland. "Behind every door there seems to be a good-looking woman in bed."

"Gangsters have a way of picking rather neatly upholstered girls," observed Mr. Whittle. "After an especially brutal murder a man deserves a little recreation."

"To some men murder is a recreation in itself," said Mr. Bland.

"I know," replied Mr. Whittle, "but those men are artists— dreamers. They come to a bad end. Our gangsters make a business of it and eventually rise to higher things, such as directing the destiny of a nice, clean city like New York."

Without any untoward experience the two gentlemen reached the Turkish bath. After parking their dressing robes they made their way to the showers and then to the steam room, which was already occupied by all shapes and sizes of men. Before going into the room, Mr. Bland studied its occupants through the glass walls. The sight made him feel sorry for the male division of the human race. How, he wondered, did men manage to grow themselves into such curious shapes and sizes, billowing out here and jutting in there? And how could nature permit such an unequal distribution of stomachs? Some of the stomachs in that room were larger than their owners. In fact, those stomachs were their owners; or at least nine-tenths of them. Mr. Bland decided he would much rather associate with naked women. He was still naive enough to think of naked women only in terms of beauty. This is perhaps the best way to think of naked women, because when a naked woman is not beautiful she is even more depressing to look at than a man.

"Looks just like a waiting-room in hell, doesn't it?" said Mr. Bland to his companion. "All that steam and all those sprawled and contorted bodies. It's just too bad."

"Let's sprawl and contort ours," suggested Mr. Whittle. "I have the bottle wrapped in my towel, but I expect the whisky will get pretty hot in there."

"So will we," replied Mr. Bland, "and that will make things equal."

Gasping for breath and already a little dizzy, they made their way through the clinging, steam-laden atmosphere of the room and, sitting down in deck chairs, added their own unlovely bodies to the naked company.

Mr. Bland found himself sitting next to an individual who was at least fifty pounds over-weight. From the expression on this gentleman's face Mr. Bland gained the impression he was not at all happy about himself. He subjected Mr. Bland's body to a long, critical scrutiny, after which he considered his own stomach dejectedly, then transferred his gaze to the lean flat belly of the recumbent photographer.

"If I was as thin as you," the fat man crossly opened fire, "horses couldn't drag me into this miserable place."

"It is a miserable place," admitted Mr. Bland, "and almost everybody in it appears to be miserable, too."

"Probably deserve to be," said the gentleman. "But I don't deserve to be miserable. What have I done?" Here he paused dramatically, then repeated, "What have I done?"

"Don't you know?" asked Mr. Bland, a little mystified.

"Of course I know," snapped the man with intense bitterness. "I've done nothing. That's what I've done. Nothing. I don't eat, I don't sleep, I don't have a good time, and still I get fatter and fatter. Bah! Men like you give me a pain in the neck."

Mr. Bland's eyes traveled to the man's neck. There was such an awful lot of it to have a pain in. Mr. Bland felt sorry he was causing the man to suffer so much. He showed the man the flask of whisky.

"Have some of our drink?" Mr. Bland asked him. "It's warm, but it's good."

"Can't drink," growled the man. "Doctor's orders. Every time I take a drink I gain another pound. A chap like you doesn't belong in here. You don't need to lose weight."

"I don't want to lose another ounce," the long man assured him in an earnest voice. "Not another ounce."

"Then you'd better get out," said the fat man, "or the first thing you know you'll become a walking skeleton."

Mr. Bland started, and then, as if the words of the fat man had reminded him to make the change, his flesh melted away, and right there before the man's very eyes he became what the man had predicted, with the slight difference that at the moment Quintus Bland was a reclining skeleton instead of a walking one.

Naturally the fat man's first reaction was that this thing could not possibly be. It was not true. At first he tried to attribute what he believed to be an optical illusion to the steam and the generally depressing atmosphere of the room. Without uttering another word he looked away from the skeleton for a full minute, feeling sure that when he turned his head again everything would be all right. In this he was disappointed, but still not greatly alarmed. The skeleton was still sitting beside him, and although it had no visible eyes, the fat man felt he was being politely but steadily scrutinized.

"Tell me," he said in a low voice, "do I look as if I'd just taken leave of my senses?"

"In this place," replied Mr. Bland, "everyone looks as if he'd taken leave of his senses. We're all mad."

"You look worse than that," continued the man in the same low voice. "To me you look exactly like a skeleton, but of course that's obviously impossible, so I'm afraid I'm a little bit mad. I hope you don't mind."

"Not at all," said Mr. Bland. "Go right ahead and be as mad as you like. It may help you to lose weight."

"Your friend over there doesn't seem to notice anything odd in your appearance," went on the fat man, "but then, he's so drunk he wouldn't find it odd if all these chairs were occupied by polar bears instead of human beings."

"This would be a tough spot for a polar bear," said Mr. Bland with forced lightness. "They'd have to drag the poor thing out."

"Well, if I don't stop looking at you," observed the fat man with the utmost gravity, "they will have to drag me out, I'm afraid. Although I realize I must be wrong about it, you are beyond doubt the worst-looking object it's been my misfortune to meet."

"What would you do if I actually were a skeleton?" Mr. Bland asked his neighbor.

"I'd run like hell," the man replied simply. "I can't run very fast since I've taken on all this flesh, but I'd do my best."

"Hey, there," came the voice of Mr. Whittle. "I say, Bland, do you realize you've turned to a skeleton?"

"Do you see it, too?" cried the fat man. "Oh, my God! And he's been letting me think I'm mad, and engaging me in conversation just as if he'd never seen the inside of a grave. What a skeleton!"

"Why don't you run like hell?" Mr. Bland asked him.

"Don't talk to me," said the fat man. "I don't know you. And I don't want to know you. I am going to run like hell."

He heaved himself out of his chair and toddled briskly across the room. At the door he stopped and pointed to Mr. Bland.

"There's a dirty, lying skeleton in that chair," he announced to the roomful of naked gentlemen. "If you don't believe me, just take a look for yourselves."

"That tears it," said Mr. Bland to his companion. "How am I going to get out of this?"

"I don't think you'll have to," Mr. Whittle answered, calmly. "Everybody else seems anxious to get out of it for you."

Mr. Bland looked up and saw innumerable large naked men striving to get themselves through a small door at the same time. The steam in the room was cut by cries of physical pain and mental anguish. Squirming bodies were trampled underfoot while others were seized in the most convenient places and dragged cursing bitterly away from the door.

"Now wouldn't you think," observed Mr. Whittle, "that grown men would have more sense than to carry on like that?"

"This place looks more like hell than ever," said Mr. Bland. "It looks like a Doré picture suddenly come to life."

Outside the room, bath attendants and husky Swedish masseurs with towels round their waists were doing their best to quell the panic that had so suddenly and inexplicably broken out. But apparently when a man has once seen a live skeleton nothing is going to change his mind until he has enjoyed his panic to the full. Finally the attendants and rubbers grew so tired of being told there was a skeleton in the steam room that they let the naked men run wild and took a look for themselves. Some of them even went into the steam room, but found no traces of a skeleton. They did find, however, two placidly intoxicated gentlemen amiably conversing while drinking warm whisky neat from a flask.

"Did either of you gentlemen see a skeleton in this room?" one of the attendants asked, feeling somewhat silly because of the ridiculous nature of the question.

"Certainly," was Mr. Bland's prompt reply. "I was a skeleton myself only a moment ago, but my bones began to warp, what with all this steam, so I got my body back again."

"He was a terrible sight," said Mr. Whittle. "You should have seen him. No eyes at all. Ugh!"

The attendants laughed, but not very heartily. It struck them that these two drunkards had an especially unpleasant brand of humor.

"How about a rub-down?" suggested Mr. Bland.

"Do you dare?" asked Mr. Whittle.

"I dare anything," Mr. Bland told him. "Just because I am occasionally a skeleton, I don't see why I should be forced to sacrifice all the good things of life."

After polishing off the bottle in what had now become their own private steam room, the two gentlemen repaired rather unsteadily to the rub-down tables upon which they virtually collapsed. Two huge, malevolent-looking individuals thereupon descended upon them and expertly endeavored to tear off their arms and legs.

"That's the catch in getting drunk in a Turkish bath," Mr. Whittle managed to get out between gasps. "When these devils find you in our condition they go on the principle that you've lost all sense of feeling and don't give a damn what they do."

"They experiment with our drunken but human bodies," complained Mr. Bland, a strained expression on his face. "This is worse than vivisection."

"It's the very refinement of torture," observed Mr. Whittle. "They never pull your limbs entirely off, but just far enough to maim you. This demi- murderer has got one of my legs about eight inches longer than the other. He'd either have to push it back or pull the other one out."

"You could live on a hillside," suggested Mr. Bland.

"Haven't seen a hill in years," replied Mr. Whittle. "Wouldn't know what to do with one. Are mountains still doing?"

"Splendidly," said Mr. Bland. "They're up and doing."

The rubber who had been buffeting Mr. Bland about took a deep breath as if preparing himself for the final assault. Several times he opened and closed his hands, flexing his vicelike muscles. Mr. Bland watched him with growing apprehension, then extended an arresting hand. But it was not the hand he had been using only a few minutes before. It was composed entirely of bone and looked more like a claw than a human hand. Both the rubber and Mr. Bland stared at it in numbed wonderment, then transferred their gaze to other sections of the photographer's person. Nothing but bare, unvarnished bones greeted their eyes. Neither of them was favorably impressed by the greeting. Of the two the rubber was the more surprised and the more alarmed. Mr. Bland was merely disgusted with himself.

"Don't touch me," snapped Mr. Bland. "Don't put even a finger on me."

The rubber's short laugh was devoid of all mirth. He edged away from the table.

"I'd like to know who would?" he retorted. "Not for a thousand dollars would I willingly lay a hand on any one of your ghastly bones."

"Thank God for that," said Mr. Bland. "A skeleton is not without some compensation after all."

"Then there was a skeleton in the steam room like the man said?" the rubber faltered, his strength seeming to drain from his body.

"Didn't I tell you I was the skeleton?" demanded Mr. Bland.

"You did, but I thought you were drunk," the man replied.

"I was and I still am," Mr. Bland told him, "but that happy fact doesn't prevent me from getting rid of my body, especially when it's going to be torn from my bones anyway."

Mr. Bland swung his legs from the table and found himself confronting the three gangsters of the morning's pursuit. Automatically he began to run, and out of force of habit the gangsters began to run after him. He dashed through a door and found himself in the swimming pool. Cries of consternation greeted his arrival. Not having the slightest idea whether he would crash like a rock to the bottom of the pool or be able to keep his skull above water, Mr. Bland launched himself into the air and plunged into the pool.

"A diving skeleton!" cried a man. "God-almighty! A swan dive, at that."

"Not bad," thought the diving skeleton as he struck the water cleanly. "I still retain my form."

A moment later his skull popped up about three inches from the placid face of a gentleman contentedly churning water. At the sight of Mr. Bland the gentleman's legs refused to do any further churning.

"I'm going to drown," announced the man, unemotionally, "and I'm glad of it."

"I'll save you," said Mr. Bland.

"I'd much rather you wouldn't," the man replied, coldly, then sank beneath the water.

Mr. Bland then began to worry about his own safety. He took a few tentative strokes and found he could swim like a fish. Indeed, the absence of his flesh enabled him to twist and turn in the water like some ghastly denizen of the deep. It was a terrible exhibition. Strong men clapped their hands to their eyes and called aloud to God in frantic voices. A man sitting on the edge of the pool hastily removed his feet from the water as the skeleton streaked by.

"I never knew a skeleton could swim," said the man to a companion.

"I never knew a skeleton," said the other. "Are you beginning to see things?"

"Look," was all the first man said, and pointed.

His companion looked, then hastily arose.

"That finishes my swim," he told his friend. "When skeletons start using this pool it's time to hurry home."

A cold plunge does not always have a sobering effect on one inebriated. Frequently it makes him even drunker. The same must hold true with skeletons. It certainly did with Mr. Bland. He had forgotten all about his implacable enemies and was having the time of his life. He had climbed to the highest spring-board and was now exhibiting himself shamelessly before a stunned group of naked gentlemen standing within safe striking distance of the exit. Through this door appeared the three gangsters, now armed to the teeth.

"There he is!" cried the man who was going to make tooth powder of Mr. Bland. "I put him in his grave once and I'll put him there again. Always spoiling my fun."

Immediately a volley of deafening explosions rang out in the swimming pool. Mr. Bland rose lightly from the springboard and neatly split the water twelve feet below. The gunmen still squeezed their guns, but Mr. Bland outwitted them by swimming under water. He emerged at the far end of the pool, dashed through a door, and found himself in a vast, dimly lighted dormitory. He was standing at the head of a long aisle with beds on either side. And in these beds were sleeping men, blissfully unaware there was a skeleton in their midst. But one man was not sleeping. His name was Joe. Joe was lying quite still in his narrow bed, and his eyes, sharp now with dread, were fixed on the skeleton of Quintus Bland, standing in great indecision as water dripped from rib to rib.

Quietly Joe thrust out an arm and shook his friend in the next bed.

"Wake up, Charlie," he said in a low voice. "There's a skeleton down there and he's all wet."

"You're right," admitted Charlie after his sleep-laden eyes had discovered the skeleton of Mr. Bland. "He's wet all over."

"But don't you realize he's a skeleton?" said Joe, annoyed by Charlie's calm acceptance of the awful sight.

"I don't," replied Charlie, "but I will in a minute. Why don't you give him a towel?"

"Me?" asked Joe, incredulously. "Why, I wouldn't give him a handkerchief."

"He could mop his skull with a handkerchief," Charlie said, musingly, "but that's about all."

"Look!" exclaimed Joe. "He's tiptoeing down the aisle in this direction."

"I see him," said Charlie. "The sly devil."

"Wonder who he's after," muttered Joe.

"Maybe the poor lost soul is looking for a bed," suggested Charlie, "or he might be looking for another skeleton—a friend. Almost everybody goes to a Turkish bath with a friend."

"What!" exclaimed Joe. "Another skeleton in this room?"

"Why not?" replied Charlie. "This room may be filled with skeletons for all we know."

"If it is," declared Joe, "I don't want to know. One skeleton is enough for me. I came in here to keep from seeing things like that."

"He's got into bed," said Charlie.

"Is there anyone else in it?" Joe asked.

"I guess we'd have heard if there was," replied Charlie.

"God, yes!" said Joe. "If that thing got in bed with me I wouldn't make any secret of it."

But the casual Charlie had been mistaken. Mr. Bland had not got into bed. He was trying to get into bed, but the man already occupying it didn't see things eye to eye with the skeleton.

"I want to get into bed with you," the gentleman awakened to hear a skeleton saying.

"With me?" he asked in amazement. "You? Do you realize what you're asking? Why, I don't want to be even in the same room with you, much less lying in bed cheek by jowl."

"I haven't any cheek," muttered Mr. Bland.

"Well, I haven't any jowl," replied the man. "So that's that, and I don't want to talk about your body."

"But, my dear sir," said Mr. Bland, "I haven't any body."

"That's as plain to see as the nose that isn't on your face," declared the man. "You can't get in bed with me, and that's final."

"I'd lie very still," Mr. Bland said, rather bleakly, "and scrunch myself over on the side."

"Scrunch yourself?" repeated the man. "Oh, no. That settles it. I could never bear that. Why don't you find a man who's passed out cold and scrunch yourself up with him? I'm nearly sober myself, since arguing here with you."

Mr. Bland straightened himself and looked hopelessly around him at all the comfortably occupied beds. In the long, dimly lighted room he was a lonely-looking figure. He thought of Lorna peacefully sleeping at home and wondered if Busy, like himself, was an undesirable skeleton. With sagging collar-bone he turned away from the bed. What could a skeleton do with the human race set against him, three members of which were actively gunning for his life? And why should everyone assume that just because a man was a skeleton he was going to start trouble? He had no desire to start any trouble. He wanted to go to bed.

As he stood there lost in thought, his chin buried on his breastbone, he became gradually aware of the fact that his feet were covered with flesh. Following his legs as they ascended steeply towards his hips, he was delighted to discover he no longer differed from his fellow men in any important respect. He turned back to the bed.

"I want to crawl in with you," he told the man.

"What again?" exclaimed the man, irritably, then stopped abruptly as his gaze rested on the figure of a naked man. "What the hell!" he exploded, furiously. "Do all you people think my bed is a public parking place? A skeleton was around here a minute ago giving me a hell of an argument about getting into my bed, the big stiff. And you're hardly any better. Go find a bed of your —"

Three snappy shots cut short the man's ill-natured tirade.

"There he is!" cried the voice of the strangler. "That guy was in bed with my girl."

The man in bed looked curiously at Mr. Bland.

"You try to get in bed with everybody, don't you?" he said. "Well, you're entirely welcome to mine. I'm going to get under it."

But Mr. Bland was hiding in no one's bed. He was sick and tired of being a target for the gunmen. Charging through a fusillade of bullets, he bore down on his enemies. One long arm shot out and snatched the covering from a peaceful spectator cowering in his bed. The next minute Mr. Bland had tossed the coverings over the heads of the gangsters. Having momentarily rendered them impotent, he proceeded to smite them with terrific punches wherever his fists could land. Then he jumped through the door and, hurrying through the deserted swimming pool, collected his slippers and bathrobe. A few minutes later he let himself quietly into Mr. Whittle's room.

Pauline had shown the grace to get herself under the covers. Mr. Bland, drunker than ever from excitement, his inflamed mind set on getting into a bed—any bed—got under the covers with her.

"Hello," said Pauline. "Do you know any funny stories?

"No," snapped Mr. Bland. "You leave me alone and go back to sleep."

But the idea of going to sleep was the farthest thought from the fair Pauline's attractively depraved mind.

Some time later Mr. Whittle appeared.

"Am I too late?" he asked, nervously, then hastily added, "Don't answer! I suspect, but I'd rather not be told."

CHAPTER 19.

A SKELETON AT BAY

The hue and cry was on. Bending low to the ground, the skeleton of Quintus Bland was running through the woods. And the woods were dark. At that moment the usually peaceful photographer would have been a dangerous man to meet. He was a fugitive from the mob, and his hand was turned against men.

The skeleton ran awkwardly. Ahead of him the black trees stepped ever higher up the steep incline until their wind-swept branches swayed among the stars.

Underbush lashed at the bones of the skeleton, reached out to trip him as he blundered on. And stones lay in wait to crush his feet as they fumbled blindly for a footing on the uncertain terror. Branches whipped against him and threatened the safety of his brittle bones. But still the skeleton ran, his breath rasping painfully through his naked teeth and an all-consuming bitterness burning where his heart should have been.

Behind him rose the sound of hoarse, excited voices, shouting through the woods. Those voices held a note of hateful triumph. Back and forth they fled across the night, troubling it with their sinister intent. Lights stabbed at the trunks of trees, and bushes thrashed viciously as the bodies of the searchers hurtled through them. Occasionally the sharp, efficient voice of a revolver stood out with disagreeable distinctness from the confused onrushing of sounds.

"Damn them all to hell," muttered the skeleton, steadying himself wearily against a tree. "Just because a man is different he doesn't necessarily have to die."

The sounds were sweeping nearer, spreading out and closing round him. He held his breath and listened, then swore softly up at the stars.

"At any rate," he reflected as he resumed his flight, "I've got one thing to be thankful for—a skeleton can't sweat."

Shivering involuntarily, he pushed deeper into the woods, the lone skeleton of a living man fleeing to escape the cruel, stupid fury of the self-righteous mind of the race.

Quite unconsciously Mr. Bland had selected an unfortunate moment for his return home. The mob was milling over his front lawn, calling aloud for his blood. On the front porch stood Lorna, and she was calling the mob inclusively and each member specifically every vile name that popped into her pretty, defiant head. Not knowing what it was all about, Mr. Bland listened to his wife with admiration. For the moment he forgot the harassing fact that his flesh was no longer with him. He was far too interested in hearing Lorna, loyally supported by Fanny and the partially drunken cook, defy this mob of masked men. When Lorna ran out of words she would turn to her two domestics, who eagerly replenished her exhausted stock with exceedingly common but telling contributions.

It was an unsavory body of men that received Lorna's taunts and insults. And it was out for an unsavory purpose—the mobbing and doing in of Quintus Bland. Its members were armed, masked, and mean—mean with the ruthless arrogance bred of numbers.

It seemed that their leader had been that morning most brutally assaulted, but not quite killed. This was too bad, for the leader and organizer of this viciously intolerant rabble, glorified under the name of the Guardians of America, was none other than Mr. Blutter, that superfluous member of the human race and flower of the advertising world.

He had been found rather badly banged up in his own woodshed, and when found he was raving wildly about a skeleton who was Mr. Bland and Mr. Bland who was a skeleton. Already rumors about a skeleton had been circulating through the village from several sources, Dr. MacQuirk being the most authentic. These rumors had come to the ears of the Guardians and were to be taken up seriously at their next secret conclave. The just retribution sustained by Blutter supplied the excuse for immediate and direct action.

With the Guardians the darkly sardonic Bland had become increasingly unpopular. He had gone out of his way to denounce them in public and to ridicule their avowed purpose to protect the home life of the nation. The delirious mouthings of a natural-born fool had been sufficient to furnish them with a pretext for going out after Mr. Bland and getting him good.

That a man should change himself into a skeleton was, to the Guardians, a sufficiently un-American act to warrant their violent intervention in the private life of their severest critic. This, together with the assault on their leader, enabled them to work themselves up to a mood in which they became dangerous and irresponsible members of the community, especially for Quintus Bland. Their sick, egotistical conception of patriotism, morality, and civic virtue made them far more undesirable citizens than the relatively honest gangsters of Chicago and New York. And because they were many while Bland was but one, the Guardians of America felt no fear behind their masks.

Unable longer to stand seeing these worthies deflowering his lawn, Mr. Bland deliberately took his skeleton through the mob and joined his wife on the porch. At the sight of the skeleton an angry buzzing sounded in the heart of the Guardians until it gained sufficient courage to swell to a roar.

"You damn' fool," breathed Lorna, "this is no time to come home. These slop-fed thugs are out to get you."

For the first time Mr. Bland noticed the pallor of his wife's face and the signals of fear in her eyes. She was afraid for him, and with reason. Already stones were falling around them and breaking the front windows. The mob was pressing forward, some of its more courageous members having one foot on the lower step leading up to the porch.

"Slop-fed thugs," repeated Mr. Bland, getting himself in front of his wife. "Lorna, my dear old love, your vocabulary grows more impressive every day. Have you called them that? If not I would like to borrow it."

"You don't seem to realize," replied Lorna in level tones, "That these masked devils have put you on the spot. Last week they dipped a girl in tar because she refused the advances of one of their members in preference to somebody else. God knows what they won't do to you. And in your condition you could never stand rough treatment."

"What have I done to them?" asked Mr. Bland.

"You're supposed to have assaulted their leader, a person who thrives under the horrid name of Blutter."

"I wish I could take the credit," said Mr. Bland. "In my heart I've assaulted that creature at least a dozen times." He paused and considered the mob. "I think," he resumed, "I shall endeavor to bewilder them."

Reaching in his pocket, he produced the long white beard and affixed it to his chin. For a brief moment an awed silence fell upon the mob while its members were recovering from the shock produced by this sudden alteration in their quarry's appearance. Then voices rose in anger as they realized they were being scorned and belittled by a skeleton.

"You swine!" shouted Mr. Bland. "You inferior grade of scum! It pains me to hear that your leader, that insufferable bore, Blutter, was not murdered outright and in his own cold blood. As soon as he is well enough to walk, I myself person-ally shall make it my business to correct this error. Now get the hell off my lawn or I'll wiggle my beard at you."

It was not a tactful speech. So far as the fate of Mr. Bland was concerned, it definitely clinched matters in the mind of the mob. There was a general scramble for the porch. The world seemed suddenly to have turned to a sea of reaching hands, but before they reached Mr. Bland he was seized from behind by three determined women and dragged into the house.

"Listen," said Lorna, speaking rapidly and very earnestly. "Please listen and stop cursing for one minute. Your presence in this house is a danger to all of us. You've got to do a bunk. Slip out by the back door and make for the woods. You know that little cave we used to play in years ago? Well, try to get to that. When things quiet down I'll come and let you know."

Disregarding his protests, she led him to the back door just as a loud crash gave warning that the front one had fallen before the assaults of the Guardians.

"Damn them," muttered Mr. Bland. "I wish I had my body back." He paused and looked at Lorna, started to place his hands on her shoulders, then quickly withdrew them. "Good-bye, kid," he said. "I'd like to kiss you if I had a couple of lips. Ah, to hell with it. I'm off."

Then with a wild yell of defiance designed to draw the pursuers away from the house, Mr. Bland sprinted across his backyard, climbed a fence, and vanished into the woods. Once he was among the trees he divested himself of his garments the better to speed his flight. For a moment he gazed thoughtfully back at his home until the sound of shouts and shooting assured him the chase was on, then he turned and ran as best he could in the direction of the little cave.

Eventually he succeeded in reaching it, but before he did so he had taken a far more serious view of the situation. There was a note in those following voices that sounded cruel and ominous—a note of blind antagonism not only against himself in the form of a skeleton but also against the way he conducted his life as a man. These men were dead set against frank and open living openly arrived at. They feared such an existence and were prepared to stamp it out. To them sin was a secret form of enjoyment derived entirely from sex. Therefore, sex was sinful, a subject to whisper about and smirk at from behind curtains. Mr. Bland realized, also, that he could not continue indefinitely being a peripatetic skeleton. Something had to be done about his condition or else he would have to withdraw permanently from all social relationships and live in the privacy of his home.

It was now late at night. The sound of his pursuers had died away in the distance. Mr. Bland had come out of the little cave and was sitting miserably at its entrance. Lorna had not shown up, and he was worried about her. The damp air in the woods seemed to have got into his bones. It was the first time he had realized a skeleton could be cold. A feeling of solitude and isolation settled down on him, and he knew fear. He was afraid of the little cave behind him. It suggested the grave or the tomb. And he was afraid of the possible dangers lurking in the woods—an unexpected shot in the dark or a sudden assault in overpowering numbers. Mr. Bland did not want to die. He was altogether too fond of Lorna. He wanted to carry on with her for some years to come, assuming his damn' unreliable body would only stick around.

Some yards off, Lorna stood and gazed with a curious expression at this skeleton who was her husband. For the first time she saw him as a man alone, sorely afflicted and brooding over his problems, in all of which she realized she played an important part. And once again she felt that tight little clutch at her throat.

"Sweetheart," she called softly, not wishing to disturb him.

The skeleton turned his blind face to the darkness.

"Sweetheart," he muttered. Then in a louder voice, "Anything serious, kid? I haven't heard that in years."

She came up to him quietly and sat down on the dried leaves of a dead year.

"You're cold," she said. "Here's a drink." She handed him a flask, which he eagerly accepted.

"I was just thinking," he said, rather diffidently, "that we could have a lot of fun—you know—you and I—if I ever got my body back. Don't you think we could?"

"I know," replied Lorna, with reassuring conviction. "There's nothing like losing your husband's body to find out how much you love him. Why, you horrid thing, I love you even as you are right now."

"Sure you're not playing futures?"

"Perhaps I am," she said, "but the present is very much with me."

"Is the coast all clear?" asked Mr. Bland. "Is it safe to return home?"

"That's just the trouble," she answered. "I can't be sure. I noticed nothing suspicious on my way here, but somehow I've a bad feeling inside me. I'm afraid for you—sweetheart." She stopped abruptly and looked at her husband with bright, defiant eyes. "Did you hear that?"she continued. "I called you sweetheart again, and I didn't hardly boggle."

"It embarrasses me a little," said Mr. Bland, "but I wouldn't mind getting used to it, although I've grown fond of being called a dirty dog."

"I'm afraid," said Lorna in a strained voice, dropping all attempt at lightness. "If anything happened to you now I think I'd go mad."

Instinctively he stretched out a hand towards her, then slowly took it back.

"Hell's bells," he muttered and rose impatiently to his feet.

There was a spurt of flame in the darkness and the sharp report of a gun. Mr. Bland whirled and made for the trees on the opposite side of the little clearing.

"Good-bye, kid," he called back. "Sweet-heart."

Another stab of flame. Lorna was running towards it. She never heard the explosion. In her ears sounded a choked cry, followed by a thrashing in the leaves. It stopped and the woods were still.

Then she found herself looking down at him. He was back in his long, lean body. Blood was flowing from a wound in his left breast. She was surrounded by a circle of masked men seen but dimly. Their lights were playing on the still body lying naked beneath the trees.

It was typical of the mind of the mob that somebody snickered, then looked slyly at the small, tense figure of the woman. She was a good looker, she was. There was something almost salaciously intimate in the situation.

"I'm not going to curse you," said Lorna in a voice of weary detachment. "If there's a God sitting in on this He has already done it for me. You are all damned for ever. Go away now. You have killed a man."

The lights flashed out as she knelt beside her husband.

"Sweetheart," she called in the darkness. Her voice broke. Lorna was crying.

The men had gone away, the sound of their receding footsteps leaving a trail of sound behind in the rustling woods.

Presently four of the men came back and carried the body down the hill. Lorna followed them, a blood-stained handkerchief clutched absently in her hand.

CHAPTER 20.

THE BLANDS COME THROUGH

Mr. Bland was not a great help to the hospital. As soon as his wound had healed he began to get funny. On one occasion when his nurse was absent and he found himself a skeleton, he deliberately removed his pajamas and slipped out into the hall on a trip of exploration.

Seeing an interne coming toward him, Mr. Bland froze in his tracks, hoping to be mistaken for a dead skeleton. The interne was new and had heard nothing about the strange case of Mr. Bland. He stopped and regarded the skeleton, then called to a passing nurse.

"What is your name, nurse?" he asked.

"Crawford, Doctor," the nurse replied.

She was quite young and pretty. The interne noted that, as internes have a way of doing.

"Well, Miss Crawford," he said with a slight frown, "can you tell me what this old skeleton is doing here? I should think it belongs in one of the lecture rooms."

"I'm sure it does," replied Miss Crawford. "He wasn't here when I passed about fifteen minutes ago."

Turning her neat back on the interne and the skeleton, she looked down the hall as if seeking an explanation. Unseen by the interne, Mr. Bland extended one hand. Miss Crawford gave a slight but convulsive start and stifled a small scream. For a moment she remained rigid in her tracks, striving to regain her composure, then she slowly turned on the interne, her face still crimson.

"Please don't do that again," she said. "A doctor should have better sense. I don't even know your name."

"I've done nothing at all," the young doctor protested.

"It may seem like nothing to you," said the nurse, "but it means a lot to me."

"I'm sure I don't know what you're talking about," the interne declared. "It must be your nerves. Your eyes look funny."

"No wonder," replied the nurse, edging back of the doctor as a precautionary measure. "Let's say no more about it."

This time the depraved Bland repeated his experiment, with slight difference that it was upon the doctor. The young man bounded forward, then with an effort regained his dignity.

"Miss Crawford," he said, "that was a dirty trick. I hope it doesn't become a habit. You actually hurt me."

It was now the nurse's turn to be mystified. "What did I do?" she wanted to know.

"Plenty," replied the interne, furtively rubbing the seat of his trousers. "You must have used forceps instead of your fingers from the way it stings. Did you use forceps?"

Miss Crawford shrugged her pretty shoulders helplessly, then looked at the skeleton. The doctor turned and got behind the nurse. Carelessly locking her hands behind her, Miss Crawford stepped aside.

"Something should be done about this old duffer," said the doctor. "If a patient came upon him unexpectedly he might receive a terrible shock."

In answer to this remark the skeleton chattered very gently in the doctor's face.

"Doctor," whispered Miss Crawford, "did you hear that peculiar sound?"

"Yes," replied the doctor. "I assumed you were making it."

"Why should I make a sound like that? It wasn't at all nice."

"Well, what you did to me," remarked the doctor, "was not exactly ladylike."

Both of them now had their backs turned towards Mr. Bland. It was a heaven-sent opportunity. Realizing it might never come again if he stood there for years, he stealthily extended two hands. As if rehearsing an act, Miss Crawford and the interne took a delicate leap of about a foot, gasped simultaneously, then placed a hand behind them and rubbed with solicitous fingers. Miss Crawford was the first to speak.

"We just couldn't have done it to each other at the same time," she said reasonably enough.

"Are you sure you didn't do it?" asked the interne. "Think carefully, Miss Crawford. I won't tell."

Miss Crawford grew furiously red.

"Do you imagine that if I nerved myself to do a thing like that to a gentleman," she demanded, "I'd be likely to forget it?"

"I don't know," said the interne, wearily, "I thought it might be a sort of friendly habit you formed during your training period, and it had become second nature. You just did it automatically."

"Regardless of color, race, or sex," the nurse added, sarcastically. "Just a cheery little greeting."

At this moment the skeleton of Mr. Bland once more claimed their undivided attention. He had been trying to hit on something that might upset them even more, and had just thought of an especially novel idea. He would pretend he was going to pull his head off, then see if their sense of thrift would prompt them to try to stop him. Accordingly he seized his skull in both bony hands and began to tug at it violently.

"Come off, you old skull," he mumbled. "Get to hell off my neck. All the time grinning and gnashing your teeth. Off you go, old skull,"

It was an upsetting spectacle. Both Miss Crawford and the doctor were stultified with astonishment.

"By God!" cried the doctor. "He's trying to get rid of his head."

"No, I'm not," said Mr. Bland. "I'm just trying to twist it off, then I'll be able to carry it under my arm and scold it from time to time."

"What with?" asked the doctor, professional interest overcoming his horror.

"Hadn't thought of that," said the skeleton. "You think of everything, don't you? I'll give it to the pretty nurse."

The pretty nurse was in such a condition that she cared little what was done to her. The young interne found himself supporting her lush body with much more than necessary coverage. He felt almost grateful to the skeleton. In the meantime Mr. Bland was once more tugging at his head.

"It's good-night for you, old skull," he muttered. "Off you go and away."

"Don't let him do it," Miss Crawford pleaded. "He's just mad at his skull now. Later on he'll wish he had it."

The arrival of his nurse interrupted Mr. Bland's fun. The moment he saw her he dropped to all fours and started to crawl busily away, his head twisted jauntily over his spine.

"Spinach! Spinach! Spinach!" he shouted, which was the most inane thing he could think of shouting.

Quite naturally these gratuitous sideshows on the part of Mr. Bland did not exactly endear him to the staff of the hospital. He was fascinated by the idea of getting hold of the ancient, fly-blown skeleton in the lecture hall. Once he actually succeeded in substituting himself for it and was carried up to the platform. When old Dr. Weiss, half blind from years of service, turned back from the blackboard to consider his companion of years—the skeleton—he was surprised to find it sitting cross-legged in his chair, idly turning the leaves of a book.

"Ha!" cried the old doctor. "I always thought that skeleton had more sense than my students. Now I know it. The class is dismissed."

As the students filed out of the hall they looked back and saw the doctor drag up another chair and start an animated conversation with what was to them the most baffling object in the world. Dr. Weiss never gave another lecture, but retired on a comfortable pension and wrote a book about a skeleton, who, after years of listening to lectures of great erudition, at last returned to life and discoursed intelligently on almost any subject.

On another occasion Mr. Bland contrived to steal the skeleton and take it to bed with him. When the nurse pulled down the covers she nearly had a fit. Mr.

Bland insisted he had just become a mother.

But as the effects of the chemical fluid in his system gradually grew less potent through a system of irrigation and dieting, these little excursions occurred at longer intervals, until finally they ceased altogether and Mr. Bland became almost a normal patient. He insisted to the end, however, that both doctors and nurses had mistaken him for the Grand Canal.

* * * * *

Since the episode in the woods Lorna had lived in the ultimate chambers of hell until her husband was out of danger. Although still her old, unedifying self, she showed unmistakable marks of strain as she sat by his bedside. Mr. Bland, now himself permanently, considered her the most beautiful woman in the world and rejoiced in the return of his body.

He reached out a casually searching hand and Lorna slapped it sharply, looking quickly at the half-open door as she did so.

"You're still a dirty dog," she told him, then bent over and placed her mouth on his.

"And that doesn't make me a better one," he said when their lips parted.

"I wonder," mused Lorna.

* * * * *

Some time later a wild scream from outside sent Lorna, in a state of happy confusion, hurrying to the door. Opening it and looking out, she saw the skeleton of Busy tapping briskly down the hall. The sight of a skeleton dog was doing convalescent patients little if any good.

Lorna quickly collected the dog and carried him into the room. After greetings had been exchanged between master and beast, Mr. Bland rose, dressed hastily, then, after a few words of admonition, placed the dog in the bed, where he promptly fell asleep. Taking Lorna by the hand, he quietly drew her from the room.

A few minutes after their unobtrusive departure the nurse arrived. When she threw back the covers of the bed her reason almost crumbled.

A small cluster of bones occupied the center of the bed.

"My God!" she cried, hysterically. "The patient's had a relapse!"

THE END

Lector House believes that a society develops through a two-fold approach of continuous learning and adaptation, which is derived from the study of classic literary works spread across the historic timeline of literature records. Therefore, we aim at reviving, repairing and redeveloping all those inaccessible or damaged but historically as well as culturally important literature across subjects so that the future generations may have an opportunity to study and learn from past works to embark upon a journey of creating a better future.

This book is a result of an effort made by Lector House towards making a contribution to the preservation and repair of original ancient works which might hold historical significance to the approach of continuous learning across subjects.

HAPPY READING & LEARNING!

LECTOR HOUSE LLP
E-MAIL: lectorpublishing@gmail.com

9 789353 367312